THE TWIN MOONS

THE CRYSTAL CHRONICLES BOOK 2

R. DAWNRAVEN

CROSSED CLAYMORE PRESS

The Twin Moons by R. Dawnraven
Published by Crossed Claymore Press

ISBN 978-1-7389024-1-5 (paperback)

ISBN 978-1-7389024-2-2 (hardcover)

ISBN 978-1-7389024-3-9 (electronic book)

Contents

For everyone who wanted more dragons.
Here's some queer dragons.

Content Warnings and Pronunciation Guide

Aelim (third elven gender) – ay-lim

Alysion – uh-lee-shun (similar to the word legion)

Anaril – ah-nuh-rill

Atharil – uh-thar-ill

Aubrillias – aw-brill-ee-us

Ayel – ay-el (ay rhymes with hay)

Belim (female elf) – bay-lim

Braemyrin – bray-muh-rin

Damis (source of an elf's magical power) – dah-miss

Damisri (elf with no damis) - dah-miss-ree

Eburnas – ee-bur-nus

Elithar (elite elven warriors) – eh-lee-thar

Eranyl (kingdom's top healer) – ee-ran-yill

Fae – fay (rhymes with May)

Fiiraania – fee-ran-ee-ya

Glendarion – glen-dare-ee-on

Hammanth – hah-manth

Hissan – hee-san

Illerias – ill-leer-ee-us

Illithen – ill-leh-thin

Illuven – ill-loo-ven

Isidyll (head priest) – ee-see-dill

Konn (junior initiates) – kown (like 'own' with a k)

Luuya – loo-ya

Lymsia – lim-see-uh

Lyrellis – luh-rell-is

Melann – meh-lahn

Mellith – mel-ith

Navir – nah-veer

Nelim (male elf) – nay-lim (nay rhymes with say)

Nyrvrin – near-vrin

Odenia – oh-dee-nee-uh

Ornthalas – orn-tha-lass

Ranwa – rahn-wah

Sevarak- seh-vuh-rack

Sera (honorific for the future royal consort) – seh-ra

Silias (ritual performed to destroy a damis)– see-lee-us

Striiya (coming of age ceremony) – stree-yuh

Sy-Sy – sigh-sigh (like 'pie')

Sylandris – sigh-lahn-dris

Sylandrian – sigh-lahn-dree-in

Tarathiel – tuh-rath-ee-el

Thaliir – thaa-leer

Thelim (elven child) – they-lim

Uhaan – oo-han (han rhymes with fawn)

Urka – er-kah ('er' like in 'urn')

Vyrmyris – veer-muh-riss

Xyrros – Zee-rohs (similar to 'zeros')

Zen-Zen – 'zen' rhymes with 'pen'

Ziiran (male dragon) – zee-rahn

Ziirar (third dragon gender) – zee-rawr

Ziiras (female dragon)– zeer-us

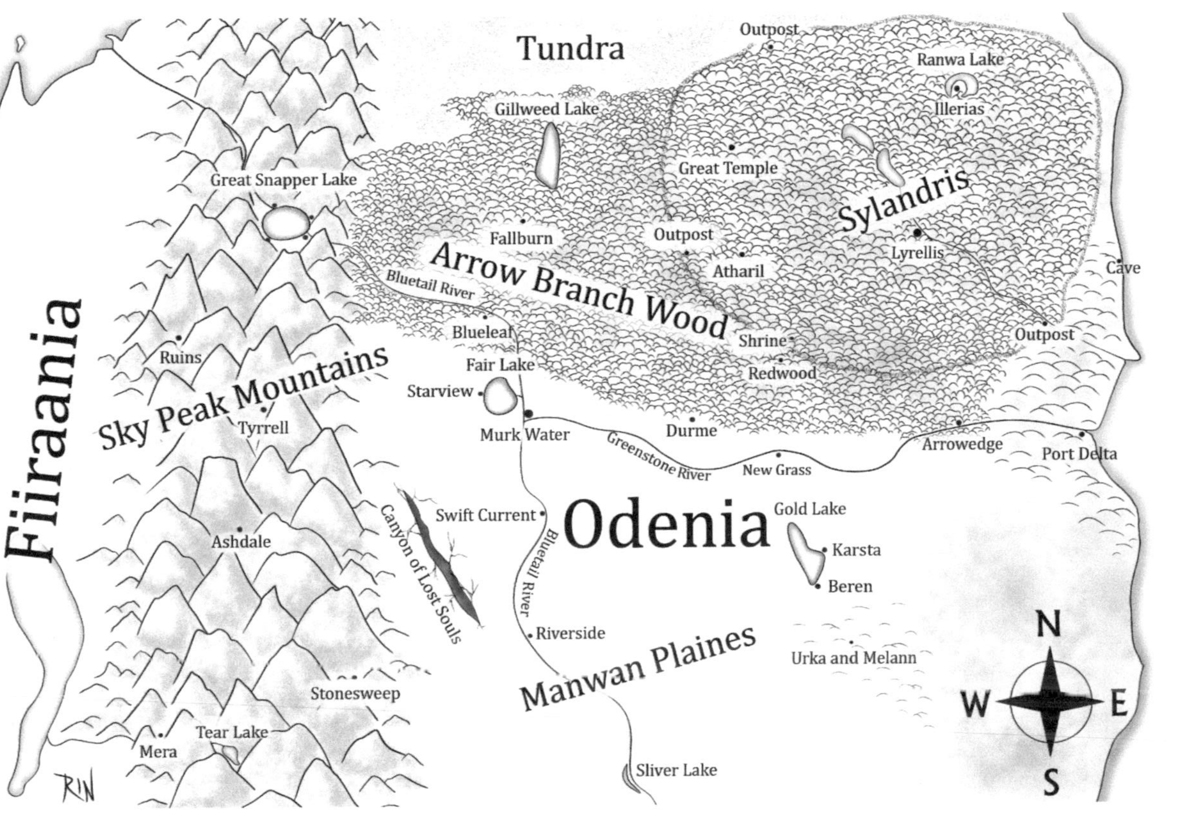

Fiiraania
Tundra
Sky Peak Mountains
Arrow Branch Wood
Sylandris
Odenia
Manwan Plaines
Outpost
Ranwa Lake
Gillweed Lake
Illerias
Great Temple
Great Snapper Lake
Outpost
Atharil
Lyrellis
Fallburn
Cave
Bluetail River
Shrine
Ruins
Blueleaf
Redwood
Outpost
Fair Lake
Starview
Durme
Tyrrell
Murk Water
Arrowedge
Port Delta
Greenstone River
New Grass
Ashdale
Swift Current
Gold Lake
Canyon of Lost Souls
Karsta
Bluetail River
Beren
Riverside
Urka and Melann
Stonesweep
N
W   E
S
Mera
Tear Lake
RIN
Sliver Lake

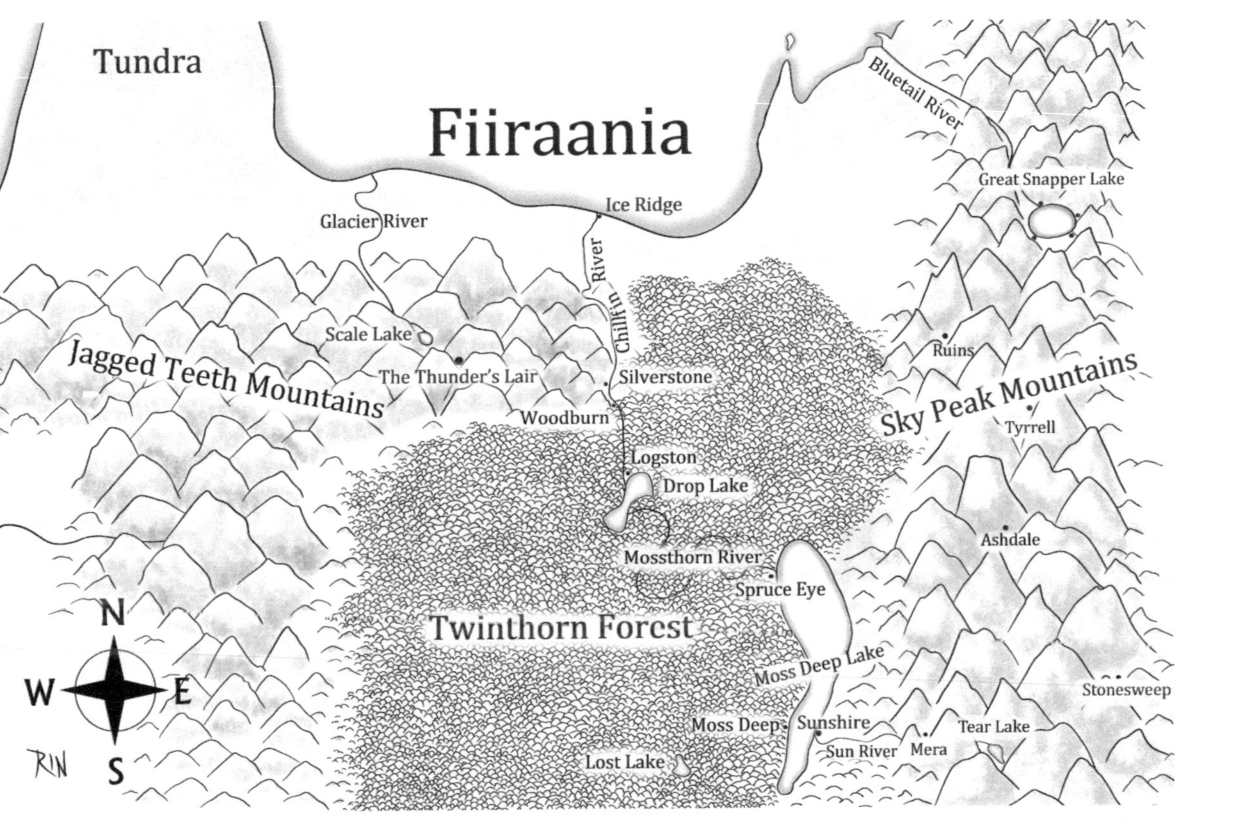

Tundra
Fiiraania
Bluetail River
Great Snapper Lake
Ice Ridge
Glacier River
Chillfin River
Scale Lake
Ruins
Jagged Teeth Mountains
The Thunder's Lair
Silverstone
Sky Peak Mountains
Tyrrell
Woodburn
Logston
Drop Lake
Mossthorn River
Ashdale
Spruce Eye
Twinthorn Forest
Moss Deep Lake
Stonesweep
Moss Deep
Sunshire
Tear Lake
Sun River
Mera
Lost Lake
N
E
S
W
RIN

Part One

Low chanting reverberated off cracked stone walls. Boney hands moved with expert precision; the motions practiced thousands of times. Pale light followed in their wake—the only light in the otherwise endless darkness. When a hand dipped low, the light passed close enough to the floor to illuminate one of the many sigils carved into the stone surrounding the caster. One by one, the sigils slowly lit up, emitting their own faint pink light.

When the last sigil activated, the hands stilled, though the chanting continued. From within the folds of their robe, the caster produced a small glass vial containing a thick, dark liquid. They uncorked it and tossed it into the air. The liquid sloshed out of the vial but didn't splatter to the ground; it remained suspended, glistening in the strange glow. The caster ignored the tinkling of glass as the vial shattered against the floor. They raised an arm, their long sleeve billowing. The liquid rained down, droplets hitting each glowing sigil. The pale light turned crimson.

The chanting grew louder as the light from the sigils solidified into misty vapour and wafted towards the caster, following the movements of their hands. It swirled around them, completely obscured them from view—had there been anyone around to observe the ritual.

As their chanting reached its zenith, the caster's hands suddenly stilled. The crimson mist continued to swirl around them. Drawing a dagger from their waist, they pricked a vein on their forearm. Blood poured, and they walked around the sigils, allowing a drop to hit each one. The vapour darkened in colour even more.

Soon.

Their chanting ceased, but they kept their mouth open, inhaling all the mist. They fell to their knees, hacking and spluttering in pitch darkness. But that did not bother them, for this part of the spell had succeeded. Rising, they left the circle of sigils, already planning the next step. Everything needed to be ready for the night, once in a millennia, when both the twin moons would be full. And it was rapidly approaching.

On the solstice, I shall regain my freedom.

ONE

PALATIAL LIFE

Alysion sighed as he made the trek from his chambers to the dining hall to meet his parents. He already knew why they had called him: to plan the *Aubrillias*—the autumnal equinox celebration—but that didn't improve his mood. He'd been hoping for one last lazy morning with Fae before things got busy with preparations. Upon returning home, his mother immediately tried to get him back into his normal routine of classes and tutoring and had arranged a similar schedule for Fae. Somehow, their lessons were never together, much to Alysion's irritation. It felt like he'd hardly seen the other elf since they had come to Lyrellis less than half a moon ago. It was starting to grate on him.

"Things can't go on like this," said a low voice.

Alysion stopped in the hallway just before the door, his father's tone on the other side making him pause. Whatever his parents were talking about, they didn't want anyone overhearing. He pressed his ear to the wooden door, hoping his aura wouldn't give him away. Since he'd handed over the crystals when they had returned to the palace, his aura had mostly returned to normal without their direct influence. They were being kept somewhere in the city until they could be properly rehidden, their auras warded to stop others from discovering them. Yet Alysion could still feel his connection to them. It was very faint, but it wouldn't be hard for him to find the crystals if he wanted.

"Someone is bound to find out sooner or later," King Illuven continued.

"What happened died with *him*," replied Alysion's mother, Queen Lymsia. "Not even his followers know about it. Captain Anaril has extensively questioned all of them."

Alysion cocked his head and frowned. His parents were discussing Tarathiel.

"Not all of them. The one you sent to Fiiraania wasn't questioned."

Ash? What about Fae's twin brother?

"Even if that boy had been told the truth, he wouldn't believe it. His trust in *him* has been completely destroyed. He would simply think it was another lie told to perpetuate his hatred of our family."

"I suppose...but if the truth did get out, things—"

"Enough, our prince has arrived." The queen's words were final.

The king fell silent.

Alysion took that as his cue to join them and pushed the door open.

His parents, both in voluminous spider silk robes of white and silver, the colours of the Brightstar line, were already seated at the polished wooden table in the private dining hall. The hall was a small half-moon-shaped room on an upper level of the palatial tree with tall windows along the curved wall, providing a good view of the garden and pond below. It was only used when the royal family wanted to dine together in private.

Alysion ambled up to the round table set for three and took his seat. The chairs were elaborately carved with motifs of leaves and vines native to the forest, and like the table, all bore the Brightstar crest.

"You're late, Prince Alysion," his mother said in the form of a greeting. Her long golden hair, a shade paler than his own but just as straight, was tied back in a high ponytail. She looked strained, but that wasn't surprising, given all the stress they were under.

"It took a bit longer than I anticipated to get here. It's been a while," he said, worrying at the burn mark on his wrist with his other hand. He'd given it to himself when he'd removed an aura-suppressing band Captain Anaril had put on him back when he, Fae, and Gale had been trying to find the crystals to stop Tarathiel.

Queen Lymsia narrowed her emerald eyes—to his relief, only in annoyance. She hadn't noticed him eavesdropping. Apparently, saving all of Sylandris from Tarathiel's plot to overthrow the kingdom by grooming Ash to be a conduit for the crystals hadn't been enough to thaw her frosty attitude toward him. Pleasing his mother was impossible, so upon returning home, he'd decided it wasn't worth the stress.

His father cleared his throat as a serving elf came in with tea. There were shadows under the king's eyes. "I imagine you know why we are all here today."

Not all of us. Alysion kept his mouth shut. Technically, Fae wasn't a member of the royal family, but since they were in a relationship, Alysion considered him one.

"The equinox is nearly upon us, and with the Great Temple lacking an *isidyll* and experienced *ayel* since Tarathiel's infiltration, it falls upon us to lead the festivities this year," his father continued, ignoring his son's moody expression.

"What's our plan?" the prince asked flatly.

"The Aubrillias will take place here in Lyrellis," explained his mother, "and the three of us will stand in for the isidyll and ayel. We have very little time to perfect performing the rites."

Alysion suppressed a groan. He'd been looking forward to spending time with Fae at the festival, but if he had to take up the role of an ayel, then that wouldn't happen. He'd be far too busy.

"Who's going to be the isidyll?" he asked. The isidyll was the spiritual head of the temple. They acted as the mouthpiece for the Divine Ancestors, the beings who had given life and magic to their people. It was an incredibly important role to fill.

"I will," replied King Illuven.

Alysion blinked. Usually, his mother wanted to be the center of attention. *Perhaps he's trying to atone for Tarathiel? But Tarathiel wasn't his fault.* Maybe it had something to do with what they had been discussing before his arrival. Whatever the reason, Alysion had other things to worry about.

"Starting tomorrow, you will have extra tutoring with Selaena-ayel in order to prepare you for the festival," said Queen Lymsia, taking a sip of her tea.

Alysion fought to keep his face straight as the server brought out their meal. Now, he wouldn't be able to see Fae until after the festival! Was his mother *trying* to keep them separated? He stared glumly at his food while his parents went over the details of their roles. Fae was going to be so disappointed.

• • ● ● ● • •

Fae did his best to ignore the stares and not-too-quiet muttering as he made his way to the large clearing on the east side of Lyrellis for his early morning swordsmanship training. Though he didn't have a *damis*, the source of an elf's magical ability, he still had the physical skills of his people. He could wield a sword just as well as any Sylandrian—providing they didn't use magic.

He quickly ate a bun smothered in lunaberry jam as he hurried along the vertigo-inducing walkways of Lyrellis. They were high in the air, woven out of the living branches of the trees and vines around them. Fae was grateful that someone had had enough sense to put up guardrails along them. Since he had no magic, he would be nothing but a splatter on the ground far below if he fell. But even with the guardrails, which were made of braided branches like the rest of the walkway, being up so high made him a little uneasy.

He reached a set of stairs that spiralled down around a tree, taking him to the forest floor. Fae let out a small sigh of relief when he reached the ground. Though his childhood home had been up in a tree, he'd spent most of his life living amongst humans on solid earth. At least he didn't have a genuine fear of heights. He couldn't imagine how he'd survive in this city if he did.

"Fae-*illim!*" a voice called out as he hurried up the path to the training grounds. The grounds were a large clearing filled with elves practicing with all sorts of weapons, from swords to staves and even bows at the far end. He approached a group of adolescent elves waiting near the edge.

The unusually short elf approaching the group—their instructor—had a scowl on her face. "Last one again, Fae-illim," she said, her disapproval of his existence evident in her tone.

Fae didn't bother to point out that he wasn't last; another pair of elves was still sauntering over to the group. But doing so would only incite Ubriel-*nia*'s anger, which he suspected she only kept in check because word might get back to Alysion. She didn't want to cross the prince.

"My apologies, nia," he said, dipping his head just enough to hide the flash of annoyance that flitted across his face.

She gave him another unsettling look that made him question to what extent Alysion's influence would protect him. "Get a sword and pair up," she barked at the group.

Fae waited until most had claimed a wooden practice sword from the shed before grabbing one for himself. They had left him the most battered one, but it still felt balanced in his hand.

The hard part was finding a partner. No one wanted to spar with the *damisri*, the elf without a damis, regardless of his affiliation to the throne or his bloodline. His parents had been high-ranking nobles before they'd been murdered by Tarathiel and his followers when they had come to kidnap Ash.

"Ornthalas-illim," Ubriel snapped, seeing that Fae once again stood by himself, "you're with the da—with Fae-illim."

Fae frowned. Since the first day he'd first set foot on the training field, Ornthalas had been determined to make his life a living nightmare.

A male—a *nelim*—wearing gold and white, the colours of the Goldbark family, stepped through the crowd. Ornthalas held his head high, as if to peer down his nose at Fae. The effect was lost since Fae was taller.

"I can't believe you're still here," sniffed the young nelim, assuming a fighting stance.

"Aly—the prince wants me to be here," replied Fae, raising his wooden shortsword. He was more familiar with the longsword, but that didn't matter here. His goal wasn't to beat his opponent, fearing it would further antagonize the nobles. Rather, he simply wanted to avoid incurring any severe injuries.

Ornthalas snorted, then sprung into action. He quickly closed the gap between them and aimed a cut at Fae's head. Fae suppressed an eye roll. Though he'd only been training with these elves for a few days, it hadn't taken him long to figure out their habits. While the nobles' moves were perfectly executed, they were incredibly predictable. It was obvious none of them had been in a real fight before. Their only advantage over Fae was their magic, which Ubriel-nia forbade them from using during these morning sessions. "You're here to train your bodies, not your damai!" she would say.

Fae waited until the last moment to deflect the blow, pretending to struggle. He didn't want to reveal the extent of his abilities to the nobles; better to have them think he was slow and unskilled.

But holding back was difficult. Ornthalas left many openings that any real opponent would take advantage of. Fae grit his teeth and let them slide by, which was almost harder than purposely leaving openings for the other nelim to strike him. At least he had some control over where Ornthalas was hitting him—a few dark bruises were better than a broken arm or a cracked skull. Oh how he missed sparring with Gale! Though her human disguise hadn't been as quick or strong as an elf, she'd been a crafty opponent. He'd learned a lot from her while collecting the crystals.

They shuffled around the field, swords clacking with each strike. Fae leapt back as Ornthalas' wooden sword came for his shoulder. He hissed as a stinging blow landed on his arm. Ornthalas shot him a smug look as he brought his sword up, leaving his left side exposed. Moving on pain-fuelled instinct, Fae stepped in to strike, all thoughts of holding back forgotten. But at the last moment, he pulled back. Ornthalas took the opportunity to come for his head.

Off-balance, Fae brought his sword up to block the strike. Ornthalas' blow glanced off harmlessly.

"Enough!" called Ubriel. "Swap partners!"

As he stepped back, Ornthalas took the opportunity to smack him in the ribs. Pain flared up his side. Coughing, he pressed a hand to the sore spot. Nothing was broken. He looked to see if Ubriel-nia would reprimand Ornthalas, but her attention was elsewhere. With each session, it was becoming evident that she wasn't above turning a blind eye to such misconduct.

Annoyed, Fae faced his next partner.

When he returned to his bedchamber after training, he found Alysion inside, looking out the window. Immediately, his mood improved. The prince was impeccably dressed in a gold tunic edged with silver embroidered stars over a simple pair of dark brown leather leggings. A red sash cinched his waist, adding a pop of colour.

"I apologize for not coming to breakfast. My parents summoned me," said the prince, turning towards him.

"That's all right," Fae replied, pulling off his clammy top. Even though autumn was nearly upon them, he'd still managed to work up a sweat in the brisk morning air.

"It's not all right. We've hardly seen each other since coming here," Alysion huffed.

Fae took his time selecting a fresh tunic. "Things will settle down once the Aubrillias is over and the captives at the temple have been dealt with."

Alysion's emerald gaze, which had definitely not been focused on Fae's toned body, dropped to the floor. "About that... I've been given extra duties for the festival."

Fae got a sinking feeling. He turned and crossed his arms over his bare chest, waiting for the bad news.

"Because we lack the necessary spiritual leaders to perform the ceremonies, my family will be doing it instead. I've been asked to stand in as an ayel."

"Will you be busy the whole time? Will we be able to spend any of it together?" Fae asked, sounding calmer than he felt. Ever since Alysion had told him about the festival, he'd been looking forward to it. Not only was it to celebrate the changing of the seasons, but it was when the boundary between the realm of the living and the dead was at its weakest. On rare occasions, the departed would cross over to visit loved ones. Which meant there was a very slim chance he might see his parents.

Alysion raised his head. "I'll be busy performing my duties the entire time."

Still riled from sword practice (the illicit strikes had only worsened with each partner), Fae clenched a shaking fist behind his back.

"I'm sorry," said the prince quickly. "I was really looking forward to it, and I know you were too." His disappointment was obvious.

Fae let out a long sigh, expelling his frustrations. "It's not your fault. You're the prince; things like this are expected of you." He closed the space between them and wrapped his arms around Alysion's slim waist. The sweet scent of lunaberries filled his nose as he rested his head on the prince's shoulder. He took a slow, deep breath, relishing it.

"The day after the festival is a rest day. We'll have the whole day together..." said Alysion, his tone suddenly airy.

"Then we'll definitely make the most of it," Fae murmured into his pointed ear. Alysion quivered, igniting something within him.

"I brought something for you," said the prince, pulling away before Fae could do any more. He produced a wooden talisman from a pouch at his waist. "It's supposed to help call forth whoever you want to see at the festival."

Fae took the talisman and held it up, studying the tiny falling leaves that had been painstakingly carved into it. The craftsmanship was rudimentary. Had Alysion made it himself?

"Of course, I don't expect it to work—"

Fae cut off his words with a heated kiss.

Alysion wrapped his arms around him, and they fell into the bed.

Two

Aubrillias

Alysion hardly had time to blink before the equinox festival was upon them. His days had been crammed with lessons to prepare him, so his morning breakfasts with Fae had been put on hold. Instead, he ate while being lectured on his new ayel duties. With all the recent turmoil at the Great Temple, the royal family needed the festival to be a great success in order to please the Ancestors and show their subjects they were as strong and confident as ever.

"We cannot allow the noble families to question our rule. We are the descendants of the Divine Ancestors, and we will not break over discovering a handful of traitors," his mother had said one morning. There was concern amongst the nobles that the deities were angry with them for not removing the fake isidyll sooner; Ash had been performing various rites and rituals for at least a decade, and he had admitted his lack of faith in the Ancestors to Alysion and Fae before leaving with the dragons. He'd merely been acting as isidyll to maintain their cover. Thankfully, the nobles and Alysion's parents didn't know about this. They believed Ash had been genuine in his role as isidyll—that only his motives had been impure. Alysion wasn't about to share this secret with anyone. It would only make things much, much worse. How could the Ancestors let someone with no faith hold such a position? The isidyll was supposed to be their representative, yet they had done nothing to correct it.

So yes, Alysion fully understood his mother's concerns. The festival had to go off without a hitch. If there was any doubt among the nobles, then the royals' rule could unravel despite their divine lineage. Though Alysion couldn't recall any incidents where the royal family had been completely overthrown, there had been instances where the nobles lost faith and made things very difficult for the monarch of the time. In most cases, that faith had only been restored once the Brightstar heir had joined with one of the noble *thelim* and ascended to the throne. Alysion had no desire to have an unwanted mate forced upon him; he'd run away to try to escape that very fate. Not to mention, he was very happy with Fae.

But Fae was an unspoken issue, wasn't he? The court wasn't pleased with Fae's presence due to his lack of damis. And they were even less thrilled that Alysion had declared him his mate. *And this is why the festival has to be perfect. If we mess up, they'll try to blame it on Fae.*

He wouldn't let that happen. Though he had yet to see it, he suspected the other young nobles were giving Fae a hard time. Especially the *belim,* since Fae had taken what many of them coveted: the chance to become queen. From what little he knew of the other adolescent elves, he'd be shocked if they weren't harassing Fae. Unfortunately, there was nothing Alysion could do about it unless someone reported it, and so far, no one had. Not even Fae. Then again, they'd hardly had time to talk at all.

Once the festival was over, he would make time.

On the morning of the festival, Alysion woke to the sound of a servant bustling into his room, urging him to get up. They set a platter of food down on the small table beside his bed and began to fiddle with the heavy silk ceremonial robes he would be stuck in all day. The main ceremony didn't take place until sunset, but as a stand-in ayel, and the prince no less, he was expected to meet the people.

Alysion shovelled down his breakfast, knowing it could be a while before he got to eat again, then let the servant dress him. If the time it took to put on the robe was any indication of what today would be like, things were not looking good.

After what felt like the entire morning, he was escorted to the training clearing where the festival would be held. Already, it was unrecognizable. A large stage had been erected at one end where he and his parents would perform various rites and rituals that evening. Stalls and booths were being set up off to one side, their owners laying out goods or preparing food to sell. The scent of cooking herbs and spices began taking over the clearing. Aside from those finishing up preparations, hardly anyone else was about. But it wouldn't stay that way for long. By midday, the place would be packed full of his people, many of whom would be journeying from the furthest reaches of Sylandris.

What Alysion usually looked forward to most was when groups gathered around bonfires to play music and swap tales after sunset. He'd never left Lyrellis until he'd met Fae, so it was one of the best ways for him to learn about the rest of Sylandris.

Alysion tried not to let his frustration show on his face as he shuffled his way across the field, taking small steps to avoid treading on the hem of his heavy robes. He'd been looking forward to snacking and listening to stories with Fae, but instead, he would be stuck under an arbor giving out blessings and praying to the Ancestors on behalf of his people all day.

Ugh.

He wasn't sure how he felt about the Ancestors at the moment. After meeting Fae—an elf without a damis—and dealing with Tarathiel, his loyalty had been shaken up. *They're better off sending their own prayers.* But as an ayel and member of the royal family, everyone believed his prayers had a better chance of being heard.

He was led inside a small tent that had been erected for him and his parents. Thankfully, they hadn't arrived yet. He sat down on a stool.

"Pardon me, My Prince, but you will wrinkle the silk if you sit. I must ask that you remain standing," said his attendant.

Biting back a retort, he stood up. Yup, today was going to be a long, long day. *Just remember, tomorrow is a rest day for everyone. You get to spend the entire day with Fae.*

Fae blinked as he beheld the training grounds, overwhelmed by how they had transformed. The clearing was usually a place of order and routine. Now, it was anything but. Elves wearing colourful silks milled about, checking out goods for sale and greeting old acquaintances. Music filled the air, mingling with the sounds of conversation. His nose was assailed by many intriguing scents ranging from food to incense. Fae knew he needed to be cautious of the incense—Alysion had warned that some could affect his mind.

Speaking of Alysion, somewhere in the chaos was his prince. Fae figured it wouldn't be too hard to find him. All he had to do was look for the largest group of people; no one wanted to pass up the opportunity to have the royal family send off their thoughts and prayers to the Ancestors. He let out a breath. Well, there was no point in seeking him out. It wasn't like they could spend any time together today. Even if he pretended he wanted to send a prayer to the Ancestors, he'd only be with Alysion for a few moments.

And judging by the looks he was getting from the elves around him, his presence wouldn't be well received by the nobles. Though the talisman Alysion had given him had been enchanted to help hide the fact that he had no aura, the palace nobles would recognize him on the spot. His strange hair stood out too much.

He decided to stick to the outskirts of the clearing. There were still a lot of interesting things to see there. And crowds weren't really his thing.

"Good day!" voices called out as he wandered into the merchant section. Many had wooden stalls decorated with all kinds of foliage—some clearly not native to the area—set up to display their goods, but a few had their wares laid out on colourful blankets. One had everything displayed on what appeared to be miniature clouds that floated chest high off the ground.

Fae didn't know where to look first. There was all kinds of jewelry, some fine weapons, mouth-watering snacks, and what appeared to be enchanted artifacts. The last Alysion told him to steer clear of; many were fakes or had unwanted effects. The Elithar were tasked with checking all the merchants before they set up, but some things always slipped through.

Fae eyed the coin pouch Alysion had given him—another apology for being unable to spend the day together—as he tried to make up his mind. He'd never had money he could freely spend before. Any coin he'd earned from working with Master Cane in her smithy, he had stashed away for his search for Ash. But with Ash found and hopefully in good hands (talons?) with the dragons, he could now buy whatever he pleased.

His stomach growled loudly, so he bought a small loaf of bread packed with herbs and drizzled with honey. It was warm and delicious, perfect on a cool day like this.

Fae sat on a stump near the edge of the trees, enjoying his snack.

This is so strange, he thought, watching the crowds. Since he'd come to Lyrellis, he'd received nothing but dark looks from the elves around him. But between the talisman, which he'd resented taking, and the influx of elves from other parts of the kingdom, he was hardly spared a second glance. The lingering stares were only because of his hair, which was currently white at the root, fading to black, then back to white at the tips. They likely just thought his hair was some sort of fashion statement for the festival.

This is what acceptance feels like.

He frowned. The elves only accepted him because they didn't realize he was different. If he were to chuck the talisman into the trees, it wouldn't take long for the haughty looks and ill-concealed whispers to come. He fidgeted with it, reminding himself that Alysion had said it could somehow help him reunite with his parents.

When the sun began to set, casting a brilliant fiery glow across the sky, the festival's mood shifted. Music continued floating through the air but wasn't as loud nor jubilant as before. Even conversation took on hushed tones. When the crowds began to gather in front of the large stage at the far end of the clearing, Fae trailed after them, careful to keep his distance from any nobles he recognized.

A flute sounded and the clearing fell silent. A strong perfumed scent filled the air. Solemnly, the royal family walked on stage, the platform tall enough for everyone to see them. Fae's eyes were glued to Alysion, who was staring out at the crowd. The prince was dressed in layers of flowing white and silver with deep violet accents. It was the first time he'd seen the prince in his ceremonial garb. His stomach did a funny flip.

King Illuven was speaking, but Fae hardly heard a word he said. Alysion looked good in silk. But he'd look better if those layers were all—

Alysion stepped forward, drawing Fae from thoughts that made his face heat up. He began to chant something Fae didn't quite understand. *Must be an old form of Illithen.*

His mother joined in, adding her voice. The two began to sway and turn about the stage, taking careful, graceful steps that gave them the illusion of floating. The king eventually joined in, his deeper tones adding another layer.

Their coordination was impressive. No one tripped or stepped on any of the flowing hems. Fae wouldn't have been able to manage it, not in those robes.

All three of them slowed and became still, their voices fading away. Silence once again fell across the crowd. The gathered elves put a closed fist to their chests, shut their eyes, and bowed their heads. Fae did the same, not wanting to draw attention to himself.

The king began to chant in the strange tongue.

Something rained down on Fae, wetting his hair. He cracked open an eye and bit back a shout. The crowd had disappeared entirely, leaving him alone in the clearing. Or nearly alone. A mist crept in, collecting in front of him. It rose up, forming swirling pillars. The falling leaf amulet around his neck twitched. The pillars gradually took on elven forms, their features sharpening.

"Ama, Dada," Fae breathed. The corners of his eyes prickled.

His dada reached out a misty hand and lay it on his head. The weightless touch was warm, radiating his parents' love.

"We're glad you survived, Fae," said his ama, smiling.

Fae, tears flowing freely, resisted the urge to hug her incorporeal form. "I found Ash. He's...safe."

His dada removed his hand, the warm feeling fading, and closed his eyes. "I feel him," the older elf murmured. "He's...in Fiiraania?"

Dada's eyes shot open, and both his parents gave him questioning looks.

Fae shifted nervously. "It's a long story, but the queen sent him as a messenger."

"A tale we would love to hear," said Ama. "But, we don't have time tonight. Already, we are being drawn back."

Fae nodded, throat tightening as their misty faces became muddled.

"We have something important to tell you, Fae," said Dada, his voice starting to sound like he was far away. "Darkness lurks in these lands. Though we are no longer among the living, we can feel something stirring."

"What kind of something?" Fae asked quickly. Mist wafted off his parents, their forms swiftly losing shape.

"It's old," said Ama. Fae had to strain to make out her words. She said something else, but it was lost as she and her mate turned back into a cloud of mist.

"The royal heir..."

"What about Alysion?" he shouted.

The mist disappeared.

Around him, the crowd of elves stirred. Judging by their expressions, he was the only one who had been visited. Heart pounding, he looked up at the stage. The royal family was leaving. Fae wanted nothing more than to seek out Alysion and tell him about his parents, but even if he was free of his ayel duties, he wasn't free of his princely ones.

Needing some space, Fae left the crowd and returned to wandering around the edge of the clearing. The last of the sunlight had faded. Fires, scattered haphazardly across the clearing, had been lit. Elves sat around them, talking and making merry. The music kicked back up again, loud and lively.

He passed close to one of the fires.

"—cursed heir."

Fae stopped in his tracks and looked at the group of elves seated near him. Cursed heir? His stomach knotted unpleasantly. His parents had mentioned an heir. Was this about Alysion?

Needing to know more, he tucked himself behind a nearby tree, his keen elven ears just able to pick out their words over the sounds of the festivities. He caught the scent of something pungent and covered his nose with his arm. They were smoking.

"There's no such thing," a female voice said.

Fae let out a breath into his arm. Not Alysion. But then...who? A cursed heir certainly sounded like something to be wary of. Fae sat and leaned back against the tree, making himself comfortable.

"'Course there is," someone slurred, clearly deep into thornberry wine. "Wanders the forest at night, looking to lead other nobles astray."

"Hah! Sounds just like our own prince, though he's not interested in nobles. Only damisri. That's a curse if I ever saw one. No wonder the Ancestors are angry."

Fae clenched his jaw.

"He's not the one I'm talking about," the first voice said. "Though they too were a member of the royal family."

"I've never heard of a cursed Brightstar," said a belim voice.

"Neither have I," said another, their tone more serious. "The king and queen can only have one child. If their thelim had been cursed, their line would have died out."

"And we would know if something like that had happened," someone else added.

"It would depend on what the curse was."

"Nobles shouldn't wander inta the forest 'lone a' night," one elf slurred, seemingly obvious to the conversation around him.

"I hear they were born a damisri. That's why they're cursed," one said.

Someone snorted.

Fae's pulse began to race. Born a damisri? It took everything he had not to barge in demand to know more. But if he did that, they might think *he* was the cursed heir—especially since they were all a few cups into the wine. Instead, he quietly got up and made his way back to the palace.

I'll ask Alysion about it when I see him tomorrow.

THREE

DUTY

Unfortunately, Alysion's day of rest did not go as planned. He was woken up not by Fae, but by Layniir.

"Pardon me, My Prince, but Queen Lymsia has requested your audience at breakfast."

"Are you sure?" he asked, emerging from the covers.

"Her request was clear."

Alysion grumbled to himself all the way to the private dining hall. He was supposed to eat breakfast with Fae, he'd promised! Though the other elf wouldn't show it, he knew Fae would be upset that he'd been stood up again. *Maybe I can eat fast and escape.*

But when he stepped into the hall and beheld his mother's expression, that tiny flicker of hope died like someone had thrown a bucket of icy water from the Silverstar River on it.

He respectfully dipped his head to his parents, noticing his father looked just as unhappy about being there as he felt, and took his seat.

"The festival was a disaster," his mother snapped before his royal butt had even touched the down-filled cushion.

Alysion didn't dare speak; he'd learned not to when she was angry. How had it been a disaster? He thought it had gone pretty well, considering he hadn't much time to learn his role. None of them had made fools of themselves on stage, and all the elves he'd sent prayers for had been grateful.

"The noble families do not believe the Ancestors have been appeased."

"Why is that?" King Illuven asked when she took a breath. "As far as I could see, everything went as smoothly as it could."

"I'm aware," she snapped. "I don't believe the festival is the issue—it's an excuse." She let that hang in the air for a moment as a servant brought out a round of spiced tea.

Illuven sighed. "What are they asking for now?"

"They want the temple to be fully operational by the winter solstice," she replied, her anger melting away, replaced by exhaustion. There were dark circles under her eyes that Alysion couldn't recall ever seeing before. Had she gotten any sleep last night, or had she lain awake worrying about this? He'd slept like a log, wiped out from being on his feet all day servicing their people.

"By the solstice? That's not possible," said his father. "A spiritual leader isn't someone you can train so easily. We were only acceptable replacements because we're the royal family."

"Some are unhappy that you were given the isidyll's role," Queen Lymsia said, "because you are not of divine blood."

His father frowned. "They knew I was taking that role."

The queen waved her hand. "It's merely another one of their excuses. What matters now is putting all our energy into dealing with our captives at the Great Temple and finding elves willing to become konn and ayel. Regardless of the nobles' demands, it's unlikely we will have a fully-fledged isidyll by the solstice. A solstice, might I remind you, that coincides with the *Luuya*." She let out a little cough.

Right, the twin full moons that only happened once every few centuries. It was a time when Elven magic was at its most powerful.

Alysion caught his mother's eye and got a sinking feeling. He would be the one standing in as isidyll, would't he? That's why he was here. Dealing with Tarathiel's captive followers wasn't something he needed to worry about. His parents and Captain Anaril were handling it.

"Since none of the nobles have volunteered to help rebuild the temple's rank of disciples, your training as temporary isidyll will begin this afternoon," she said.

"What!?" Alysion exclaimed. "Today is for resting! I—" His voice trailed off as his mother's expression tightened.

"There is no time for rest. Selaena-ayel is expecting you." She coughed again and took a sip of tea.

Alysion frowned. *What a terrible day this is turning out to be,* he thought bitterly as the servants brought out their meal. Well, maybe he'd have enough time before meeting the ayel to see Fae.

No, not maybe. He would make sure he did.

• • ● ● ● • •

When Alysion didn't show up to breakfast, Fae figured the prince had overslept and went to wake him up. He knocked on Alysion's door, the polished wood decorated with vines and stars, but got no response. Knowing the prince was sometimes a heavy sleeper, he pushed open the door. The bed was already made.

He blinked. "Alysion?"

Silence.

He checked the small attached washroom but it too was empty. There was no sign of Layniir either.

Fae furrowed his brow. Where could he have gone? Had they made arrangements to eat somewhere else? No, he would certainly remember that. Fae looked around to see if Alysion had left him a note, but the prince's quill was dry. Strange.

Mentally, he reviewed the list of activities they had planned to do today, wondering if Alysion had mixed something up. Hmm, but breakfast always came first, no matter what.

He bit his lower lip and went to check his own room just in case the prince had turned up.

It was empty.

Fae sat on the edge of his bed, unsure of what to do. There had to be a good reason for Alysion to miss their date. The last time he hadn't shown up his parents had called him away for an important meeting.

Ah, that's it.

A servant bustled past his open door and Fae hurried to catch them. After an awkward conversation in which the servant refused to look at him—something most of them did—they confirmed the prince was with his parents. Then they abruptly turned and hurried down the hall as if they couldn't escape him fast enough.

Fae tamped down his rising annoyance and returned to his room. *It's not Alysion's fault. He's the prince. His duties have to come first.* He flopped onto his bed and sighed, trying to force the tension out of his body as he exhaled. Ugh, was he ever going to see the prince? He could count on one hand how many full days they had spent together since coming to Lyrellis.

Maybe Alysion wouldn't be with them for long. They were his parents after all. Perhaps they just wanted some private time with him unrelated to running the kingdom. But Fae couldn't imagine that happening. The impression he got from the queen was that she didn't have time for that sort of nonsense. So whatever it was, it must be important.

If that were the case, there would be no point in laying around here.

He got up, scribbled a note for Alysion, and made his way to the royal library—a place he had yet to visit since coming to the city. Something had been niggling at the back of his mind since last night, and he wanted to check it out. It wasn't a coincidence that his parents had shown up to warn him about an heir just before he'd overheard drunken elves rambling about the same thing. Maybe he was being paranoid, but after all that had happened with Ash and Tarathiel, he didn't want to overlook this. And if the cursed heir turned out to be nothing more than a tall tale told by tipsy elves, at least he'd learn something interesting.

The library existed in the hollowed-out interior of a massive tree. The front desk was located on the same level as the aerial walkways, made up of circular floors of books with huge windows extending above and below it. Each floor held its own genre.

Fae had no idea where to begin. Did he head upstairs to look under myths and legends? Or maybe he should look through records of mysterious disappearances? In the end he decided to scour the Brightstar lineage. If this elf had been real, there would be a record of them there.

He made for the stairs.

"There you are," huffed a familiar voice, causing him to pause. Alysion. "Do you know how hard you are to find because you don't have an aura to track?"

"I left a note," Fae said more stiffly than intended as a sudden spike of annoyance shot through his chest.

"Oh…sorry," said Alysion, dipping his head.

The way the sunlight filtering through the massive windows hit his golden hair dazzled Fae. He would have run his hands through it, but he didn't want others to see. The nobles weren't the only ones who disapproved of their relationship.

Alysion led him to a nearby table and then plunked himself down in a chair. "My parents summoned me without warning *again*. I wasn't even awake when the message came."

"It's all right. They must've had a good reason for it," Fae said, taking a seat.

Alysion visibly stiffened up.

Uh oh.

"They had a reason but *I* don't think it's a good one," the prince said, fidgeting with a strand of golden hair.

Fae didn't get a chance to respond before Alysion went off on a tangent about various nobles, the Aubrillias, and the Great Temple. He found it all a bit hard to follow until Alysion got to the real issue at hand.

"They want me to be the isidyll at the *Eburnas*—the winter solstice!"

"Isn't that moons away?" he asked, flinching when a librarian stuck their head around a corner and gave them a dirty look.

"Yes, but I have to start training immediately," Alysion said, lowering his voice.

"You mean tomorrow?" A pit formed in his stomach.

"I wish! I have to meet with an ayel *today*," the prince huffed, crossing his arms. "Right now, actually, but I wanted to see you first."

Fae stared at him, mixed emotions swirling around his chest, dragging him down. "Well, don't keep them waiting," he said, fighting to keep his voice even.

"I'm sorry. I don't want to do this. I tried to get out of it, but once my mother makes up her mind about something, nothing can be done about it."

Fae sighed. Would they ever get any time together? "It's fine. You're the prince. This is just how things are. We knew it wouldn't be easy for us when we decided to be together. Hopefully, once the solstice has passed, things will get better."

A hand touched his shoulder, and he turned to see the prince standing beside him. Emerald eyes gazed into his own boring brown.

"I really am sorry," Alysion said softly. "I was looking forward to today…"

Fae laid his hand over Alysion's. His skin, while chilled from the autumn air, was soft. "It's not your fault."

He would tell Alysion about his parents another time.

• • ● ● ● • •

Sword practice the next morning went just as well as it always did, meaning all the young nobles did their best to beat the snot out of him. Fae wanted nothing more than to put one of them in the dirt, but doing so would only make things much, much worse for himself. Still, it was a struggle. And it didn't help that he was still feeling down about Alysion's new isidyll training.

He ducked to avoid his opponent's cut, an obnoxious nelim named Glendarion Skyshade, who would have been attractive if it weren't for his shoddy attitude. Glendarion swung at him again, forcing him to leap back. Fae quickly adjusted his stance and brought up his sword.

There was a loud *thunk* as their wooden blades met.

Glendarion leered at him. "I can't believe you're still around, damisri. But I suppose the prince is allowed to keep whatever pets he wishes."

Fae did his best to ignore him—not an easy task, given they were barely an arm's length apart. He tried to break away, but his adversary wouldn't let him.

"What's it like being the only one to warm the prince's bed? I bet..."

Fae suppressed a snort and tuned him out. Really? That's how low these nobles were willing to go? Pathetic. He'd suffered through worse from the adolescent humans back in Redwood. And some of them he'd slept with.

"Oi! Are you listening?" Glendarion finally broke away, sword quickly dipping down and around Fae's.

Fae whipped his sword around to knock the blow aside. The force of it caused Glendarion to lose his balance, leaving him wide open. Taking him down would be easy.

Fae started to move, but something suddenly hit him in the side, knocking him off his feet.

Damn!

As he got his legs back under him he thought he saw Ornthalas turning away. Annoyance flared up. Did he have to watch out for *every* elf out here? *You would in a real fight,* he reminded himself.

He quickly rolled as Glendarion's blade came up high. They were supposed to avoid heads, but everyone conveniently forgot that rule when sparring with him. And, like with the illicit magic, Ubriel-nia never seemed to notice.

Glendarion was coming for him, so he assumed a defensive stance. His side ached. Thankfully, nothing was broken. He avoided the incoming sword and struck out with his own. To his and Glendarion's surprise, his blade connected with the noble's shoulder.

Glendarion's eyes sparked with rage. "Big mistake," he hissed.

Before Fae could react, he was hit by a powerful gust of air that slammed him down hard on his back, knocking the wind out of him. A sword touched his neck.

"The only good damisri is a dead one," Glendarion sneered quietly, looming over him.

Fae took a deep breath to calm the emotions building inside him. First they gang up on him, and now they use magic when explicitly told not to? This was sword practice, not spell practice! He tried to push the sword's tip away, but Glendarion didn't move.

"You can stay down."

There were a few titters from the elves nearby. Fae glared at him as he forced the blade away and stood. It was then he realized he was shaking.

Thankfully, Ubriel-nia signalled it was time to stop. He didn't know what would happen if they kept going.

By the gods, I need a break from all this, he thought as he made his way back to the palace. Though it had been stressful, part of him missed travelling around with Alysion and Gale. It had just been the three of them, and Gale would have happily given them alone time if they had asked. Not to mention, they had been far away from these snotty elves.

Ugh, if only he could get away to someplace like Redwood for a few days. And if Alysion came too, even better. The prince hadn't spent much time around humans while hunting for the crystals. One stop had resulted in the town of

Ashdale being destroyed by a volcano, something that still bothered the prince to this day.

Wait a minute... An idea slowly formed, one he needed to share with the prince. Unfortunately, he had to wait until that evening to tell him, but Alysion was completely on board when he did.

"The problem is that we have to convince my mother," Alysion said, stifling a yawn. "She won't let us traipse off to Odenia at such an important time."

"We'll come up with something."

Four

The Library

Having once again grown weary of the nobles' judging looks, Fae decided to hide himself away in the library to research the cursed heir. Luckily it was large enough that he could easily spend the day there without running into too many elves. He went down to the lowest floor where the historical records were kept, intending to bury himself in scrolls whose ink was so faded that they were nearly illegible. *Don't they have spells for preserving this stuff?* At least the room was well-lit by the massive windows and magical lights.

As he stared at the ornate shelves of scrolls and books, he wished someone had mentioned when the cursed heir had been alive in order to give him a starting point. Or even their gender. Anything to narrow the search.

Fae sighed. If only his parents had been able to tell him more.

At least the documents were organized by family, date, and topic. Of course, the Brightstar section was massive, and narrowing his search to just the records regarding their divine lineage still left him with a few shelves to go through. Resigning himself to the task ahead, Fae made himself comfortable at one of the elegant wooden tables and unfurled an ancient scroll sealed with the Brightstar crest.

It wasn't long before he abandoned it, unable to read it between the faded ink and looping hand. He put it to the side to try again later and pulled another from his stack.

A few scrolls in, he was nearly ready to give up entirely. Whoever had written them liked to go on and on about the most trivial things, regaling each Brightstar as if they were the Ancestors themselves. *Well, I suppose they sort of are.* No wonder Alysion had been so obnoxious when Fae first met him. He was glad their adventure across Odenia had helped the prince mellow out.

After scanning a few more scrolls, he got up and wandered the aisles, stretching his sore legs. So far, he hadn't found the slightest hint of a troublesome heir.

Maybe I'm going about this the wrong way.

One of the elves at the festival claimed that the cursed heir was a member of the royal family, but another had said the royal line would have died out if that were the case. Fae frowned. The royal family could only produce one thelim. Alysion had said it was to prevent succession wars. Maybe the heir wasn't a member of the royal family after all? Nobles could have multiple thelim if they wished. Fae sighed, feeling like he'd wasted his entire morning.

He chose another family at random—Redstalk—and pulled their records before wandering back to his table. He stopped dead. Someone dressed in a dark grey tunic with vibrant sky blue accents sat in his seat. Their head shot up at the sound of his footsteps.

Confusion passed over their features, their storm-grey eyes lingering on his hair. Fae knew they were trying to detect his aura. Disgust would cloud their face as it did on everyone else once they realized he was a damisri.

"You must be Fae, Prince Alysion's new...partner," they said, pushing away a long strand of pale hair that had come loose from the messy bun perched on their head.

Fae nodded, his face expressionless while he waited for the coming outburst.

"Ah, pardon me. My name is Mellith." They inclined their head, then looked down at the pile of scrolls. "I suppose you are working here."

"Yes," Fae said stiffly. What was a noble around his age doing down here? The only elves he saw this far down were the librarians who liked to shoot him disapproving looks when they thought he wasn't looking.

Mellith got up, but instead of leaving like Fae wished, they sat in the other chair. They were short, their head hardly reaching his chest. "Do you want some company?"

No. "Sure." Despite the fact he was Alysion's *sera*, the future royal consort, the nobles didn't treat him as such. He didn't want to bring Mellith's ire down upon him by refusing their offer.

"What are you researching?"

Wary, Fae returned to his seat and laid the new scrolls on the table. "During the festival I overheard something about a cursed heir that wanders the forest, targeting nobles. It's a ridiculous tale, but all myths are founded in truth. I want to know more about this individual."

Mellith listened intently, their eyes not leaving him as he recounted everything he'd overheard. He tried not to fidget as he spoke.

"At first, I thought the heir was a member of the royal family, but then I remembered they can only have one thelim." He pushed away the Brightstar scrolls. "The heir must be from a different family, but I don't know where to start."

"They can only have one child?"

"That's what Aly—Prince Alysion told me." Wasn't it common knowledge? Maybe not. Perhaps not every noble needed to have extensive knowledge of the Brightstars. Still, wasn't it obvious they could only have one?

"Well if that's the case, then you're right about having to look at other families." Mellith grabbed one of the Redstalk scrolls and started skimming.

Fae's gaze rested on them for a beat longer, looking for a family crest. He couldn't find one. Just who was this elf, and what were they up to?

With a second set of eyes helping, it didn't take long to get through the Redstalk records. While still lengthy, they weren't as bad as the Brightstar scrolls. Still, Fae didn't know how much more he could take of this. All the nobles believed they were the gods' gifts to the world.

Fae leaned back in the chair and rubbed his eyes, having finished looking through the final scroll in the pile. The sun had started to set, filling the sky with vibrant colours. The shelves cast long shadows across the floor.

Mellith had started cleaning up the records. Fae could hear them moving about the shelves, the scrolls rustling as they were put away. While there were a fair amount of *aelim* in Lyrellis (a few attended the morning weapons training), Mellith was only the second aelim Fae had actually met, the first being Captain Anaril.

Fae gathered up the last of the records and put them away. When he returned to the table, Mellith was there waiting for him.

"Thank you for helping me out," he said.

"You're welcome. It's a shame we didn't find what you're looking for."

Fae shrugged. "There are thousands of cycles of history here, and it's entirely possible I don't find anything. The heir could be nothing but a myth." But he didn't believe that. It couldn't be a coincidence that both his parents and the drunken elves had brought up an heir.

"Will you be here again tomorrow?" asked Mellith.

Fae hesitated. If Alysion didn't have time for him again, then yes. But he wasn't sure if he wanted Mellith around. They'd been super helpful, but they had to have a motive. Were they just using him to get closer to Alysion? They weren't here for him, that's for sure. No noble would willingly spend most of their day in the presence of a damisri. Besides, they'd hardly spoken a word to each other, having been so wrapped up in their search. Fae didn't know which family they belonged to—or anything else about them, for that matter.

"Fae?"

"Ah—I don't know yet. It depends on what Prince Alysion is doing."

Mellith nodded. "All right. I'll see you around then." They dipped their head respectfully, the first time anyone had done it without obvious disgust, and ascended the stairs.

Fae stood alone amongst the polished shelves, mind whirling as the setting sun slipped below the trees.

• • ● ⬤ ● • •

With Alysion busy with his extra isidyll training, Fae spent the next few evenings continuing his hunt for the heir. To his surprise, Mellith showed up again on the third day.

"Sorry I wasn't able to come sooner. I got roped into a project." They wore the same grey and blue tunic as before with dark leggings, but this time their hair was pulled up in a tidy looking bun.

"It's all right," said Fae, not looking up from the beaten scroll he was pursuing. This one contained information on the Greyleaf family. Apparently, Tarathiel had been the last of their line.

His stomach twinged unpleasantly. The queen had warned him and Alysion that the Brightstar line would end if Alysion did not produce an heir. Alysion had readily accepted that responsibility, proclaiming his love for Fae. Queen

Lymsia hadn't been pleased, but she had let them go at the time. Fae wasn't convinced that had been the end of it. He had a sneaking suspicion that the queen was trying to keep them apart by scheduling them (mostly Alysion) so many lessons. But he had no proof of this.

"Find anything?" Mellith asked.

Fae shook his head. "Not yet."

"Maybe we'll get lucky today." They strode off between the stacks.

Fae watched them go, wondering why they were helping him, then returned to the scroll. The writeup on Tarathiel was brief. It was little more than a short paragraph that proclaimed him a traitor for using shadow magic and letting a dragon through the wards. But it made Fae pause. As someone who couldn't use magic, was shadow magic really all that bad? Any magic could be used for nefarious purposes; it all depended on the wielder's intent. His brother had shown him that.

He sighed and rolled up the scroll, gaze drifting to the window. A dull grey autumn sky greeted him. How was his twin doing? Hopefully Gale and the dragons weren't giving him too hard of a time.

Mellith returned with an armload of scrolls and books. "Is something wrong?"

"I was just thinking of someone."

"Oh? The prince?"

He shook his head. "No, my brother. I hope he's doing okay."

"Is he here in Lyrellis?"

"No, he's away travelling. What about your family?"

"My family is in Illerias. They sent me here to study."

A handful of the young nobles Fae had seen around were from outside Lyrellis. Apparently it was a big deal to be selected to study in the royal city.

"But enough about me," Mellith continued. "We have an heir to find."

Fae wanted to know more about this elf who not only tolerated being in his presence, but had actively sought him out. Yet he couldn't bring himself to press them. Mellith was the first noble to show him any iota of respect; he didn't want to ruin it by being nosy.

He pushed aside the Greyleaf scroll and reached for a book emblazoned with a crest of two songbirds in flight: the Sunlarks.

Thump.

The Greyleaf record hit the floor.

Fae frowned. The scroll hadn't seemed that heavy when he'd grabbed it off the shelf. He picked it up and weighed it in his hand, comparing it to some of the other scrolls. Despite being smaller it *was* heavier.

"What's wrong?" Mellith looked up from their reading.

Fae unrolled it a bit, pinched the paper, and then did the same to another scroll. The Greyleaf one was thicker almost like—

"Do you sense any magic on this?" Fae held the scroll out to Mellith.

Mellith hesitantly reached out and took it. They closed their eyes, concentrating much like Alysion had done when they had been collecting the crystals. His heart panged. He missed the prince.

"I feel something," Mellith murmured. "I'm not sure what. The aura is stale."

From what he knew of Tarathiel, Fae wouldn't put it past him to have hidden something in the scroll. "The paper is thick, like two pages that have stuck together."

Mellith nodded. Fae fell silent, letting them focus.

The scroll flickered with violet light.

"Oh!" Mellith's eyes snapped open. "Shadow magic! I wasn't expecting that."

So Tarathiel *had* done something to it.

"I'll try again," said Mellith. "Shadow magic is...not something I'm used to working with."

The scroll flickered again, like it was fighting against whatever Mellith was trying to do. "Come on," they mumbled under their breath, eyes squeezed shut.

A shadow slowly peeled away from the record, then fell to the table without a sound. Mellith opened their eyes and set the Greyleaf scroll beside the dark one.

The shadow scroll slowly lightened until it was a dull brown. The paper resembled dry leaves, the sort that turned to dust when stepped on. Fae was afraid to touch it, fearing it would do just that. He gingerly picked it up and flipped it over, revealing a wax seal. The crest that had been stamped into had long been smoothed away. But that didn't matter. Fae knew in his gut that this was what he'd been looking for.

FIVE

FIIRAANIA

Though Ash had only lived a small portion of his life with his twin, he already missed Fae. He'd only just reunited with his brother—whom he'd believed dead until very recently—and they'd had less than a day together before being separated again. At least this time he knew that Fae was alive and well. And he would return once his mission to see the vorais, the leader of the dragons, was complete.

He and his two dragon companions had just passed through the Sky Peak wards back into Fiiraania, leaving their Elithar escort behind. Despite what Drath, or rather, Tarathiel, had told him, there wasn't a mob of angry dragons waiting to ambush any elves who crossed over. In fact, as far as he could tell, they were alone in the western foothills.

Sevarak, the red dragon accompanying him, knelt as he slid off her back. In Odenia she'd disguised herself as the dragon watcher named Gale and had travelled around with Fae and the prince. The silver dragon with them, Nyrvrin, who'd simply gone by Cane, was the one who had found Fae the day their parents had been murdered by Tarathiel and his followers. Cane had been hiding as a human blacksmith in the small town of Redwood near the Sylandrian border.

The two dragons had snuck through the Sky Peak wards to look for a copper dragon who had gone missing decades ago. The official story was that Tarathiel had lured the missing dragon across the border to destabilize the Sylandrian throne. Tarathiel had done many terrible things and told many lies in his time, but luring a dragon through the wards simply didn't align with his beliefs and motives. Yet the story he'd told Ash about the copper's demise was almost as hard to believe. He'd claimed that Queen Lymsia had been the culprit.

His feet hardly touched the ground before he felt auras approaching. Strong auras could only belong to one thing: dragons.

"Damn, that was quick," huffed Sevarak. "We'll pretend you're our snack. It's the only way you'll get through this."

"Snack?" He didn't have time to argue. The approaching dragons had them in their sights and were preparing to land.

The foothill they were on suddenly felt very small as three dragons touched down and folded their wings. The leader of the group, a bronze *ziiras*—a female dragon, Ash reminded himself—stared at him with blazing orange eyes. With his magical prowess Ash figured he could take her on, but their objective wasn't to get into a fight. It was quite the opposite.

The two flanking her, a small green ziiras and a gold *ziiran*—a male, kept their attention on Sevarak and Nyrvrin.

Ash was suddenly knocked to the ground. A scaley red foot pinned him there. Ruffled but unhurt, he lay still, letting Sevarak and Nyrvrin take the lead.

"What's that doing here?" asked the bronze.

Sevarak and Nyrvrin had been teaching him their tongue on the flight over. Speaking it was tricky since he wasn't a dragon, but he'd picked up a bit just by listening.

"A snack. Found him in the mountains," said Sevarak.

The bronze narrowed her eyes and lowered her head to give him a good sniff.

Ash whimpered and pretended to cower.

"Not much of a snack," replied the bronze, raising her head to study Sevarak. "Aura seems kinda strong, though."

"Eh, isn't much different from the others I ate."

Ash withheld a snort. He'd only known Gale—er, Sevarak—for a short time, but she didn't strike him as an elf-eater. Or even a human-eater.

"Snacks aside," she continued, "we're on our way to report to the vorais. Just stopped for a quick break and then we'll be on our way."

"It's been a long time since I've had any elf," said the bronze ziiras, completely ignoring Sevarak.

"I'm not in the mood to share," snapped Sevarak. "If you want one, convince the vorais to let you cross over."

The bronze bared her teeth. Clearly, the vorais didn't grant just any dragon that privilege, and with good reason.

"Won't eating elves set them against us?" she asked, switching tactics. "Surely you're smarter than that." The two dragons beside her tensed, ready to spring into action. "You should let it go."

So you can eat me instead? As if. He didn't like where this was going. Ash didn't want to be caught in the middle of a fight, especially one where some of the dragons had no qualms about eating him.

"We're not foolish enough to pick off elves that would be missed," Sevarak growled. "This one's a straggler, found it wandering alone in the mountains."

The bronze snarled. But instead of lunging like Ash thought she would, she merely signalled to her companions. "We'll be reporting you," she snarled as the three dragons turned and took to the skies.

Ash let out a breath he hadn't realized he'd been holding.

"Good riddance," Nyrvrin huffed. "Thought that was going to get nasty."

Sevarak removed her foot from Ash's back. "Braemyrin's full of nothing but hot air. She'll tell the vorais we're back but whether or not she mentions Ash is a mystery. Old Korvran'll just think she's lying to make herself seem important. They won't smell any elf on my breath!"

Ash got up and dusted himself off. He decided not to dwell on whether or not the bronze would tell the vorais since he had bigger problems to worry about. Literally. If he was going to meet the vorais he needed to blend in with the locals. And unlike Nyrvrin and Sevarak who'd had talismans to help them turn into humans, Ash only had his own magic to rely on. Turning into a dragon would be a challenging task for even the most skilled of elven sorcerers, but hopefully he could pull it off with his extra power.

Technically, some of the magic should have been Fae's but he'd unknowingly absorbed his twin's damis while they were still in the womb. Fae had been left with nothing and branded a damisri, while Ash had magic that rivalled that of the royal family. And the royals, namely the queen, weren't too happy about it.

"Right then, let's get this going!" said Sevarak. "I wonder what colour you'll be!"

Scale colour was the last thing on Ash's mind as he sat and assumed a meditative pose. Though he cared nothing for the Ancestors (what had they ever done to help him and his family?), he'd still taken his role as isidyll seriously. Cultivating his magical prowess had been one of them.

Closing his eyes, he focused on calming his mind. His dragon companions seemed to catch on because they kept quiet. Entering a trance-like state, he pictured himself transforming: his hands growing talons, wings sprouting from his back, his clothes and skin hardening and taking on a gem-like sheen. He delved into his magic, letting it flow through his body. Aura flooded all his senses, obliterating everything. If anything was changing, he couldn't feel a thing.

Then, from somewhere far away, he heard a snort. The flow of magic faded, and sensation returned to him. His body felt heavy, but that wasn't usual after meditating. Slowly, he opened his eyes, both nervous and excited to see if he'd been successful. Everything was red. Confused, he lifted his head, but it was only Sevarak, her large snout right in his face.

"D-did it work?" he croaked.

"Humph, see for yourself," she said, thwacking him with her tail. It should have sent him sprawling, but instead it thumped harmlessly against his side.

Ash scrambled up, clumsy and awkward like a new-born uhaan. His new wings threw him off balance, and he had no idea what to do with his tail. It took a moment to get control of his limbs and steady himself.

Raising one of his front feet, he examined his scales.

"White? Don't see that colour around here," said Sevarak. "Usually the ice dragons to the north are white."

"He's not completely white," said Nyrvrin. "Look."

As Ash moved his scales reflected different colours, sometimes blue, sometimes pink.

"Great, he's a giant pearl," snorted Sevarak. "So much for being discreet!"

"Quit being dramatic," huffed Nyrvrin. "No one will notice. There are other white dragons around."

"Not many," she muttered.

Ash was too busy examining his new form to pay them much attention. He was smaller than either of them, but they were at least a few centuries older than he was. They'd both survived the Syl-Raanian War.

"At least he managed to shift his aura. Feels dragon," said Sevarak. "Hey Ash, try breathin' fire!"

Ash looked up at her, clueing in that she was no longer speaking Illithen. Good, the language spell he'd woven into the transformation had worked, too. He wouldn't get anywhere with only a rudimentary understanding of their tongue. "How do I do that?"

"Don't worry about it right now," said Nyrvrin, shoving Sevarak. "We need to move. The residual aura from your transformation is going to attract unwanted attention. We need to get you up in the air."

Ash picked at the ground with a talon. He would rather have learned to breathe fire than to fly. With fire he wasn't in danger of plummeting out of the sky to his death. But he had no choice. Dragons flew; there was no way around it.

Walking around in his new body was an odd experience, but it paled compared to dealing with the strange appendages coming out of his back. He felt very foolish, hopping around on the ground like a rabbit while trying to get his wings to flap in sync. He beat them slowly, then quickly; one went down, and the other went up. No matter what he tried, they simply didn't want to cooperate. All he managed to do was stir up a lot of dust that had them all sneezing.

"Training him is a lot different from training a hatchling," observed Nyrvrin.

"Yeah well, we can't push him off a cliff. He's too big to catch," said Sevarak.

Ash was glad for that.

It was nearly midday before he achieved any liftoff, and by then, he was too exhausted to do anything else. In the meantime, Sevarak had gone and caught some prey. She dropped something bloody and hairy at his feet.

"Do I cook it?" he asked hesitantly.

Sevarak rolled her golden eyes. "No, you want to eat it like that. Some dragons will flame their food, but we want you to get used to eating like this first."

Ash sniffed the carcass, some sort of herbivore with silvery-blue fur and antlers. The metallic scent of blood was strong, as was the creature's own musky odour. It didn't smell as bad as he expected. Perhaps his transformation had changed more than his outward appearance.

He looked up at the two older ziiras, each pulling apart their own meal.

"We don't have all day," said Sevarak.

"Quit rushing him," huffed Nyrvrin.

"The vorais will wonder what took us so long. Braemyrin will have already alerted him to our return by the time we arrive."

"Korvran can wait."

Ash ignored their bantering and opened his jaws. The bloody scent immediately got stronger. Resisting the urge to close his eyes, he bit into the furry mess. Blood gushed into his mouth, the coppery tang not entirely unpleasant. The fur tickled his tongue, but he found that he didn't mind it. He tore off a chunk and swallowed it.

There, he'd done it. He'd had his first piece of meat and he didn't feel like gagging. He took another bite. Then another. Soon only a pile of bones remained.

Ash's full belly made him drowsy. He wanted nothing more than to curl up in the sun and sleep. *What's wrong with me?* But instead he resumed learning how to fly, determined to figure it out before nightfall.

To his delight, he managed to take to the air shortly before sunset.

Running down the hill, he suddenly sprang up and unfurled his wings. Angling them as Nyrvrin instructed, he felt air catch beneath them, filling them. He began to pump them. The ground slowly fell away. Sevarak and Nyrvrin appeared on either side of him with pointers and words of encouragement. They kept their distance, giving him space to wobble about like a baby bird. They did a lap around the hills, and by the end he'd found a rhythm.

Landing was another story. It wasn't graceful, but he considered it a success since he didn't land on his face. His companions looked pleased.

They set out at dawn the next morning, having slept tucked between the foothills. Ash was hungry—"Are dragons always this hungry?"— but Sevarak promised they would catch something along the way.

Flying, while incredibly tiring, was freeing. With his wings, he could go anywhere his heart desired. Well, anywhere that didn't involve passing through an Elven barrier. And the view was fantastic. He'd never seen the world from so high up, and couldn't help but marvel at the land far below them.

For a few days, they flew over an expansive forest fully decked out in its fiery autumnal cloak of colour and dotted with shining blue lakes. From their height Ash couldn't judge how large it was. Size and distance were very different when one could fly.

"The humans call it the Twinthorn Forest," explained Nyrvrin. "A small smattering of them call it home. There are a few logging towns—you can see the smoke there...though most avoid it. Quite a few nasty things lurk between the trees."

"Nasty if you're a human, that is," added Sevarak, making a low rumbling in her chest that Ash now knew marked amusement. "We don't have to worry about much down there."

He'd been under the impression that the dragons lived near the Sky Peak mountains, but after spending days flying over the lake-riddled forest, it was clear they kept away from the elves' wards. He didn't pick up any strong traces of aura until they were close to their destination.

"Ah, there it is!" said Sevarak, speeding up. "Been a long time since I've been back here!"

Night had just fallen. Ash strained his eyes to make out the dark smudge on the horizon. He struggled to keep pace with her, but his wings were as heavy as lead. He may have figured out the rhythm of flying, but he didn't have stamina. They'd had to stop every few hours to let him rest, prolonging their journey.

The dark streak ahead turned into a chain of rocky mountains.

"The Jagged Teeth range," said Sevarak.

"Stay close to us and try not to speak for now," said Nyrvrin. "Not all dragons are welcoming to newcomers."

"And don't mention elves," added Sevarak.

Ash nodded, his stomach starting to knot unpleasantly.

As they approached, numerous dragons rose from hiding places to surround them. Silently, the dragons guided them along. Neither Sevarak nor Nyrvrin reacted to this, which was a good sign. Yet the thought didn't calm Ash's quickening pulse. Could the dragons smell his concern? He took a deep breath, but couldn't detect anything beyond their dry, smokey scents. For such large creatures, he was surprised by how little scent they gave off. *Just like lizards.*

They wove their way into the mountains. Heads poked out of caves as they passed. Ash didn't have time to take in things properly. Their escorts were in a hurry.

They were guided to a large ledge halfway up one of the prominent peaks with a huge cave opening up behind it. Most of their escort left, but a few remained, surrounding them on the ledge. Many stared at Ash. Even with all his isidyll training, he couldn't help but fidget. Had he messed up his spell? Did he smell like an elf? Was his Elven aura noticeable?

"Ah, the brave spies return."

A sapphire blue dragon strode out of the cave, moonlight glinting off his sharp horns.

Both Sevarak and Nyrvrin tensed.

"Vyrmyris," said Sevarak, her tone making Ash's scales prickle uncomfortably. "We're here to see the vorais."

Vyrmyris' silver eyes narrowed and he flicked his tail. "Korvran is unable to see you. I will hear your reports."

Six

Unease

Vyrmyris' eyes slid to him. Ash had the strong urge to sink his teeth into the sapphire dragon's long neck. Something about the larger ziiran rubbed him the wrong way. Perhaps it was the way Sevarak had flared her nostrils when he'd appeared. Or maybe it was how he carried himself, as if he was the most important dragon around. It reminded him of Tarathiel. Ash would have to watch himself with this one.

"What do you mean Kor—the vorais can't see us?" growled Sevarak.

"He's resting," replied Vyrmyris, his lip curling in amusement.

By their expressions, it was obvious neither Nyrvrin nor Sevarak believed him.

"And who is this dragon?" he asked, his attention back on Ash.

Ash tried to look submissive but wasn't sure how to do that. He kept his head and tail low.

"Ranath," said Sevarak, using the name they'd decided for him on the flight over. After having been Ash, then Navir for so long, what was another name? Part of him was relieved to start over with a new identity. Only Nyrvrin and Sevarak knew what he'd done back home, and they weren't about to tell anyone. "He's related to me. Comes from a thunder far to the south. We met up with him on our way here."

"South? Isn't the south warm? He looks like an ice dragon."

"Yeah, we have ice dragon lineage way back," she explained. "Sometimes it shows up in our scales. Ranath here breathes fire."

To Ash's relief, Vyrmyris didn't ask for a demonstration.

"Keep an eye on him," the blue dragon warned.

"Will do!" said Sevarak, playfully whacking Ash in the side with her wing. He stumbled but managed to stay on his feet.

"Follow me," said Vyrmyris, turning and leading them to another cave nearby.

A short tunnel opened into a spacious cave large enough for all four dragons. Vyrmyris leapt up on a ledge and looked down at them, eyes little more than slits. "Your report." It wasn't a request but a demand.

"Korvran was explicit in his orders. We are only to report to him."

Now that they were away from prying eyes, the mood quickly shifted. Tension prickled in the air around them, making Ash's scales itch uncomfortably. He wouldn't be surprised if this ended in bloodshed.

"I am the *korais*, working right under the vorais, selected by Korvran himself. You will give me your report." Vyrmyris' last few words ended in a low growl.

Sevarak rolled her eyes.

"We've learned that Hammanth is no longer with us," said Nyrvrin, her tone achieving a level of neutrality.

"Dead?"

"Yes. From what we found and heard, he attacked some elves and they fought back. The fight ended with his death."

The large ziiran bared his teeth. "His death means war!"

Ash, who had been taking the cave's stalagmites and stalactites, snapped his attention back to Vyrmyris.

Nyrvrin sighed. "No, it doesn't! From what we found, Hammanth—"

"Don't tell me it wasn't unprovoked!" snapped Vyrmyris. "He was lured across the border by those scheming *thaliir*!"

Ash frowned, knowing the word was an insult but not quite understanding it.

"We won't deny he was lured," said Sevarak quickly. "We even found the one responsible for that. BUT. That elf has also passed on, killed while fighting his own people."

Ash awkwardly shifted his folded wings. Bringing up Tarathiel was like reopening a deep wound. He'd trusted Tarathiel, who had shoved a knife in his back by murdering his parents and stealing him away as a young thelim. He'd lied about the royal family being responsible for the crime, and about Fae being alive (though in Tarathiel's defence, he hadn't known that Fae had survived).

Yet despite all this, Ash still didn't believe Tarathiel had brought Hammanth through the wards.

When he and the two dragons had met with Queen Lymsia before departing for Fiiraania, she'd told them everything she knew about Hammanth's death; that Tarathiel had somehow brought the dragon through the wards and forced them to attack. She hadn't been present, but her mate, King Illuven, had fought Hammanth alongside Tarathiel. Despite that, Illuven had kept silent while the queen told their version of the event. There were a few instances where Ash had thought the king would say something, but in the end, he hadn't.

Illuven had been close to Tarathiel. If not for the royal family choosing him to become king, he and Tarathiel would have been lifelong mates. Surely, he knew the truth of what happened with Hammanth. But if he did, why was he still with the queen who had painted Tarathiel as a traitor?

The story Tarathiel had told him seemed much more plausible. It certainly explained some of Tarathiel's desire to overthrow the royal family. If Tarathiel had indeed been telling the truth, then Queen Lymsia was the one who had broken the treaties by bringing Hammanth across the border. And if word got out, war *would* be upon them.

Ash looked up at Vyrmyris, who was listening intently to Nyrvrin. Smoke curled from his nostrils, forming a sinister cloud above him. This dragon could never learn the truth. He'd only just met Vyrmyris, but there was no doubt in his mind that this dragon would do everything he could to start another war with Sylandris. He would keep the queen's secret and let Tarathiel take the fall. His heart panged. Hate and guilt for the elf who'd raised him swirled within him.

Vyrmyris snarled, showing off white teeth as long as knives. He crouched low on his perch, tail lashing from side to side. "The thaliir will pay for their crimes! They have broken their own treaties!"

Both Sevarak and Nyrvrin looked tense, as if expecting Vyrmyris to spring at them. Judging by the look on his face, he wanted nothing more than to do just that.

"That's not your decision to make," said Nyrvrin calmly. She clearly had more to say but held her tongue.

Vyrmyris growled.

"I think this discussion is over," said Sevarak. "We'll talk to the vorais tomorrow." She turned and left the cave.

"Fine, you're dismissed," the blue ziiran growled.

Ash hurried after her, not wanting to be around the grouchy korais a moment longer.

The two ziiras led him to a smaller cave the next mountain over. Twigs and rocks littered the narrow entrance, and the floor was coated in a layer of dust. The cave was large by elf standards, but with three dragons occupying it, it felt small. Thankfully, there were ledges for some of them to sleep on.

"Ah, home," said Sevarak. She took a deep breath, then suddenly sneezed. Ash jumped as fire shot from her mouth. "Needs a cleaning," she sniffled.

They quickly set to work pushing out all the debris that had blown in during their absence. Sevarak flapped her wings, creating a gust of wind that blew away most of the dust.

"That blue dragon, he doesn't like you, does he?" asked Ash as they finished tidying up.

"Nah. We've butted heads with Vyrmyris since we were young. He's spent a long time pushing for us to go to war with your—with the elves again. He's not happy with the treaties and the Sky Peak wards," explained Sevarak.

That sounded familiar. If not for the racial hate between them, Vyrmyris and Tarathiel would have gotten along well.

"Why is he unhappy with them?" Ash asked, making himself a nest out of rocks and branches on the floor. He wasn't to deprive the ziiras of their ledges.

"He believes an outdated ideology that dragons are superior to elves," said Nyrvrin, climbing onto the largest ledge.

Ash snorted.

"Exactly," said Sevarak, squeezing beside Nyrvrin on the ledge. It looked rather cramped with two full-grown dragons on it. Ash was suddenly wondering if he should climb onto a ledge in order to free up the floor for them. "As you know, near the beginning of the *Saarantivas,* the Syl-Raanian War, the vorais was killed before the situation with the death of the elf-child was resolved. The killer, a nasty beast called Zagarrin, was unhappy with the vorais' decision for the dragons to take responsibility for the child's death. Apparently, many felt this way because although Zagarrin had illegitimately taken the role of vorais, he had a lot of support. Not only did he and his supporters spread the idea that dragons are a superior species, but they believed that we should control all the lands between here and the eastern sea."

"But the dragons could freely cross the Sky Peak mountains," said Ash, frowning.

"Yes, but the lands east of the Sky Peaks have always belonged to terrestrial peoples," explained Nyrvrin. "Though we could come and go as we pleased, we didn't have any large lairs like this." She gestured with a wing to the cave-riddled mountains outside. "Zagarrin wanted full control of the lands and their people. The humans and dwarves with their limited magic didn't pose as much of a threat as the elves. It only took burning a few dwarven cities for them to flee underground. The humans at that time didn't have as many cities as they do now—just one or two little towns where the rivers forked."

"You have to remember that many dragons have a taste for terrestrial snacks," Sevarak cut in. "Though many vorais throughout the ages have tried to discourage the eating of sentient peoples, it's a temptation many can't resist."

"And Zagarrin said the dragons could eat whoever they wanted," said Ash.

"Yup," replied Sevarak. "That's what led to the kidnappings and whatnot." Ash growled.

"And that damned Vyrmyris holds Zagarrin up on a pedestal."

"But the current vorais wouldn't go for that, would he?" He picked at the ground with a claw.

"No, Korvran has no desire to break the treaties. He'd try to be friends with elves if he could."

Ash let out a breath.

"I'll never understand why he chose Vyrmyris to be korais," huffed Sevarak.

"I think it was to keep an eye on him," said Nyrvrin. "As korais, he doesn't have as much freedom to wander about and stir up trouble."

"In theory," Sevarak said. "I think it gives him more influence. It—" Her head snapped towards the cave entrance, and she let out a low growl. "Who's there?"

Ash leapt to his feet, teeth bared. Was it Vyrmyris?

The dragon at the entrance was small—too small to be the nasty korais. Sunlight glinted off their deep amethyst scales as they stepped inside, keeping their head low in submission. Ash's mind raced. Had they been listening? Were they a spy for Vyrmyris? He hadn't been discussing anything overly sensitive with Sevarak and Nyrvrin, but still...Ash didn't like spies unless they were working for him.

"What are you doing sneaking around, Xyrros?" Nyrvrin asked calmly. Sevarak stopped growling. Ash forced himself to relax.

Their yellow eyes met his for a heartbeat as they looked up at the two ziiras. Ash's gut squirmed.

"I saw you return and was curious about the newcomer. I thought maybe I could show him around since he's from the far south," said Xyrros.

"I suppose you two are around the same age," mused Sevarak. "Might not be a bad idea for Ranath here," she gestured to Ash with her snout, "to make some friends. I doubt he wants to be stuck with us all the time."

The dragon in question did not want to go off with a stranger. "I don't—" A large yawn cut him off. He was exhausted.

"Come back in the morning," said Nyrvrin.

The young dragon dipped their head and backed out, never once taking their eyes off Ash.

SEVEN

XYRROS

"**F**ollow me!"

Xyrros showed up right at the crack of dawn. Normally, Ash was used to waking up early, but his body ached all over from flying. The last thing he wanted to do was more of it.

Xyrros excitedly leapt from the mouth of the cave, their wings snapping open in a smooth, effortless motion. Ash followed suit, but his takeoff was far less graceful. As he unfurled his wings, one hit the side of the mountain. He dropped for a few heart-stopping moments before he caught the air.

"Ranath, are you all right?" Xyrros appeared beside him.

"I'm just tired from our trip." Not a lie, but not the whole truth. "And I haven't eaten yet today." Ash couldn't believe how hungry he felt; it was like his stomach was trying to devour itself. As isidyll, he'd sometimes fasted for days on end to cleanse himself and strengthen his aura. He'd never been this hungry during those times.

The amethyst dragon's face lit up. "I know a great hunting spot!"

Ash's stomach plummeted. He'd never hunted before. He didn't want them to witness his pathetic attempt—they would realize he was an elf right away.

I'll pass it off as being tired, he thought moodily as they winged their way through the mountains.

Following Xyrros proved to be a challenge. They were quick, and could skillfully dodge other dragons. On his part, Ash could hardly keep up and nearly got into a few collisions, earning him dirty looks. He didn't like how some expressions turned to confusion when they saw the colour of his scales. At least, he hoped it was his scales they were noticing and not something else.

"Wait up!" he hollered after the speeding purple blur.

Xyrros angled a wing and swung back towards him. "Ah, sorry," they said.

"I don't know my way around," Ash said stiffly, eyeing the eager *ziirar*. As with elves, dragons had three biological genders. Some species, like humans and dwarves only had two at birth—a defect in Ash's opinion. Sometimes individuals were born in the wrong body and would use magic or potions to obtain the biology that was right for them.

If Xyrros noticed his tone, they didn't show it. "We're nearly there."

They flew around a squat mountain covered in tall, straight trees, and landed in a small clearing near its base, pine needles crunching underfoot. The evergreens around them had a sharp but sweet scent. It was very different from the leaf-bearing trees that made up Sylandris' massive canopy.

"Don't we need to be up in the air to hunt?" asked Ash.

"Normally, yes, but here the trees are too close together. What we're hunting today you can't see from the sky."

Ash frowned, disliking the sound of that. Had this dragon led him here for some other reason? He squashed the urge to growl. *Sevarak and Nyrvrin trust them*, he reminded himself.

"What are we hunting?" he asked.

"You'll see," Xyrros said quietly, slipping into the trees.

Ash didn't think he would ever see. Moving around on the ground in this body was awkward. His wings bumped trees, causing needles to rain down upon him, and he kept whacking things with his tail. With how much noise he was making, every living thing on the mountain had to know they were here.

Xyrros kept casting him strange looks over their shoulder. Ash didn't blame them; he knew he looked ridiculous.

"You sure you're all right?" they asked after a third batch of needles fell on him.

Ash shook himself, flinging needles everywhere. He heard a low growl and saw Xyrros shielding themself with a wing.

"Ah, sorry."

"Wait here if you're too tired. I'll catch one for us," Xyrros offered.

"I'll come with you." Ash needed to learn to hunt whatever it was they were looking for. After all, his excuses would only hold out for so long before someone started questioning his abysmal skills.

"All right, just try to be quiet." Xyrros wove through the trees, much like the feathered tree serpents of Sylandris. Ash followed after them, mindful of where all his new limbs were.

Xyrros quickly disappeared from sight, but Ash's improved nose could follow their scent—a mix of smoke and something that reminded him of the spice of firegrass. He saw a flash of purple ahead and slowed to a stop.

Xyrros had something cornered up a tree. Ash followed the angry hissing and spotted a shape on a branch about halfway up. Before he could figure out what it was, Xyrros leapt up at it. Ash sucked in a breath as they crashed through branches, needles flying all over the place. If Xyrros felt any pain, they didn't show it. They only had a mind for one thing: clawing the rest of the way up to the large spotted cat hissing above them. Compared to a dragon, the cat looked small, but Ash knew it could easily take down an adult human, or possibly an elf, had it been one of the aura-blessed cats.

The cat took a swipe at Xyrros' snout, razor-sharp claws bouncing harmlessly off their tough scales. Xyrros opened their mouth wide. The following *crunch* made Ash's stomach churn unpleasantly.

When Xyrros dropped to the ground, the cat hung limply in their jaws. They laid it at Ash's feet.

"There you go! They're tricky to catch because of the trees, but it's well worth it. The meat is delicious."

Ash eyed the cat. He'd had no problem eating the various hooved herbivores Gale and Cane had caught him, but eating another hunter was strange. Feeling Xyrros' eyes on him, he gave it a sniff. A pungent, salty musk assailed his sensitive nose, making his eyes water. He sneezed.

"They can be a bit smelly. But go on, try it!" Xyrros urged him, eyes shining.

Ash couldn't back out now. He didn't want to disappoint them after they'd gone to all this effort. Positioning himself so he couldn't see its head, he sunk his teeth into its shoulder and tore off a bloody chunk.

Xyrros was right. It was delicious. Since the cat was all muscle, the meat was tough, but it had a rich tang he never would have expected. Ash eagerly began to devour it, not noticing that Xyrros had left until the other returned with a deer.

He quickly stepped away from what remained of the cat. "My apologies, I didn't—"

"Don't worry about it," said Xyrros. They lay down and started chomping on their catch, bones cracking between their teeth.

"You can have the rest of this. You caught it," said Ash.

Xyrros made no move to get up. "I caught it for you. Next time, you can return the favour."

After they had eaten their fill, Xyrros led him on a slow tour of the region. They pointed out other good hunting spots, caves to avoid because they contained cranky old dragons, and which rocks were the best for sunbathing. Now that his belly was full, Ash wanted nothing more than to pass out. Preferably in one of the nice, sunny spots they'd passed. The urge surprised him. Did dragons always want to nap after a large meal? Or did some of this have to do with hi s affinity for light magic?

"What do you know about the Saarantivas?" he asked as they did another lap of the region around Sevarak's cave to familiarize him with the area. He'd only ever heard about it from Tarathiel, but Ash didn't believe for a moment that Tarathiel had told him was correct—that dragons were nothing more than bloodthirsty beasts. Already, he'd seen that they weren't. Or most of them, anyway. Hopefully, Vyrmyris and Braemyrin were exceptions.

"I hatched after the war," said Xyrros. "The older dragons don't like discussing it. They don't like reopening old wounds."

"What do you mean by that?" asked Ash. He didn't like how he had to flap his wings three times for every beat of Xyrros'. Xyrros wasn't much larger than him, so hopefully his flying muscles would strengthen quickly.

"Some dragons are upset with how things ended. They don't agree with the Sky Peak wards."

But what do you think about it? Were they on Sevarak and Nyrvrin's side? Or Vyrmyris'? Vyrmyris reminded him too much of Tarathiel. If Xyrros supported him, then Ash wanted nothing more to do with this young ziirar.

Xyrros must have sensed his question. "I'm not happy about the wards. I would love to see what's on the other side, but I understand why they are necessary. Maybe one day we will be free to cross the mountains."

It was a miracle that Xyrros couldn't hear his mind working. Were they telling the truth? Ash wasn't skilled enough at reading dragon body language to tell. He would have to keep his guard up.

"Coming from the south, I suppose your family didn't participate in the war," they said.

"No, we didn't." Yes they had. His grandparents had nearly lost their lives fighting the dragons off. "I've heard stories about it but never directly from a dragon who had been there—or their descendants."

They flew around Sevarak's mountain and were met with a brilliant golden sky as the sun started to dip below the peaks, which took on a fiery hue. Ash stared, awestruck.

"Do you not have sunsets like this in the south?" Xyrros asked, slowing so they could admire the view.

Panic flared. Had he just given himself away by looking at a sunset? He took a slow breath, calming his mind just like he'd done when he used to meditate in the Sacred Hall. "There are fewer mountains and more trees where I live."

Xyrros nodded. "I'd like to see the south one day. But with how things are right now..."

Alarm shot through him. What did they mean? Were they referring to Vyrmyris, or was something else going on? Only his years of being isidyll allowed him to keep his expression neutral.

Xyrros didn't elaborate. Instead, they launched into their telling of Saarantivas. Their story, while not as detailed, matched the one Sevarak and Nyrvrin had told him.

"Defeating Zagarrin was no easy task. The elves managed to do it using powerful magic. Of course, they can't take all the credit. Our own rebels worked against him."

Powerful magic—the crystals. Supposedly, they had been created for the sole purpose of defeating Zagarrin, but Ash didn't believe that. Though his aura hadn't properly bonded with theirs, he'd gotten the impression that they were older than that. Even Tarathiel had believed that they predated the Saarantivas.

"What?" asked Xyrros, giving him a questioning look.

He'd completely spaced out.

"Ah, nothing. Who became vorais after Zagarrin?" he asked.

"Korvran."

Ash wasn't surprised to hear that.

"Korvran signed the treaties with the elves. I believe he helped cast the wards."

No wonder Vyrmyris was so angry. Had the wards been solely created by the elves, then he could understand the dragon's frustration. But the dragons had helped...

As they returned to the cave, Ash could only hope that Vyrmyris was full of nothing but hot air.

PART TWO

Unclean. Blight. Words like these had followed Calandriel throughout his first half-century of life. And now that the *Striiya*—the coming-of-age ceremony—was nearly upon him, the nobles' whispers had only gotten worse.

Have we angered the Ancestors? Why has such a child been born? And to the royal family no less...

Calandriel was born to Illyndria and Thalaniel Goldensky, Queen and King of Sylandris. As crown prince and descendant of the Ancestors, he should have been loved by their people. But they reviled him.

Unlike his mother and all the preceding Goldenskys, he did not have an affinity for light, fire magic, or even water magic. Instead, a strange darkness embraced his aura, making itself known not just in his magic but also in his unusual jet-black hair. No other elf in Sylandris had dark hair; it was not a trait the Ancestors had passed down to their people. But his hair may have been overlooked if not for his inability to use any other type of magic. And this drove him and his parents mad, for even the most low-born elf could wield each form of magic, with an affinity for one kind over the others.

The nobles believed it meant he wasn't blessed by the divine entities, that somehow, the royal family had lost the Ancestors' favour. This, understandably, put his parents on edge. If the nobles believed the royal family had fallen out of favour, they would swoop in to "restore balance" by forcing one of their heirs to join with him. It was the perfect excuse to elevate their social standing by placing one of their own in the royal family. It made Calandriel sick.

The queen and king told their people that he simply had a rare affinity for shadow magic and a strong connection to the world of dreams. But Calandriel had never been able to manipulate dreams. He wasn't able to enter and influence them as the scrolls said.

And so he spent every moment he could spare going through all the historical records he could get his hands on, looking for information about his magic. But he'd never come across a situation like his. No Goldensky like himself had ever existed. A handful of nobles had accessed the realm of dreams via the aural plane, but they could still use other forms of magic. And judging by the lack of note—for it certainly would have been marked—their hair hadn't been black.

No, the magic that Calandriel could perform was entirely different. The shadows reaching out to him didn't belong to the world of dreams.

As he learned at a young age, they belonged to the realm of death.

His first experience with his magic had occurred during his seventh suncycle. He and his parents had descended to the forest floor to see the pond that wrapped around part of the base of the tree that made up their home. They hoped that "exposing him to the Ancestors' blessed realm" would help lighten his hair.

Calandriel wasn't sure about that. His parents had already tried a few things to change his hair, and so far, none of them had worked. He didn't see how going for a stroll around the pond was going to help. Unless of course it was a magical pond. But he didn't think so. His tutor had told him that Ranwa Lake which almost completely surrounded Illerias was magical, but they hadn't mentioned anything about the water directly below his home.

Nevertheless, he was excited to leave the palace. His parents rarely let him outside, stating it wasn't good for his health. As a young thelim, he'd believed them, but as he'd approached adulthood he'd realized it had been to keep him hidden away from the nobles.

They'd hardly set foot on the forest floor before nobles flocked to his parents, nearly tripping over themselves to greet the rulers of their realm. Not a single one spared Calandriel a glance. That was fine by him. He didn't like the looks they normally shot his way. Even at such a young age he knew something was wrong. He hid behind his parents' voluminous robes—an easy task since they seemed eager to keep him out of sight as well. As the group chatted about boring things he didn't understand, something flitted across this field of vision. Curious, he followed the flapping shape away from his occupied parents.

The flying thing was small, and it was slowing down. The insect landed on a flowering bush, slowly opening and closing its black and yellow wings. It had a long, curled proboscis for drinking nectar. An *ayflit*! Calandriel had never seen a real one before, just drawings in books. He marvelled at its thin, delicate wings, like the soft pages of a book. As he observed, the ayflit curled in on itself and dropped to the ground.

"Oh no!"

Carefully he poked the ayflit, hoping it would hop right back up.

The insect didn't move.

Worried, he poked his head out of the bushes, looking for his parents. The group of nobles still surrounded them. He was alone.

As carefully as he could, he scooped up the ayflit in his tiny hands and put it back on the flower. To his dismay, it fell to the ground again.

"What's wrong?" he asked, lip starting to quiver. Why wouldn't it move? It was so pretty!

He tried putting in on the flower again, but to the same result. "Why won't you f-fly?" Tears welled up in his eyes. He picked up the ayflit and held it to his chest as he started to sob.

What was wrong with it? He just wanted it to fly!

He sat down and cried in the bushes. He didn't stop until he felt something—like someone was putting a comforting blanket around him. But when he looked up, there was no one there. Nor was there any blanket. What was going on? He sniffled. It felt like something was touching him. Maybe touching wasn't the right word; the sensation seemed like it was under his skin.

Then, something fluttered against his hands. Hands that were lined with a strange pink glow. Surprised, he dropped the ayflit. It fell into his lap, smoking faintly.

Oh no, he'd somehow burned it!

Before he could burst into tears again, the ayflit twitched.

Calandriel went still. Was it okay? Slowly the insect uncurled and rose to its feet, giving its wings a few slow flaps. Much to his surprise, it lifted off and landed back on the flower.

It was okay!

Delighted, he watched it until it flew away.

He stood up and stretched. It was probably time to return to his parents. They'd want to know all about the ayflit! He scurried back to them. They'd hardly moved, though the elves around them had changed.

"Ama, ama!" he said, tugging at his mother's flowing sleeve.

The queen blinked and looked down at him. The crowd went silent.

"What is it?" she asked.

"I saw an ayflit. It was licking a flower!"

"Was it?"

"Yes!" He hunched over like the stiff insect. "Then it did this and fell off the flower. I couldn't get it to fly, or even move. It made me sad, so I held it and cried. And then I felt something, like a...a..." he didn't know how to describe it. "Maybe like a hug?" He hugged himself and straightened up. "I looked at the ayflit, and it was aaaaall smokey! I thought it had caught fire. But then it started to move again!"

When he met his parents' eyes, neither of them was smiling. The crowd of nobles had gone deathly silent. Calandriel didn't understand.

"What—"

"I think it's time we go back inside," his mother cut in. He reached out to take one of her hands, but she clasped them behind her back instead.

It was a long time before his parents let him out of the palace again.

EIGHT

RIFT

Morning sword practice was quickly turning into the bane of Fae's existence. The nobles, led by Ornthalas, did everything they could to humiliate him. Fae found it harder and harder to resist knocking them down a few pegs. The incidents of illegal magic increased, and soon they were doing so in plain sight of Ubriel-nia while the older elf simply observed with an impassive expression. Fae tried to convince himself that it was good training, because in a real fight his opponents would be using a mix of steel and magic. Yet it didn't make him feel any better. He spent most of his time getting hit, never able to properly defend himself. Actually landing a hit on his opponent was now a far-off dream.

It didn't help that a rumour was going around that the queen was feeling unwell. It had started hardly a half-moon after the equinox, and had quickly gained traction. The nobles were quick to point their fingers at him, whispering none too quietly to each other whenever he came within earshot.

"They never should have brought him through the barrier!"

"Of course Queen Lymsia is getting sick. The damisri is polluting the air!"

He did his best to ignore it, telling himself it wasn't true. But a small part of him worried that there was a kernel of truth to their words. Was he the cause of the queen's illness? He never saw Queen Lymsia but that wasn't unusual. He never saw King Illuven either, and there were no rumours about his health going downhill. *You don't even know if the queen is ill!* Alysion would be able to tell him. He'd track the prince down after morning practice.

On the training grounds, the whispers quickly turned to loud accusations, carrying across the clearing to where older elves drilled. Fae rolled his eyes at their childish behaviour.

He took his usual battered wooden longsword off the rack and waited for Ubriel-nia to assign a partner to him.

"Haelyn-illim, you're with the damisri," Ubriel called.

A lick of anger sparked in his chest. He wasn't surprised that Ubriel-nia believed the rumours, but that she would address him as such…they all knew he wasn't reporting their actions to Alysion.

There was a grumbling amongst the group and a tall belim stepped over to him. Her hazel eyes, level with his own, openly displayed her displeasure. Fae tried not to notice the whispers as the other pairs spread out across the clearing.

He assumed a ready stance and locked eyes with his opponent. Haelyn did the same, a scowl on her face. "You are a disgrace to our people," she hissed just loud enough for him to hear.

The spark of anger he'd nearly put out flared up, hot in his veins. *Calm down*, he told himself as Haelyn sprang into action, quickly closing the distance between them. Her double-edged sword swung towards his head.

All right, if that's how it's going to be…

Fae waited until the last moment to bring his own blade up, making it seem like he was struggling.

The practice swords *thunked* loudly as they collided.

Fae held his stance as she came at him again, going for his legs since his arms were still protecting his chest and neck. Just what he wanted her to do. As she went for his knees, he leapt back at the last second, tucking his legs in to avoid the swing. The blade swished as it brushed against fabric. Had it been a real sword, it would have sliced a hole through his pants. Fae could have moved a bit sooner to avoid the cut altogether, but he didn't want to break her illusion of control. The attack left her head unprotected, but Fae still held back.

He landed and immediately had to parry a few rapid strikes, each blow a bit harder than the last.

"Are you going to fight back?" she hissed as their swords locked, her face right up in his as they struggled to overpower each other. "Or is this all you can do, damisri?"

His anger spiked. Who was she to talk? She wasn't that much younger than him, yet her skills were still rough. Fae broke away, quickly sidestepping as her blade came down. She struck at him again. "I don't see how someone like you could have possibly helped our prince at the temple," she spat. "I have no idea what he sees in you."

Something in him snapped.

Her blade came at him again. Fae easily avoided the hit. Haelyn frowned and brought her wooden sword around for another cut. Fae's own came up with lightning speed, easily knocking it aside.

As she slowly recovered, he aimed a cut at her chest, forcing her to leap back. She cleared his blade but landed very unbalanced. Her blue eyes went wide as Fae rushed in and sent her sword flying. He didn't see it land as he flicked the tip of his sword up under her chin, careful not to accidentally poke her.

"Is this better?" he asked. Damn, that felt good.

Her expression turned from shock to rage as he removed his blade and stepped back. That's when Fae noticed their patch of the clearing had gone quiet. He turned to see that all eyes were on him. No one looked pleased. His stomach twisted unpleasantly.

Ubriel-nia came to stand before him, her face oddly devoid of emotion. Fae didn't take that as a good sign.

"All of you get back to training," she snapped, her gaze on Fae. "Haelyn-illim, quit laying around and collect your sword."

There was a soft rustling sound as Haelyn did as she was told.

"I suppose I should congratulate you for your first win," Ubriel said, not sounding pleased about it. "But don't let it get to your head."

"Thank you, Ubriel-nia," Fae said, dipping his head. When he looked up, she was walking towards one of the other pairs, muttering something about luck. His stomach loosened up. But then he felt eyes boring into the back of his skull. Right, Haelyn. They hadn't been told to stop so it was time for another round.

Fae decided that it would be unwise to best her again. He caught others shooting him dark looks every now and then when Ubriel's attention was elsewhere.

He spent the rest of practice focusing on taking as little damage from Haelyn as possible. She was out for his blood; he could tell by how hard her blows were landing. Even though they used wooden swords, the weapons could still leave nasty bruises and break bones, and Fae had no desire to return to the palace in pieces.

The end of morning practice couldn't come soon enough. When it finally did, he didn't linger.

Fae changed into some fresh clothes and set out to find Alysion before he had to meet with his etiquette tutor. Etiquette lessons were by far his least favourite to attend—after sword practice, of course. His tutor was stuffy and had a voice that could put a raging dragon to sleep. Thankfully, the lessons were only every few days since the same elf tutored other families.

Fae first tried Alysion's door, but unsurprisingly, he received no response. Unbothered, he started down the hall, senses alert for any sign of the prince.

If only I had a damis, I could track his aura.

Too bad he hadn't paid attention to where any of Alysion's lessons were being held. The place was massive, and Fae wasn't even sure if Alysion was in the palatial tree.

Ugh, what a pain.

He wandered the polished wooden halls, avoiding nobles as best he could. They didn't make it easy; they swarmed all over the place like ants. Every time he turned a corner he risked running into a pair of them, if not more. Whenever that happened, he quickly walked past them, feeling their disapproving eyes burning into his back until he was out of sight. He supposed the upside was that they couldn't sense him coming, so he could duck around corners when he knew they were near.

He soon found himself in a narrow hall lined on either side with life-sized wooden statues of elves. Each was seamlessly fused to the floor, as if they had magically sprung from the wood—which he realized they had. Fae approached the one nearest him. The proud belim looked a lot like Alysion. And so did the next one. And the next. They were the Brightstar rulers of the past. In the walls between the statues there were small alcoves. Each one held an artifact. He didn't need to be able to sense aura to know they were magical.

Fae walked the length of the hall. Though he had already ruled out the cursed heir as being a Brightstar, he couldn't help but check each statue and artifact.

He reached the oldest statues, in just as pristine condition as the newer ones, but found nothing that would help him solve the mystery.

Oh well, it'd been worth a shot.

He was about to step through the far exit when voices made him pause.

"Queen Lymsia will never allow a damisri to become the sera," said a deep voice.

"That's why she's fallen ill. The damisri must be exiled from Sylandris to appease the Ancestors and regain her health," said another.

The floor jolted beneath his feet. Was the queen actually sick? Panic flitted across his chest. He needed to find Alysion *now.*

He strode quickly back down the hall of statues, resisting the urge to break into a run and put as much distance between himself and the gossiping nobles. It was bad enough that the young nobles were doing it, but the adults were too?

Caught up in his thoughts, he hardly noticed the elf striding purposefully down the hall towards him.

"Fae!"

His head snapped up, and he beheld familiar emerald eyes.

"What are you doing here?" Alysion asked curiously. He peered past Fae at the statues.

"I was looking for you," he replied.

"You won't find me in here until I'm dead," Alysion sniffed.

Fae snorted, and much of the morning's tension left his body. Simply being in Alysion's presence had a calming effect. It was a shame he was about to ruin it. "I have something to ask you. It's about your mother."

Alysion's face immediately hardened. "What about her? Has she done or said something to you?"

"No, she hasn't." But everyone else has. "I've heard rumours that she's unwell. Is that true?"

Alysion checked to make sure there was no one else around. "Yes, it's true. We haven't made a formal announcement yet, but everyone seems to know at this point. I think she's just stressed and overworked. Between keeping the influential families happy and dealing with the temple incident..."

Fae put a hand on his shoulder. He wanted nothing more than to wrap his arms around Alysion and hold him close. It had been too long since he'd even seen the prince, never mind held him. But he wouldn't risk doing that here.

Alysion, clearly unconcerned, gave him a light peck on the cheek.

Fae's face heated up. "What if someone sees?"

"What are they going to do about it? I'm the prince."

"I guess." The warmth from the kiss quickly evaporated. Clearly, the prince had no idea how his subjects treated Fae. But Fae didn't have the heart to tell him. From this close, he could see that Alysion looked strained. He didn't want to burden the prince with his silly problems when Alysion already had so much on his plate.

"I miss you," said the prince as they left the hall of statues.

"I miss you too." Fae resisted the urge to entwine his hand in Alysion's.

"Once the Eburnas has passed things will get better."

"Only if a proper isidyll is appointed," Fae countered. *And if your mother gets better.*

"We'll find one. It's one of our top priorities. The families aren't too pleased that we're currently without."

"They seem to be unhappy with a lot of things all the time."

Alysion shrugged "That's nobles for you. They're never happy."

The corners of Fae's lips quirked. "Have you spoken to your mother about my idea of visiting Ashdale?"

Alysion looked out a window and sighed. "I have. She was not open to the idea of us disappearing for a few days. Not when there is so much work to be done."

Fae's heart sank. He wasn't surprised, but a part of him had hoped the queen would relent.

"I'll try speaking with her again, and I'll make sure my father is around when I do."

"All right," said Fae, trying and failing to hide his disappointment.

"I'm sorry, I really want to go too. But speaking of going, I have to get to my next lesson. They don't like it when I'm late."

"It's fine. I have to go, too." He knew all about moody instructors.

Alysion gave him a quick kiss then took off down the hall. "I'll make more time for you, I promise," he called over his shoulder.

Fae watched him go, touching his lips as if to hold on to Alysion's fading warmth.

Nine

Ashdale

Alysion kept his face neutral as the Swiftstream family cornered him and politely presented their heir. Though they didn't outright say it, he knew choosing an auraless elf to be his sera rubbed the nobility the wrong way.

As much as he wanted to snap at them, he held his tongue. They were already upset with his family; it would do him no good to antagonize them further. He just hoped they weren't harassing Fae, though he wouldn't put it past them to do so. *But Fae hasn't mentioned anything.* Yet, it would be very much like Fae to keep it to himself. He'd ask him later. *Ugh, if I ever get to see him.*

So far, he hadn't been able to keep his promise of making more time for Fae, nor the promise about speaking to his mother about visiting Ashdale. Whenever he thought he had a spare moment, his mother was summoning him for something. But as frustrating as it was, he couldn't fault her. Her cough had worsened, keeping her in bed most of the day. It fell to him and his father to pick up the slack, adding to his already overcrowded schedule.

He didn't have time to entertain the nobles like this.

"I'm very sorry, but I must be going," he said much more calmly than he felt, dipping his head respectfully to the Swiftstreams. "We want this year's solstice celebration to be a great success to please the Ancestors."

The elves grumbled but reluctantly parted to let him by. He caught dark looks as he walked past.

Once out of sight, Alysion let out a sigh, shoulders sagging. "They're growing more persistent," he muttered under his breath. It was no secret that most believed Sylandris had fallen from the Ancestors' favour. Between the incident at the temple and his mother's illness, he couldn't really blame them. If his faith in the Ancestors hadn't been shaken up when he'd met Fae, then he would probably agree with them.

But their solution was to have him choose one of their heirs to be his sera. That was something he would never do. He loved Fae, and didn't believe for a moment that taking a different sera would solve anything. It certainly wouldn't heal his mother, whose illness even the *eranyl*, the court's most powerful healer, couldn't cure.

"The queen's illness is nothing like I've ever seen," the eranyl had said. "Something is sapping her aura but I cannot determine a cause or source." They hadn't mentioned the Ancestors but Alysion knew they'd been on the eranyl's mind.

Sensing auras in a room ahead, Alysion picked up his pace, not wanting to be delayed by more pesky families. But he slowed as he neared, hearing voices.

"The damisri is the cause. If it was thrown out of Sylandris, the queen would heal."

Alysion stopped dead, hands curling into fists.

"We've offended the Ancestors by allowing it to stay, and they're making their displeasure known. It's only time before the illness spreads to our prince."

His vision went red. They thought Fae was the cause of his mother's illness? Ridiculous! If the Ancestors didn't approve of Fae's existence, they would have gotten rid of him long ago.

"We don't need..."

The nobles were still talking but Alysion couldn't hear them. *How dare they accuse Fae!* Shaking with anger, he stepped through the door.

Two pairs of eyes snapped towards him. A mix of surprise and guilt flickered across the young nobles' faces before quickly disappearing.

"My Prince," said the one bearing the Goldbark crest, bowing.

The other bowed as well but kept silent.

"Don't ever let me catch you speaking of Fae-sera like this again," Alysion said, voice icy. "He is not the cause of my mother's illness. If I hear of this again, you will be punished."

"Of c-course, My Prince," said the Goldbark, bowing low.

His companion did the same.

"Get out of my sight."

They couldn't get away from him quick enough.

Alysion closed his eyes and leaned against the wall, taking a moment to calm his boiling blood. *I need to see Fae.* No. First, he needed to speak with his mother.

• • • ● • • •

Fae moodily tucked himself away in the library, wanting to be alone. Alysion had promised to make time for him, yet they still hadn't managed to meet up. The memory of the soft kiss from the other day did little to lighten his mood. If anything, it only made it worse.

"Will I ever get to see him?" he wondered aloud.

"Who are you talking to?"

Fae nearly fell out of his chair as Alysion stepped out from between some shelves.

"Wh-what are you doing here?"

The prince frowned. "And here I thought you'd be pleased to see me."

"Of course I am!" He sprang up and wrapped his arms around his prince.

"I bring good news and bad news," said Alysion, returning the hug. "Which do you want first?"

Fae let go and crossed his arms. "The bad."

"My mother is sending my father and I to the Great Temple to help Captain Anaril deal with the last of Tarathiel's followers."

Fae stared at him blankly.

Alysion's voice dropped. "She's not feeling well enough to go herself."

"Who's going to look after Lyrellis while you're gone?" Fae asked, voice also dropping to a near-whisper.

"She has a few trusted nobles that will help her."

"How long will you be gone for?"

"I don't know. Until Captain Anaril is satisfied with the information we get, I guess."

Fae stared at the polished wood floor. That could be a while. The captain had been at the temple since the incident. If the traitors hadn't spoken by now, Fae didn't think they ever would. He didn't see how Alysion's presence was going to help.

"But my mother's health isn't the only reason I'm going," Alysion continued. "I said I'd go in exchange for our trip to Ashdale."

Fae's head snapped up, his brown eyes meeting Alysion's emerald. "Really?"

"Yes. I argued that we would go to Ashdale before the temple. It was incredibly difficult to convince her, but my father stepped in. There's a catch—"

Fae wasn't surprised.

"Some of the Elithar will be accompanying us, and we will be going disguised as humans. It would be strange for a band of elves to show up unannounced in a human town. We don't want the Queen of Odenia to hear of it; it would raise too many questions."

"Shame the captain won't be coming with us. Can you imagine them suppressing their aura and pretending to be human?"

Alysion snorted.

"When do we leave?"

"Tomorrow. My mother wants me back as quickly as possible so I can head to the temple."

• • • ● • • •

As they emerged through the gate, the battered town of Ashdale appeared before them. Queen Lymsia had insisted that they travel by magical means in order to save time. They couldn't open a gate to Odenia within the Sylandrian wards, so they'd ridden their uhaan to the border, then opened it on the Odenian side.

"Looks like the townsfolk have made some progress cleaning up," said Fae, as they rode into town. While collecting the Fire Ruby, the volcano had erupted as a result of the crystal's influence, nearly burning himself, Alysion, and Gale to a crisp. Alysion still blamed himself for the incident.

A thick layer of cooled lava covered the north-western side of town, leaving it completely unhabitable with little that could be salvaged. Other areas had been consumed by fires, and buildings all over town had been reduced to rubble by falling rocks. Everything, even the areas that had been tidied up, was covered in a layer of choking grey ash. Even the slightest breeze disturbed it, spreading it all over.

Fae accidentally breathed in a lungful and had to sit for a few moments while he hacked it up. The group was quick to cover their mouths to shield themselves from it. Though disguised as a band of travelling human sorcerers, they had to limit the amount of magic they used to maintain their cover.

"They have..." said the prince, his expression falling at the extent of the damage.

Fae put a comforting hand on his shoulder. "Let's find Mitchy and see what they need help with."

Mitchy was Gale's friend whom they had met when they had last come through Ashdale. She'd been helping everyone evacuate until the very end. Gale had reassured both elves that she had survived the eruption. Fae suspected that she, too, was a dragon in disguise.

Mitchy's two-story house looked worse for wear. It hadn't been buried by lava or smashed by rocks, but it had clearly been burnt. Part of the blackened roof had even caved in.

"Her wards are gone," said the prince.

"Can you feel her aura?" asked Fae.

Alysion furrowed his brow. "Around here, it's stale, but she's still in town. Follow me."

They found the brown-haired, browned-eyed woman near the center of town organizing teams.

Her eyes narrowed as they approached, but she relaxed once she recognized them. "What brings you here?" she asked, stepping away from the wooden crate she'd been using as a desk.

"We're here to help clean up," said Alysion. "Since, well, you know..."

Mitchy nodded. "Glad to have the help." She peered past him at the half-dozen Elithar who had magically altered their ears and faces to appear more human. They wore talismans to help suppress their auras. "More like you?"

The prince nodded. "We're not much, but we have some magic to spare."

"Any help is appreciated," she said, giving him a small, warm smile. She grabbed a hastily-drawn map of town off the crate. "If you're willing to split up, I could use some of you here, and the rest of you here," she pointed. "You can hitch your uhaan over here for now."

"Sure thing," said the prince, who relayed orders to the Elithar. The warriors weren't pleased about splitting up, but this was what they had come there to do.

"If you don't mind me asking," said Fae, hanging back as the two groups left. "Are you like Gale and Master Cane?" It really wasn't any of his business, but his curiosity needed to know.

"Yes, I'm *like* them," she replied with an amused smile. "It's been my job to carry messages back and forth between Gale, Cane, and the vorais. Gale asked me to act as a messenger between you and your brother." She reached into her sooty apron and handed him a plain metal ring. "I have its partner. It'll flash if I have something to pass along. I don't know how well it'll work on the other side of the Sylandrian wards, but the Sky Peak wards aren't enough to thwart it. Try sending me a message once you've returned home."

Fae slid the ring onto his finger. "Thank you."

"I'm glad you dropped in. You've saved me the hassle of trying to deliver it."

They spent the entire day moving chunks of rock that were too big and heavy for non-magic users to move on their own. The townsfolk were in awe of—and grateful for—the Elithars' power, frequently pausing their own cleaning to observe. Perhaps they got some sort of satisfaction watching the rocks that had flown into town fly back out of it. Fae certainly did.

Since Fae didn't have a damis, he and Sy-Sy carted away rubble with the townsfolk. It was exhausting work but it felt good to help out. Fae only wished there was more he could do for them.

He and Sy-Sy were hauling away their final load of the evening when he overheard something that made him pause.

Two dusty women stood near the growing pile of rubble, chatting while they caught their breaths.

"Seems like the queen's ill," said one with dark hair and skin that reminded him of Gale.

"Ill? How can that be? She's got magic! That's why she's the queen," replied the fairer one.

"Could just be a seasonal cold. Fall and spring are the worst times for it. She has better things to use her magic on."

Fae's panic rose until he remembered they weren't talking about Alysion's mother. Still, it was troubling that the Queen of Odenia was unwell. He unloaded his cart and turned towards the women.

"How long has she been ill?" he asked.

They both looked at him. The fair one immediately turned red.

"About half a moon, they say," said her friend.

That was long for a cold. "Hope she gets well soon. It's not normal for Her Royal Majesty to get sick," said Fae.

"Could be she caught something only magic users can get. They'll have her sorted out soon enough!"

"True," he said, turning his cart around and heading back. "Have a good evening."

"You too!" said both women, one reply squeakier than the other.

As it turned out, the threat of keeping the group split was a great motivator for the Elithar to magically repair Mitchy's house.

"If you can fix it, you can all stay there," she told them. The warriors did not want to be separated from their prince and quickly returned it to a livable condition. Mitchy was thrilled.

Fae was pleased as well because the room he and Alysion shared had only one bed. And unlike the last visit, where he'd slept on the floor, he could squish into it beside his beloved prince this time.

"I heard something interesting today," said Fae. He nearly melted when Alysion tucked his blond head into the crook of his neck. The bed was too small for both of them. But they would make it work.

"And what was that?"

"I spoke to some women who said the Queen of Odenia is not feeling well." He played with a strand of Alysion's hair, marveling at how silver it looked in the dark.

Alysion's brow furrowed. "Really? That's...interesting."

"It's normal for humans to get sick, even their rulers. But it's lasted longer than normal, plus the timing is strange. The women said the queen can use magic, so something like a cold wouldn't be an issue."

Alysion nodded. "That is strange."

"Do you think it's somehow related to your mother's illness?"

"If what you say is true, then it's possible," said the prince. "I'll look into it when I can."

Fae felt a flutter of pride. In the past Alysion would have made some snide remark about the Odenian queen's inability to cure herself with her human magic. It was a real testament to how much the prince had grown during their travels. He gently kissed the top of Alysion's head, wishing they could do more. But he didn't want the entire house hearing them.

• • • ● • • •

"I don't want to return home," Alysion complained on their final night.

They'd only been in town for a few days, as long as Queen Lymsia would allow. Fae had hardly said more than a handful of words to the prince aside from discussing the state of the town. Cleaning up had been a bigger task than either of them had envisioned. They worked hard all day, then passed out after a quick cuddle in bed. They would be taking a gate back to Sylandris first thing tomorrow morning. It was frustrating.

"I don't want to either," said Fae, sliding into the small bed beside Alysion. "I thought we'd have more quality time together—Elithar chaperones aside."

"Mmm," replied the prince, moving to make space for him.

Fae looped an arm under Alysion and pulled him close, burying his face in the crook of the prince's neck. He could nearly hear Alysion's mind working. "What?"

"I bet I can persuade the Elithar to let us ride home," said Alysion, curling up against him. "Even if it's just as far as that awful canyon. That would give us a fair amount of time together."

"Your mother will be furious if we're late."

"My mother," Alysion huffed. "I'll deal with her."

To their delight, Alysion convinced the Elithar that his mother had allowed them to ride to the canyon. If the hardened warriors saw through the prince's lie, they showed no evidence of it. After scrounging up some provisions and saying farewell to Mitchy, they rode out of town. Once they were far enough away, the elves dropped their disguises. With Ashdale still in a state of repair, very few travellers would be coming this way.

The Elithar spread out around them. Two stuck close while the other four rode out of sight.

"How do you feel?" he asked Alysion.

"Better," said the prince. "I hadn't realized how much the destruction of Ashdale had been weighing me down." His posture was much more relaxed now compared to the stiff ride through Sylandris to the gate. "The town still has a ways to go, but it's good to know they'll be okay in the long run. From what I gathered, not many lives were lost."

"That's good," Fae nodded.

"I still feel bad about it, though."

"So do I. But like Gale said, there was nothing we could've done about the eruption. The magic was already in motion. We helped out and that's what counts. Maybe we can come back again soon."

"Maybe," said the prince. He didn't sound hopeful.

Fae took a deep breath, enjoying the crisp mountain air. The ash coating the land had started to wash away. If it wasn't gone by winter, it would disappear with the distant spring melt.

Their ride through the Sky Peak mountains was much more leisurely than last time. The Elithar weren't chasing them down, and Tarathiel's followers didn't ambush them near the foothills. The Elithar were efficient chaperones, but Fae would have gladly traded them for Gale. They were nowhere near as entertaining and only spoke to him and Alysion when spoken to. Sometimes, he swore he could feel their eyes on him, judging him for being a damisri. If not for Alysion, he knew they would leave him behind.

That aside, he enjoyed the ride. It was nice to spend quality time with the prince. They spent much of the trip complaining to each other about all their lessons, though Fae was careful not to bring up how the nobles treated him. He was not looking forward to returning to Lyrellis and dealing with their nonsense. Why did they all have to act like they were next in line for the throne?

Days passed, and they left the foothills, venturing onto the strip of open grassland separating the Sky Peak mountains from the canyon. About a day's ride in, Fae noticed that Alysion was stiff in the saddle again.

"What's wrong?" he asked, leaning over to him. Though most of their guards were nothing but pinpricks in the distance around them, he didn't want them listening in. Elves had excellent hearing by nature, more so when heightened by magic.

"Maybe it's just me, but I don't remember the canyon's aura feeling so...wrong."

Fae looked up at the dark smear across the land far ahead of them. He wasn't close enough to feel the canyon's draining influence yet, but he knew magic users were more sensitive to it.

"Maybe it feels different because you don't have the crystals?" he suggested.

Alysion frowned, thinking, before his expression relaxed. "I suspect you're right."

Fae put a hand on his shoulder. "If it makes you feel better, I don't feel anything strange or different."

"Well, you don't feel anything magical at all," said the prince absentmindedly.

"Oh?" asked Fae, removing his hand.

Panic flashed across Alysion's pretty face. "Ah, sorry, that's not what I meant!"

"I know." Fae looked back towards the canyon. "You're right. I don't feel anything, and that's a good sign."

But as they got closer, Alysion's expression became increasingly concerned. The Elithar must have sensed something, too, because they moved in close, forming a tight circle around their charges.

It wasn't long before Fae felt the canyon's depressive influence dragging his mood down, just like before.

Yet Alysion insisted that something was off and tried to convince their chaperones to let them get closer. To Fae's relief, the Elithar wouldn't have it. As the canyon slowly got closer, moods worsened. They all halted their mounts.

"It's too dangerous, My Prince. The canyon is not a place for you. It is time to open the gate," said Thalian, the belim warrior in charge of the group.

Alysion rolled his eyes when her back was turned. "We made it through last time."

"I nearly died," Fae reminded him, not wanting to relive that experience. They'd accidentally triggered some ancient magic that had caused the shadowy river in the canyon to rise. The rising mist had nearly consumed Fae, and it had caused the memory of the day his parents had been killed to resurface. The incident had also exposed his secret to his companions, that he was a damisri. Alysion had not taken the news well.

"But we all survived in the end," said the prince.

It was Fae's turn to roll his eyes.

The Elithar opened a swirling gate. Alysion begrudgingly rode through it, Fae following close behind. They appeared on the Odenian side of the Sylandrian wards. Immediately, the oppressive air disappeared. Fae took a steadying breath.

As they passed through the wards, another gate opened up before them. One of Queen Lymsia's attendants came through and asked Fae and Alysion to dismount. Fae's stomach plummeted. This didn't bode well. They handed their uhaan over to the Elithar and followed the attendant through the gate into the throne room.

Both the queen and king sat on their woven wooden thrones. King Illuven wore riding clothes and looked dishevelled, like he'd rushed to meet them. Queen Lymsia, on the other hand, looked as impeccable as ever in her voluminous silk robes. Fae never would have known she was unwell. More concerning was her icy expression. It would have made Captain Anaril proud.

"So, you've finally decided to return," she snapped. "I never would have let—" Whatever she was about to say next was lost to a bout of coughing.

Beside him, Alysion's brow furrowed.

Ten

The Ancestors

The strange scroll that Mellith had magically extracted from Tarathiel's family record lay on the table before him. Between his studies and the trip to Ashdale, Fae hadn't had a chance to read it. He'd been eager to open it, yet at the moment, he wasn't in the mood.

He leaned back in the polished wooden chair and stared out one of the tall windows. The leaves on the trees that made up Lyrellis had turned, making it seem like the city was on fire. Grey clouds blotted out the sky, reminding him that winter was on the way.

Fae rubbed his eyes.

He'd tried to convince Alysion to let him accompany them to the temple, but the prince had shaken his head. "As much as I would love for you to come, it'll be really boring. Plus you can't miss your lessons. My mother won't approve."

At the time, Fae had nodded in agreement. He didn't want to annoy the queen and give her a reason to throw him out of Sylandris. But his heart ached. Even though they'd only returned from Ashdale a few days before, he already missed his prince. Alysion was the only one who didn't make a face like they'd stepped in something smelly when he was nearby. Well, the only one save for Mellith.

Fae wondered what they were up to. He never saw the aelim anywhere save for here in the library. They didn't attend morning weapon practice, and he never heard anyone mention their name. Perhaps because they were from another city, they were being mentored elsewhere.

"Hey there!"

Fae sat up.

Mellith was striding towards him. As usual, he couldn't see a family crest anywhere on their outfit.

"Oh, are you reading the scroll?" they asked.

"I was just about to."

A ray of sunlight pierced through the clouds, brightening the room.

"Mind if I join you?"

"Go ahead."

Mellith sat in a vacant chair. "Is something wrong?"

"Ah, no. I'm fine." His mood must have crept into his voice.

"I thought you'd be buried in that scroll by now. You were so eager to learn about this heir," they said.

"I think I'm just tired. It's been very...hectic around here lately."

Mellith gave him a look, then nodded. They weren't convinced.

"What do you know about the Ancestors?" Fae asked. He wanted—no *needed*—to know their stance.

Mellith blinked. "The Ancestors? Is there something specific you want to know?"

"Not exactly. I've just noticed that not all elves have the same..." he searched for the right word, "...knowledge about them."

"Ah, I suppose it's because you hear about them from the prince who has a biased view."

"Sort of." Alysion rarely spoke about the Ancestors and when he did, it usually wasn't in the reverent tones one would expect from their descendant. Fae knew it was because of him. His existence as an elf without a damis had shaken Alysion's faith in them to the point where he was starting to question their very existence. Fae wasn't sure if that was a good thing, but so far, the Ancestors hadn't done anything to reprimand Alysion. And they'd allowed his own continued existence even without their divine gift of magic.

Unless his presence really was the cause of the queen's illness.

Mellith crossed their arms, looking pensive. "Keep in mind that I come from another city."

"Of course."

Mellith looked around then leaned forward, their voice dropping to almost a whisper. "To start, a handful of us don't believe that the Ancestors are the creators of our people."

Oh? Interesting. He raised a brow, questions flooding his mind, but nodded for them to continue.

"Now, that's not to say that they're not the oldest recorded forebearers of the Brightstar family. But some—and they keep very quiet about this—don't think they are actually deities at all. Powerful sorcerers for sure, but not higher beings."

Fae nodded. "I don't think that would go over very well with most of Sylandris' population." Saying things like that would be the fastest way to ostracize yourself.

He wanted to ask if Mellith personally shared that belief, but refrained, as their expression betrayed nothing. They'd put themselves out on a limb by telling him this, and he didn't want to push it and ruin their trust. Part of him was flattered that they felt they could share this secret with him.

But of course they can tell me; I'm the elf who's the least likely to tell anyone else. I'm already hated by most of the kingdom.

"But if they don't believe the Ancestors are divine forebearers of our people, then who is?" he asked quietly.

"They don't believe any god or higher being created us. They aren't too sure where we came from."

"But we came from somewhere," Fae said. "We didn't just pop out of nothing—neither did our damai."

Mellith shrugged. "That's just what they think."

Fae leaned back and sat in silence, trying to make sense of what he'd just learned. If this were true. it would completely upset Sylandrian society. He couldn't fathom the implications of that.

But a thought did occur to him.

"Back home," Fae started, "there aren't any elves like me, are there?"

Mellith's expression fell. "No, there aren't."

He wasn't surprised, but he still felt a pang of disappointment. It wasn't as though Mellith came from another kingdom. Illerias and all of Sylandris were under the rule of the Brightstars. No one there would tolerate a damisri like himself.

"So then, if the Ancestors don't—" Fae's words died when he heard the soft swishing of fabric in a nearby aisle.

He and Mellith exchanged a panicked look.

One of the assistant librarians poked his head around the corner. When he caught sight of Fae, he gave him a dark look, then left without a word.

Fae ignored it, too caught up in what he'd just learned. Elves that didn't hold the Ancestors above all else? He had to know more about them. Perhaps he'd find something about it here in the library. There had to be a section somewhere on heretical practices. *I might learn something about the heir there, too.*

"Oh shoot, I need to go," said Mellith, standing up. "Forgot I need to meet with a tutor."

"That's all right."

"You get on that scroll and let me know what you find!" they said, hurrying down the aisle.

Fae unfurled the battered scroll in front of him and read the first line.

I was born to Illyndria and Thalaniel Goldensky, Queen and King of Sylandris.

Fae blinked. What? Goldensky? He must have read that wrong. He skimmed the line again. The name Goldensky didn't change. He sat back, stunned. The royal family hadn't always been the Brightstars? How was that possible?

"I thought they were direct descendants of the Ancestors..." he mumbled aloud. Had the royal family simply decided to change their name one day, or had something else happened...was there credibility in what Mellith had told him about the Ancestors?

He read the next few lines, needing an explanation but the scroll didn't elaborate on that subject. Instead, it delved into the individual's—Calandriel's—experience with a strange form of magic.

Fae's skin prickled uneasily as he learned about the death of an ayflit and its subsequent revival. Magic that could bring back the dead? Impossible. This had to be a work of fiction—that would certainly explain the name Goldensky. But then why would Tarathiel have gone to such lengths to hide the document?

As he made his way through the scroll, Fae felt a sort of kinship with the prince forming. As a damisri, his parents had kept him hidden away from the rest of society. In his case, his parents feared someone would try to harm him.

Calandriel, on the other hand, had been hidden because the royals thought his existence was angering the Ancestors. It certainly angered the nobles, much like Fae's presence was now.

He set down the scroll and took a few breaths, not realizing how tense he'd gotten. It was eerie how similar his situation was to Calandriel's. They were both seen as blights upon society due to something beyond their control. The prince hadn't chosen to have a strange magic, just like Fae hadn't chosen to be a damisri. In his case, it had been an accident; Ash had unknowingly absorbed all his aura while they'd been in the womb.

Clearing his mind, Fae resumed reading. It ended with small Calandriel being taken back inside. He frowned. That couldn't be all of it, he had so many questions. Fae turned the scroll over, expecting more, but found nothing.

I'll ask Mellith to check it again. Maybe it hadn't given up all its secrets. He needed to know more about this strange magic. It certainly wasn't shadow magic. Alysion had experienced first hand what shadow magic could do while they'd been searching for the crystals. He'd been dragged into the realm of dreams and memories by the Shadow Amethyst on a few occasions. But never had they encountered anyone reviving the dead. The spirits in the Canyon of Lost Souls were the closest thing that came to mind, but they'd been mere spectres, not living flesh.

No, Calandriel's magic was something else entirely.

Well, I've certainly found the cursed heir.

• • ● ● ● • •

A few days later, a thin layer of snow fell, coating the city. Normally, Fae would be making his way down to the clearing for his daily sword beating, but instead he was sullenly leaving the throne room. He'd gone to see Alysion and King Illuven off as they left for the Great Temple. It had taken everything he had not to follow them through the gate.

He desperately wished Alysion hadn't gone. He wanted to talk to the prince about what Mellith had told him and what he'd read in the old scroll. Talking to Mellith was helpful, they were ecstatic about his discovery and had lots of ideas and theories, but it just wasn't the same.

It didn't help that the nobles were more openly gossiping about their relationship. They claimed the prince was growing bored of him, and that's why Alysion never had time for him. Fae knew it wasn't true, but it did little to lessen the sting.

If only I could go with them... But the queen had forbidden it. Besides, he'd only get in their way. What help could an auraless elf be in a temple full of traitorous sorcerers?

Not feeling like doing anything, he returned to his room. He was about to flop onto his massive bed when the ring Mitchy had given him flashed. Two letters materialized in front of him.

A spark flared in his chest as he snatched them out of the air. One was from Mitchy, chastising him for not immediately sending her a message like he'd promised. Her tone reminded him so much of Gale. The other was from Ash, and Fae eagerly ripped open his brother's letter and devoured its contents.

The writing matched Mitchy's letter, as if Ash had dictated his words to her. *Well, it would be difficult for a dragon to hold a pen.* Ash seemed to be doing fine, which was more than Fae had expected, considering everything his twin had gone through. Gale and Cane had taken to him right away, which was unsurprising, but still a relief. They'd made it safely into Fiiraania, and so far, none of the dragons suspected that Ash was an elf—not even the young dragon showing him around. Unfortunately, they hadn't met with Korvran, the vorais yet, but they'd spoken with the korais, Vyrmyris, who was second in command. Ash's writing gave the impression that Vyrmyris was a dragon to be wary of, but he didn't say why in case the message was intercepted.

Rejuvenated by the letter, Fae sat at the desk and started one of his own.

He wrote about the nobles and their petty dramas, how his lessons were going, and how he rarely saw the prince. He mulled over whether or not to include anything about the queen's mysterious illness since that information could be very dangerous in the wrong hands. *But two queens are ill...*

Frowning, he finished the letter to Ash, leaving out the queens' illnesses for now. He hastily scrawled another for Mitchy, inquiring about the Odenian monarch's health. Perhaps the dragon in disguise could shed some light on the strange illnesses affecting the two rulers.

ELEVEN

CROUCHING CATS

Ranath and Xyrros flew side by side, looking for their first meal of the day. Having to hunt for food constantly was a chore. While living at the temple, Ranath had never had to worry about where his next meal was coming from. Now, he had to work to eat, and his dragon body demanded food more frequently than he liked.

At least I don't have to worry about cooking it.

Having to hunt all the time meant he learned quickly, and Xyrros was a good teacher. He'd told his companion that he wasn't used to hunting northern prey, so he struggled to keep up—which technically wasn't a lie. Xyrros easily accepted it and enthusiastically took it upon themself to teach him how to catch everything edible in the mountains. The spotted wildcats were tricky, but Ranath's scales protected him from their sharp teeth and claws. Birds were the hardest to catch since they were small and agile. Flaming them with his breath was tempting, but that often resulted in an inedible, charred mass.

"We only eat birds if there's nothing else around," Xyrros said. "Notice how there aren't many large birds in these mountains. We've scared them off."

Carrion birds were abundant, but he was advised against hunting them.

"They cleanup whatever we don't eat," Xyrros explained as they winged around a mountain. "By doing so they prevent illness from infecting other prey. Sometimes, you'll see them pecking around in a dragon's cave if the owner prefers to eat their kills at home. But they also defecate on themselves. Something about keeping their bodies cool."

Ranath snorted in disgust. He'd eat his meals far from the cave.

They angled their wings and landed on the rocky side of a mountain. Each day, his flying muscles grew stronger, and he felt more at home in his new body.

Ranath lifted his head and scented the air, the dry smell of rock filling his nostrils. But there was something else mixed in. And that something went beyond his sense of smell: the faint trace of magic.

Lyngrax were a species of silver-furred feline that lived above the treeline, preferring the cooler temperatures and exposed rock, but would creep lower if they were hungry. Unlike their spotted cousins who lived lower down, these cats were much more intelligent and could use magic. They were also tastier, as Ranath discovered when Sevarak brought one home for him.

"I don't normally hunt lyngrax," said Xyrros. "Between the colour of their pelts and their magic, they essentially melt into their surroundings, becoming invisible."

"Invisible but still solid," said Ranath.

"True. Sight won't be of too much use. You have to hunt them by smell and aura."

They spent a portion of the morning seeking out the lyngrax. Xyrros was right—tracking them was difficult. Even when Ranath managed to pick up a scent trail, the cat kept ahead of him, using its knowledge of the rocky terrain. He had to admit defeat when its scent disappeared into a narrow crack in the rock that his scaly bulk wouldn't fit through. But Xyrros soon found them another to follow.

The lyngrax did not go down easily. Ranath suspected their eventual success was because there were two of them and only one of it. The cat's ability to blend into the environment was impressive, and he couldn't see it even as it moved. It was also smart enough not to attack their scale-covered hides. Instead, razor-sharp claws nicked the soft membrane of one of his wings. He was shocked by how much the tiny tear burned. *Magic*, he surmised.

They settled on a sunny patch of rock to enjoy their hard-earned meal. It had been well worth the effort.

"What's life like down south?" Xyrros asked once they'd filled their bellies. They lazily licked their talons clean.

Ranath, gnawing on a bone to clean his teeth, didn't reply right away. He'd never been to the southern regions. "Well, there are fewer mountains and more trees," he said, trying to recall an old map he once saw. "It's also warmer. Even further south, there's a desert, but I haven't visited it."

"And most of your family is there?"

"What remains of it."

"Ah, sorry," Xyrros said quietly.

"It's fine. Our parents are gone, but my nest-mate is still alive."

"Are you close?"

The question was rather personal, but Ranath found that he didn't mind. He got up and stretched.

"Not as close as I would like. We were separated when we were young and only recently reunited. Then I came here." He missed Fae more than he expected. For many suncycles he'd believed his twin to be dead. They'd hardly had a day together before he'd left with Sevarak and Nyrvrin for Fiiraania at the elf queen's orders. He wanted to get to know Fae again. Aside from his hair, which had been blond when they were young, how much had he changed? What had stayed the same? They'd been young thelim when Tarathiel had attacked. His mood soured.

Home.

What was home? He'd spent most of his life at the Great Temple, pretending to be the spiritual leader of Sylandris. When he returned, he'd have no place to go. *I suppose I could find our family home.* But would Fae join him? He suspected not. Fae was with the crown prince of all people. He frowned, worrying his claws in the dirt.

Fae had no damis. How did the court react to that? Hopefully, they weren't being too hard on him. Being a dragon was a lot simpler. Sure, there were some squabbles, but usually over things like food or sunny rocks, none of the mind-play he'd witnessed between the ayel or the court nobles. Usually, a dragon's biggest concern was whether or not they'd eaten enough, not how much they could raise their social status. Vyrmyris was an exception. A potentially dangerous exception.

Xyrros nodded. "That's unfortunate. Were you close to anyone else down there?" Their silver eyes gleamed in a way that had him shifting awkwardly. It was a if they were trying to peer into the very essence of his being.

No one needs to see that.

"Not really," Ranath said. Being isidyll meant that everyone had kept a respectful distance from him. He'd never had any friends at the temple. Though Tarathiel had overseen most of his development and training, he'd never truly considered him as a parent.

And good thing I didn't, he thought bitterly. Tarathiel's betrayal still hung over him like a dark cloud.

Xyrros began to clean their teeth with a talon, making the deep rumbling sound in their chest that meant a dragon was content. Ranath had never made that sound, but Sevarak and Nyrvrin made it frequently when they were together.

The two of them sunbathed for a bit longer before Xyrros stood up. They stretched, muscles flexing, before dropping into a crouch. "All right," they said. "Let's see what you can do."

Ranath stared at them, noticing how the sunlight reflected off their deep amethyst scales. It dazzled him. "What do you mean?" he said, meeting their eyes. His stomach fluttered. Had the meat upset it?

"I want to see your moves! How you fight."

What? He forgot about his stomach. "I don't—"

"Of course you do. Come on." They flexed their talons.

Ranath had extensively trained in magic but only a little bit with with steel. "Just in case," Tarathiel had said. He'd never physically fought anyone before. Not like this.

"Are you sure?" he eyed their talons and fangs. "Someone could get seriously injured." And that didn't include adding fire to the mix.

"It'll be fine. I trust you."

A jolt shot through him. Xyrros trusted him? Why? He was a stranger from a strange land, hiding secrets that would jeopardize his life. Ranath didn't trust them, and he swore he never would. Trusting others only ended in pain.

"I still don't think this is a good idea," he said, slowly rising to his feet.

"We'll stay on the ground for now."

He blinked. Why would—of course. Dragons usually fought in the sky. "On the ground will do." He copied Xyrros' crouch, suddenly very aware of his body. Already a moon had passed since he'd assumed this new form. He'd mostly gotten used to it by now, but on the odd occasion he forgot where his tail or wings were.

Xyrros slunk around him like the cats they hunted, their body low. Ranath stayed in place, keeping a close eye on them. He watched their movements, looking for some sign that they were about to pounce. When the large felines attacked, their leg muscles tightened as they gathered power for the leap. So Ranath tried to focus on their legs, but Xyrros started pacing back and forth in front of him, not getting any closer. What were they doing?

"Come on. Come get me!"

Ranath narrowed his eyes, tail lashing from side to side. He waited until they were in the right spot, then leapt towards them with all the power he could muster. Talons outstretched, he hit nothing but air. Landing awkwardly, he whipped around, looking for his target.

"Not bad, but you're too slow," said Xyrros beside him.

Ranath huffed. How had he missed? He'd timed it perfectly with their movements! "What can I do better?" he asked stiffly, irked by his failure. At the temple, failure had never been an option.

"Copy what I do."

They crouched beside him; he mimicked their form.

"Keep your tail still. Unless you're using it as a distraction or for balance, you're just wasting energy."

He hadn't realized it was moving.

"Tuck your wings in more. I think they're slowing you down."

He doubted that but kept his comments to himself.

Xyrros straightened and studied him closely. Ranath held his position, pulse quickening as their eyes roamed over him. He felt oddly exposed.

"That looks better," they said. "Let's try again." Xyrros went back to stalking in front of him.

Pushing the strange uneasiness away, he sprang again. His front claws hit something, but that was all. He wasn't sure what he'd touched. Landing much more gracefully, he turned to Xyrros. They flicked a wing at him.

"Much better! Maybe practicing on a full stomach was our mistake."

"Perhaps," he replied, forcing his lip not to curl in frustration. He would have to practice his fighting skills alone. He couldn't allow this to happen again in front of Xyrros. Maybe he'd ask the ziiras to train him.

"Let's do this again tomorrow. Before we eat."

Oh. He wouldn't be ready by then. He opened his mouth to decline, but at the sight of Xyrros' eager expression, the words died on his lips. "Sure. Maybe we can make a routine out of it." Ugh! What was he saying?

Xyrros bared their teeth in excitement. "A good plan! We should head back now before we're missed."

The two of them unfurled their wings and took to the skies.

Twelve

The Secret

During the flight back to the caves, Ranath's mind drifted, eventually settling on Fae and his lack of damis. The library at the Great Temple had been extensive, and as isidyll, he'd had access to the restricted levels. But he'd never come across anything like Fae's situation. Yet Tarathiel had been knowledgeable about it. *He must have removed that information from the library so I wouldn't find it.*

Tarathiel had revealed that Fae didn't have a damis because while in the womb, Ranath had absorbed it, taking all their magic for himself. His stomach twisted with guilt. *There has to be something I can do for him.* Yet in all his decades at the temple, he'd never encountered anything about *creating* a damis—all elves were born with them. Even non-elves who could use magic had their aural cores from birth.

"Xyrros," he called over the sound of rushing air. "Have there ever been any instances of a dragon being unable to use magic?"

Xyrros furrowed their bony brow. "Not unless it's the effect of a curse or the result of great harm," they said.

Not the answer he was hoping for, but Ranath wasn't surprised.

"Did any of them ever regain their abilities?"

"If the curse is lifted they can. But if the loss is due to injury, then I don't believe so." They gave him a curious look. "Why?"

"I was just thinking about a dragon back home. I wondered if any dragons here might know something that could help them."

"One of the elders might know, or possibly the vorais," they said. "Korvran's technically not an elder yet but it's his job to keep an eye on everyone. He's been vorais for a long time."

Not an elder yet? But Korvran had been alive during the Saarantivas which took place centuries ago! How old did a dragon have to be to be granted that title?

Ranath nodded. "Thank you." He didn't expect to gain an audience with Korvran for something like this. Sevarak and Nyrvrin still hadn't been able to meet with the vorais, and their needs were much more important than his. Every time they tried, Vyrmyris shooed them away. It was making the two ziiras very grouchy. He would have better luck asking someone else. But that was a project for tomorrow.

Ranath said goodbye to Xyrros and returned to the cave. There was an unfamiliar scent around the entrance, but no one was inside, not even Sevarak or Nyrvrin. The two older dragons were likely out hunting.

Ranath used the opportunity to experiment with his draconic magic, enjoying the challenge of remastering his own aura. He was learning a lot about dragons, and himself, in the process.

Calling forth magic from his damis was the same, but it didn't always behave how he wanted. It was like he was a thelim again, his magic doing whatever it pleased.

Once, when he was very young, he'd accidentally set their tree on fire. It had taken Ama and Dada a long time to convince him it had been an accident and that he shouldn't fear his abilities. Fae's unwavering confidence in him had really helped lift his spirits. Back then, he didn't know he carried the power of two damai.

"Ranath, come quickly!"

Recognizing Sevarak's voice and scent, he hurried out of the cave.

"What's going on?" he asked.

All around them, dragons took to the air.

"Vyrmyris has an announcement to make," she said stiffly.

That couldn't be good.

They joined the throng heading for Korvran's cave.

When they arrived, dragons had already landed on the rock-strewn ground below it. Sevarak found Nyrvrin and the three of them landed in an empty spot near the front that seemed to have been held for them. With the changing moons, Ranath had come to realize that Sevarak and Nyrvrin were important dragons, and being spies in Sylandris had only raised their popularity amongst most of the thunder. But there were a few—Vyrmyris' followers Ranath guessed—who gave them dark looks whenever they flew by.

A rocky ledge protruded from the entrance to the vorais' cave; on it stood Vyrmyris. Ranath immediately tensed. He flexed his talons, digging them into the ground. The way the korais held himself, despite the extra limbs and scales, reminded him of Tarathiel. Even his expression was similar.

Vyrmyris flicked his wings and the crowd grew silent.

"I have called you all here on our dear vorais' behalf."

Sevarak made a low sound, as if she was suppressing a snort. Vyrmyris, up on the ledge, didn't hear it. The blue dragon's silver eyes gleamed as his gaze swept over the crowd.

"Korvran is ill."

He paused as shocked murmurs rippled across the gathering.

"While I do not doubt he will recover, he cannot properly lead us at this time. As korais, it is my duty to take charge. Effective immediately, I will be leading the thunder until Korvran has recovered."

A few dragons roared their approval, the noise bouncing off the mountains, making it sound as if many more had joined in. Braemyrin, the bronze ziiras they'd encountered when they'd come through the Sky Peak wards, was the loudest.

But a quick look around showed that many more were in shock. Beside Ranath, both Sevarak and Nyrvrin had gone still as statues. His heart began to beat faster. He narrowed his eyes and studied the korais' face, but like Tarathiel's, it betrayed nothing.

What are you planning?

• • • • • • •

"Though he says he's in charge, he still can't do anything drastic without Korvran's approval," said Nyrvrin once they had returned to their cave. She had cast a spell to prevent anyone from eavesdropping—including Xyrros as they were prone to wandering in.

"Still, he's going to take the opportunity to further his goals," said Sevarak, who paced angrily about. "If he can persuade enough dragons, it won't matter that Korvran is vorais. He'll have enough power to do whatever he wants."

"Which is to go to war with the elves," said Ranath, curled up in his nest.

Both ziiras' expressions softened as they looked at him.

"Yeah..." said Sevarak, stopping in her tracks.

"We won't let that happen," said Nyrvrin.

"He doesn't have a good enough reason to. Most of us have accepted the terms of the Saarantivas."

"But with your report, he might," Ranath said.

"How so?" asked Nyrvrin. "There's nothing in our report that would provoke a war. The elf at fault has been—" she paused, "dealt with."

Ranath shifted uncomfortably, but not at the mention of Tarathiel's suicide. Already they'd seen Vyrmyris using the cause of Hammanth's death to stir up trouble.

"Your report isn't accurate," Ranath said slowly.

"What do you mean?" asked Nyrvrin. Her tone was calm, but her wings twitched.

"Are you suggesting the Queen of Sylandris lied to us?" Sevarak huffed.

"Not just to you," he said quietly, "but to all of her people."

"What do you know?" Nyrvrin asked cautiously.

Ranath reached out with his aura and tested the enchantment on the cave to ensure no one could hear. He sensed auras outside, but none seemed close.

"While Tarathiel was the one who killed your friend, he wasn't the elf who brought him across the border," he said quietly.

Both ziiras stared at him with the force of a storm. If he hadn't known them so well, it would have been unsettling. He picked at the rocky floor with a claw.

"You can't tell anyone. If you do..."

They nodded.

"Queen Lymsia was the one who brought Hammanth through the wards."

The colour drained from the older dragons' faces.

"Don't ever say that around here again," said Sevarak, gold eyes darting around as if Vyrmyris was about to materialize in the cave. "If anyone got wind of that…"

"War would be upon us," finished Ranath.

PART THREE

B y his second decade, Calandriel had figured out what had happened to the ayflit that fateful day. The insect had died, for they only lived a few short days, but his magic had restored its life. Once he'd pieced that together, he started doing experiments.

He hid away in the lowest level of the Sylandrian library where the oldest records of their people were kept. No one ever went down there save for the library staff. And that wasn't a frequent occurrence.

Calandriel started with small things: insects, a potted plant that had completely shrivelled up. He touched the dead and shut his eyes. Reaching into his damis, he called forth the soothing energy. It covered him like a blanket, enveloping him and whatever he held. He didn't need to see to know that his hands and the dead were both outlined in a faint pink light, that a misty vapour rolled off him. He kept his eyes shut until he felt the fluttering of life—the soft touch of a leaf, the twitching of tiny limbs.

Once he was confident in his abilities (he kept a few bugs around to monitor to see if there were any side effects), he moved on to larger creatures like birds and lizards. Lizards were easy, but birds proved to be a bit trickier. Not because they were hard to restore, but because they immediately took off and zoomed around the library, screeching in a panic. More than once, he'd nearly been caught when a librarian came down to investigate all the noise.

Regardless, he developed a fondness for birds. Corvids were his favourite—they reminded him of himself. Plus, they were usually the calmest when they woke from their not-so-eternal sleep. And a lot of them ate dead things, which he found fascinating. There was nothing better than finding a dead crow or raven to work on.

In order to collect specimens, Calandriel snuck out of the palace once a month on the night of the new moon when the sky was at its darkest. Night didn't bother him. He could see just as clearly as if it were midday, if not better. He would collect as many intact animal corpses as he could find. Reviving animals that had been freshly killed was easier than those whose bodies had started to rot, but with enough practice, he got the hang of that, too.

One night, he specifically set out to find a skeleton. He'd never revived something so far gone and wanted to test the limits of his abilities. It took nearly the entire night, but eventually, he stumbled upon an owl pellet containing the bones of a lizard.

"I think all the bones are here," he muttered to himself, carefully dissecting the pellet and putting the bones in a spider silk bag. He snuck into the library at the first opportunity. Making sure the coast was clear, he laid the bones out on the table. After discovering what his magic could do, he'd taken it upon himself to read as many books on anatomy as he could. He wasn't sure if his magic would correctly assemble the bones and didn't want to risk it. Once satisfied they were in the correct places, he closed his eyes and touched the tiny skull.

Nothing happened. Calandriel frowned and opened his eyes. The usual pink mist surrounded his hand and the bones. His shoulders slumped. Maybe it wasn't possible to bring back an animal so far gone—a shame, but he wasn't surprised. Just as he was about to cut off the flow of magic, the bones twitched.

Calandriel immediately redoubled his efforts.

Come on, come on.

The entire skeleton began to vibrate, rattling against the wooden table. *Tap-tap-tap.*

He scrunched up his face in concentration. The pink grow rose up his arm as he drew on more of his power, darkening to red.

The skeleton rose off the table. The vapour swirling around it began to take shape, forming a tail, legs, filling out the belly and head. Before long a shadowy replica of a lizard floated in the air before him, semi-opaque dark mist clinging to the skeleton in place of flesh.

Fearing it would fall apart when he did, Calandriel removed his hand from the tiny skull, severing the magic. The lizard fell back onto the table. To his delight it began to scurry about, just like a real lizard.

Calandriel had found some old records about shadow magic users calling on the shadows to create illusions, but they hadn't mentioned anything about bones being a necessary component. And the illusions were completely controlled by the caster. While Calandriel could feel a connection to the lizard, something he hadn't noticed with the fleshy creatures he'd revived, he hadn't woven any intention into his magic. The lizard was moving of its own volition, behaving as it had in life.

"I cannot regrow lost flesh, but I can still give life." He'd never tried working with a corpse that was missing organs or a limb, not wanting the reanimated creature to suffer should things end poorly. While hoping for success with the skeleton, he hadn't been too hopeful. This result, a wispy little lizard, was beyond what he'd expected. He watched it scurry around the table, a dark little tongue poking out every now and then. It was adorable.

He put his hand on the table and urged it to climb up his arm. It did so without any hesitation. *Interesting.* He could control it if he wanted to.

The lizard was practically weightless. It rode on his shoulder, tickling his ear as he set about cleaning up. Reviving the lizard had taken more out of him than he'd expected, and he was exhausted.

As he was returning a scroll to a shelf he heard a small clatter. The invisible tether tying him to the lizard must have disappeared, and when he looked down, tiny bones were scattered around his feet. The spell hadn't been permanent. Calandriel's heart panged at the loss. He carefully picked up the bones, vowing to bury them outside later. He wouldn't try to pull the poor creature back from the void again. That would be cruel.

He returned to his chamber, mind whirling with all the possibilities today's experiment had opened up. If he kept practicing, he was sure he could make the shadow creatures last longer. Unlike flesh creatures, he suspected the shadow creatures would never have a full lifespan, since they were magically tied to him.

Perhaps that's why I'm so tired. My life energy may have been helping to sustain the lizard's.

Yes, more experiments were in order.

• • • ● • • •

The Striiya was only a few days away.

Calandriel was making his way back to his chamber for the night when he passed by his parents' room. His senses, always more acute after the sun had set, picked up their angry tones through the thick wooden door. They were arguing about him. Again.

They always fought like this; behind closed doors and in front of his face. While they pretended to like him when others were around, he knew they despised him more than anyone. His existence put their leadership—and his mother's integrity—into question.

"We cannot recognize that thing as our heir," his father hissed. "The nobles will turn on us if we do. Already we've lost their faith…"

"Of course we won't acknowledge him," his mother snapped. "I will not let him undermine our divine lineage. We will have another heir."

The hall swayed. His mother had never spoken about him like this before. Not in his presence.

"And what if the next turns out like the first?" asked his father.

"That *will not* happen. Unless you have something you need to tell me?" Queen Illyndria's voice had dropped dangerously low. Even through the door, the tension in the air was palpable.

"Of course not. You're the one who carries the Ancestors' line. Perhaps it is you who carries tainted blood—"

Smack.

"You dare?" The queen's voice dropped so low that Calandriel could hardly hear it.

His parents' words were knives to the heart. Though they had never shown him any genuine affection, he had always done his best to please them. He'd always suspected he'd never ascend to the throne but imagined it was due to his parents giving in to the nobles' demands. Calandriel hadn't realized just how much they hated him. And each other. His existence had driven an irreparable wedge between them.

"Simply revoking his right to the throne won't be enough," said the king, pulling the conversation back to safe ground. "Everyone is demanding his banishment."

Calandriel's stomach hit the floor.

Banishment? Only those who had committed the most heinous of crimes were banished! Faint wisps began to roll off him.

"The Ancestors have been so silent...even the isidyll claims they can no longer commune with them," mused Queen Illyndria. "We must eliminate the shadow that darkens our land in order to regain their favour."

Calandriel grasped his head, taking sharp breaths. The mist thickened, quickly filling the hall.

"*Silias* and banishment may not be enough to appease them," said the king. "We are the royal family; the Ancestors' bloodline must be kept clean."

Calandriel's blood turned to ice. No, they wouldn't—they couldn't!

"What's—?"

Bang!

The door to the room flew open. There stood his parents, their eyes taking in the shadowy mist choking the hall before settling on him. Their cold expressions confirmed everything he'd overheard. They were going to kill him.

"I—" The words died on his lips as a beam of gold light shot towards him like an arrow. He threw himself to the side as the spell whizzed past, piercing through the rolling mist. Pale eyes wide, he looked at his parents. Their expressions remained unchanged as they both sent bright spells streaking towards him.

Instinctively, he threw up his hand. The mist swirled around him like a twister, deflecting the magic and sending it shooting down the hall. A loud *boom* resounded as the spells hit the far wall.

When the mist settled, a large bird made of his father's signature white-hot fire dived towards him, talons extended, beak open in a piercing cry. He threw a bone into the air and conjured a shadowy bird of his own. He didn't get to see them collide with loud, hair-curling screeches, for golden arrows were streaking towards him. Calandriel leapt out of the way, letting out a pained cry that rivalled the birds' as one pierced his shoulder, sharper than any metal. He clutched at the wound as the arrow flickered into nothingness, leaving behind a terrible burning pain.

But his parents weren't about to allow him to nurse his injury.

He called on the shadows and plunged the hall into complete darkness.

"You will not escape your fate!" his father hissed from somewhere beside him. The king made no attempt to hide the disdain in his voice.

There was another loud screech and his bird exploded. The bone clattered to the ground, broken in two.

Anger suddenly flared up inside him. "My fate? How is this my fate?" he spat back. It was the first time he'd spoken against his parents. "This is not my fate!"

Scorching heat blasted past him, missing him by a hair's breadth. He needed to keep quiet if he didn't want his parents to find him.

"You never should have been born! Your existence is a dark stain upon our people!"

His mother's words only fanned the flames of his anger. He'd spent his entire life trying to please his parents, but his efforts had been in vain. All it had done was delay the inevitable: they despised him and would stop at nothing to be rid of him. Permanently.

A blinding flash of light blasted away the shadows. Squinting, he made out the form of his father's bird streaking towards him. He threw up his arm. Pain shot through him as the bird's burning talons sunk into his skin, bringing the smell of burning flesh to his nose. The creature suddenly disappeared as shadows enveloped it, extinguishing the magic. The shadows wound around his arm, soothing the pain.

Movement caught his eye. He scrambled out of the way as more golden arrows flew towards him, striking the wall where his head had just been.

"You've been practicing your forbidden magic!" snarled Queen Illyndria. "It's no wonder the Ancestors won't respond!"

The Ancestors, the Ancestors! All they cared about were the blasted Ancestors! He was sick of it.

Calandriel deflected more spells. Tch, of course he'd practiced his magic. The calm embrace of the shadows had always been there for him, unlike his parents and the damned Ancestors! The shadows, along with the creatures brought back to life, were the few things in his life that didn't judge him.

"Then our assumption is correct. We must rid ourselves of you," the king said, eerily calm.

The bright auras around him shifted. His parents were putting everything they had into one final spell, one that would end him on the spot. He lashed out with every ounce of magic he had. The spells collided and exploded. He was thrown against the wall by the blast, momentarily stunned. Head swimming, ears ringing, he shakily rose to his feet. Down the hall, his father was doing the same.

He looked around for his mother and saw that she, too, had been knocked down by the explosion. But unlike his father, she made no attempt to get up. Calandriel took a shaky step towards her, feeling a flicker of relief when he sensed her aura. The queen was only unconscious.

His father's enraged cry broke him from his stupor. The king turned towards him, eyes blazing with hatred the likes of which Calandriel had never seen before. Without a second thought, he wrapped himself in a cloak of shadow and leapt out a window, shattered glass twinkling around him like stars as he fell.

THIRTEEN

THE GREAT TEMPLE

A few moons had passed since the battle against Tarathiel and his followers, so the repairs of the Great Temple were well underway. All the chunks of wood and broken branches had been cleaned from the courtyard, and the damaged trees that made up the various towers were being healed.

Alysion and King Illuven were given the isidyll's quarters. It was the very room where Alysion and Fae had come out to his parents about their relationship after the fight. And where Ash had lived. It filled Alysion with many painful emotions.

This was also the first time Alysion had been with his father without his mother hovering around. It was very strange. After all, he didn't know much about his father aside from the king had told him of his relationship with Tarathiel.

And Tarathiel was the reason they were here: to interrogate and punish his remaining followers for their crimes against Sylandris. They had quickly discovered that a handful had been loyal to Tarathiel directly, and not to Ash as the isidyll. The job was made harder by the fact that not all of the ayel and konn had been fully aware of what was happening. Some had been left completely in the dark about Tarathiel and Ash's true motives. Since the incident, the Elithar had been working on weeding out the conspirators from the unknowing followers and tracking down the handful that had escaped.

"All are now accounted for," said one of the warriors, leading Alysion and the king down a set of compacted dirt steps to the holding cells beneath the Verdant Hall. The Great Temple, being a place of worship, didn't have a prison, so the Elithar had built one. There'd been some debate about moving the treasonous elves to Lyrellis, but in the end, it was decided that it would be safer to keep them here. The royal family didn't want all the details of their betrayal reaching the people, and there was no way to move a hundred elves discreetly.

"We are keeping the 'ayel' separate from the rest. Though they are without their leader, they remain incredibly devoted to his plot."

Their leader. Alysion glanced at his father. The king's face was devoid of emotion. Alysion wasn't sure how he did it. If Fae ever betrayed him (not that he ever would), he wouldn't be able to hold his composure. His father could do it because he'd done it for centuries. Alysion's heart panged. He would make sure nothing ever happened to Fae, which meant he had to convince his people that Fae wasn't an insult to the Ancestors. And to start that off, he had to ensure these elves were dealt with appropriately and that a new, capable isidyll was found before the winter solstice.

He had a long, hard road ahead of him. But it would all be worth it if his people accepted Fae.

They passed through a magical barrier at the bottom of the stairs, one of many in the subterranean prison, and into a circular cavern. Tunnels branched off of it, leading to different holding cells. Alysion could see more barriers faintly distorting the light at each mouth.

The Elithar led them down the tunnel opposite the stairs. Alysion's skin prickled as they passed through the shimmering wards. The earthy tunnel twisted and turned like the large feathered serpents living in the forest above them. Every so often, they turned down a tunnel and passed through another ward. Alysion, stomach unhappy from all the barriers, wondered if they were still within the temple grounds. He tried to keep track of all their turns but knew he'd never find his way back on his own.

The tunnel eventually opened up into a small antechamber with a heavy wooden door opposite them. Two pairs of warriors were stationed at the door. A fifth—Captain Anaril—approached them.

"My King. My Prince."

Alysion assessed the captain while they greeted him and his father. They had sustained some nasty injuries while fighting Ash—injuries that would have felled a lesser elf. He saw no signs of pain, no wincing, no limping, no favouring limbs. As far as the prince could tell, the captain was in peak condition. Impressive.

"Let us not tarry. We are about to begin today's interrogation," they said.

"These are his 'ayel'?" King Illuven asked.

"They are, My King."

Alysion gazed at the door, stomach twisting. He knew they'd come specifically for this, but he wasn't sure if he was ready. He'd never interrogated criminals before. A hand touched his shoulder. Alysion looked at his father.

"Are you ready?" the king asked. His father had to be just as nervous as he was. These were Tarathiel's followers, after all.

Alysion took a steadying breath and nodded.

"Very well." Illuven met the captain's gaze. "Let us begin."

They were in a small circular stone room with two doors, one they'd just come through and another that presumably led to wherever the prisoners were being held. It was dark, dingy, and smelled of musty earth, nothing like the bright, wooden rooms of his home. But Alysion supposed this was the best they could do, being so far underground. Or maybe it was meant to put the prisoners on edge. He certainly found it unsettling.

An elf was escorted into the room and forced to kneel before them. Alysion could see aura-suppressing bands on not just one of their wrists—like they'd done to him and Gale near the Glimmering Forest during the hunt for the crystals—but on both, along with their ankles. The Elithar weren't taking any chances.

Judging by the tattered state of the false ayel, the Elithar had been interrogating them for a while. Yet they would not speak beyond spewing insults. Not even when Anaril sent a jolt of magic through them—the same spell they'd used on Fae when they'd been caught outside the Glimmering Forest. It made his stomach churn.

The prisoner was swapped for another. This one took some convincing—with magical methods that had Alysion looking away—to get them to talk. Though clearly not news to the Elithar, they admitted that Isidyll Navir (clearly guided by Tarathiel) had convinced them that the Divine Ancestors wanted the royal family overthrown. That there was a darkness festering in Lyrellis that must be eradicated. And once the Brightstars had been ousted, they would seize control and work towards bettering their people. Though what precisely the issue with the Brightstars was, they wouldn't say. Or maybe couldn't say. Alysion couldn't read the prisoner's expression.

The next elf revealed that Tarathiel had wanted to go to war with the dragons.

Alysion, pale from watching the interrogations, furrowed his brow.

Why? The Syl-Raanian War had ended centuries ago. Why had Tarathiel harboured such a great hatred towards them? While searching for the crystals, Alysion had seen some of Tarathiel's memories. In the earlier ones, the elf had shown a great dislike of the dragons. Something about them not being adequately punished for starting the war. Alysion could understand his frustration, but Tarathiel hadn't participated in the war; he either hadn't been born yet or was a very young thelim at the time.

The false ayel kneeling before them was hauled away, pulling Alysion from his wonderings.

Another prisoner was brought in, a belim this time. Her piercing gaze met his and she bared her teeth.

"Well, if it isn't our precious prince," she said.

Alysion was instantly transported back to when Tarathiel's followers had taken him.

"You're one of the ayel that kidnapped me!"

Beside him, his father frowned.

"Ah, he remembers," she said.

He'd been unconscious when the fake ayel brought him to the temple, but he recalled seeing her face when Ash first took the crystals before Fae had shown up to save him.

Her head suddenly snapped like she'd been struck across the face. A dribble of blood leaked out of the corner of her mouth. She looked at the captain and spat a mouthful of it towards their feet.

"You are not to speak to him," said the captain, their voice even.

The elf narrowed her eyes at Anaril.

It was then that Alysion noticed she wasn't wearing any of the silver aura-suppressing bands. A chill swept over him. She had no aura. She'd already undergone the Silias, the ritual that destroyed one's damis. Normally, an elf would be cast from Sylandris immediately following the ritual, but this follower was important enough that they kept her for questioning.

The interrogation began. She didn't provide much more information than the prisoners before her.

The lack of progress was frustrating. They needed to have the prisoners dealt with before the winter solstice. If the Eburnas wasn't perfect, the nobles wouldn't be convinced that the Ancestors hadn't forsaken the royal family. And if that happened, Alysion would be forced to join with a noble belim. Ugh.

"Did you think the Ancestors would approve of this?" he suddenly asked her. All eyes turned to him.

The kneeling belim looked to Anaril for permission to speak, a hint of amusement on her face. The captain gave the slightest nod of their head.

"You can't believe for a moment that the Ancestors care about what we do," she said. "We took over this temple and operated out of it for decades. They did nothing to stop us."

Alysion bit his lip. His faith in the Ancestors had never been strong, and it had only weakened once he'd met Fae.

"The Divine Ancestors are nothing but a thelim's tale," she snorted.

From the corner of his eye, he saw the captain move. Alysion raised a hand to stop them.

What she said was blasphemous, but he couldn't help but wonder if she was right. What had the Ancestors ever done for him? For Fae? What if...what if they didn't exist at all? Was it possible? But, his family was descended from their line. What did that mean? The ground swayed as his mind whirled with possibilities.

He needed air.

Ignoring his father's concerned look, Alysion strode from the room. He hurried back down the tunnel, wanting to get above ground as quickly as possible.

But at the first intersection he came to a stop. He peered down the gloomy side tunnel. It didn't look familiar, but that didn't mean anything. He didn't recognize tunnel ahead of him either.

Damn. He had no idea how to get back above ground. *If only I had the Earth Emerald...* The crystal would have been able to show him the way.

He crossed his arms and leaned against the rocky wall, not wanting to go back to the interrogation room.

Alysion reached out with his aura to see if it would help. Two suddenly brushed against his consciousness. One aura belonged to one of the Elithar; his father or the captain must have sent them after him to make sure he didn't get lost. The second was much more faint and didn't seem to belong to an individual. It felt similar to the wards the warriors had set up, but it wasn't their handiwork. The magic felt...off.

Frowning, Alysion closed his eyes and honed in on it. It seemed to be coming from the side tunnel. He opened his eyes and glanced back towards the interrogation chamber. The warrior sent after him hadn't caught up yet. Curiosity piqued, Alysion headed down the tunnel.

The aura slowly but steadily grew stronger with each step. He soon came to a fork and paused. If he followed this and got lost, he'd have a rough time finding his way back, especially if there were any wards ahead.

I'll just mark my route.

Calling on his magic, he drew a star on the wall with his finger. He made no visible mark, but the magic's aural signature lingered. Alysion continued, marking every turn.

He passed through a few more of the Elithars' wards. Did the aura belong to something they were guarding? Perhaps it was a magical artifact they'd confiscated.

The aura suddenly started to fade. Alysion came to a stop. *Focus!* He walked back down the tunnel. The aura grew stronger for a handful of steps, then weakened. *Hmm.* He walked up and down along the stretch, but the aura's pattern of strengthening and weakening did not change.

There must be something here.

He touched one of the walls and walked the stretch again. Nothing changed. He did the same with the other wall and stopped. The aura was emanating from the wall. Alysion tilted his head and surveyed the rock. It looked no different from any of the others. Perhaps there was another tunnel running alongside this one? Given how much of a maze this place was, it was possible.

Brow furrowed in concentration, he pushed his aural consciousness into the wall. The strange aura flared brightly in his mind's eye. Intrigued, he followed it, his consciousness passing through the earth like his body would through air. Alysion couldn't help but feel a spark of pride for how his aural abilities had improved. Before he'd bonded with the crystals, tracking auras like this would have been well above his head. And now he could do it without their help.

The aura flared up again. Though he couldn't physically see what was there, he knew he'd found a room. A room that had contained traces—albeit stale and fading—of Tarathiel's aura. His concentration slipped, but he managed to hold on to the aura.

Heart racing, he checked for other auras, for signs that the Elithar or any of the false ayel had set foot in the room. Nothing. Aside from the magic in the room, Tarathiel's was the only one.

Alysion's eyes flew open as he pulled himself back into his body. He had to tell his father and the captain. If that truly was a hidden room, one Tarathiel had used to do his plotting, it probably contained all of the elf's secrets.

He turned back towards the interrogation chamber but stopped after a few steps. No, he should confirm his theory first. There was no point in dragging the captain and his father away from their work for nothing. They didn't have time to waste.

Returning to the spot, Alysion placed his hand on the wall. He closed his eyes, concentrating, reaching deep into his damis. If he had the Emerald, boring through the rocky wall would be a breeze. But he didn't. He had to rely on his own abilities. Praying the strange aura wouldn't put up too much of a fight, he began to reshape the wall, compressing and compacting earth and stone to form a tunnel.

It was slow going and hard work. Earth magic was something he didn't have a lot of experience with—even when he'd been in possession of the Emerald. It didn't help that the wall was protected by magic.

After what felt like an eternity, he stopped to take a break. He wiped the sweat from his forehead and slumped against the wall. The tunnel was only a few paces deep, resembling a deep alcove. Dismayed, Alysion felt for the aura. It was stronger than before, but he still had a ways to go.

By the Ancestors, I'm never going to make it!

He wanted to give up, return his father and forget, about the room. But he couldn't. Whatever was in there could be really important. Steeling himself, the Prince of Sylandris straightened up and resumed his efforts.

After what felt like hours, he eventually broke through.

The room was pitch black. But the darkness was nothing compared to the unsettling, oppressive aura that nearly overwhelmed him. This wasn't shadow magic—Tarathiel's natural affinity. This aura was dark and twisted.

Alysion took a moment to catch his breath then used the last dregs of his energy to conjure a handful of bright flames.

The room was small. Shelves covered the walls, nearly obscuring them from view. A battered, but sturdy wooden desk occupied the center of the study. Skin prickling from the unsettling aura, Alysion made for it. Unsurprisingly, its drawers were sealed with magic. Which meant there were secrets inside.

Undeterred, he checked out the shelves. They were packed with books, scrolls and an assortment of strange objects. There were dried herbs, bones that still had shriveled patches of flesh clinging to them, and crystals whose luster and aura seemed pale in comparison to his. There was jewelry that gave off weak auras and squishy things in dusty jars that he didn't want to examine further. None of the objects seemed to be the source of the strange aura. Which meant the source of the twisted aura had to be Tarathiel himself.

But how? Why? Alysion didn't recall Tarathiel's aura feeling like this during the fight at the temple. But then again, he'd been in a pretty sorry state. Perhaps he'd overlooked it.

He stood near the desk and concentrated on the aura. It didn't feel like shadow magic, but he didn't have a lot of experience with it. When the Shadow Amethyst had bonded with him, he'd gotten a sense of peace and serenity, like the night sky itself had come down and wrapped him in a velvet blanket. The aura in this room felt completely different. It was thick and oppressive, his chest tightened just from being there. But something about it seemed familiar. Something unrelated to Tarathiel. Yet try as he might, Alysion couldn't place it.

As he turned to leave, not wanting to linger any longer than necessary in such a place, something caught his eye.

An old book stuck out on its shelf, as if the last reader had hurried to put it away. It was strange given that the rest of the study was immaculate and orderly. Alysion willed his flame to float in the air beside him, and reached for it. The books were so tightly packed that he ended up dropping the tome. As he picked it up, pages fell out of it. Worried that he'd damaged it, Alysion scooped them up and laid them on the desk.

His brow furrowed when he opened the book. The pages didn't match. The loose sheets weren't as yellow as the rest, and the writing differed. The text in the book had been produced by a spell that allowed one to make many copies easily. However, the sheets were hand-written.

He quickly skimmed them. The writing seemed to be about branches of magic and concepts that didn't fit in with what Alysion knew. Or maybe his head was too fuzzy from the aura to make any proper sense of it. He needed to get out of here.

Alysion rolled up the sheets, shoved them into his tunic, and then returned the book to the shelf.

When he set foot back into the main tunnel, the entry behind him immediately resealed itself.

Good riddance, he thought as the unsettling aura released its hold on him. His chest loosened up, and his mind cleared.

He hurried back to inform his father and the captain of what he'd found, deciding to keep the sheets a secret for now.

Fourteen

Letters

After spending the morning acquiring new bruises, Fae returned to his chamber to change into something fresh before his history lesson. He was still holding back on the nobles; the alternative wasn't worth the risk, and he didn't need another reason to upset them. But their nonstop taunts about how Alysion didn't care for him and would be better off without him weren't helping. The worst part was that he was starting to believe them.

Alysion had been away at the temple for a while, and Fae hadn't heard anything from him. He knew the prince was busy; he and the king had quite a mess to clean up. Still, it would be nice to get a letter. Fae had debated sending one of his own, but his magical ring would only send letters to Mitchy, not to anyone he wished. His heart panged. He missed his prince. Hopefully Alysion's return would dispel the doubt that was beginning to gnaw at him.

The ring flashed, drawing his attention to where it lay on his desk. A letter appeared, floating in the air above it. He snatched it up, expecting it to be from Mitchy, who had yet to reply to his message about the queen's illness. To his surprise, it was from Ash. Like the last letter, it was partially coded just in case it was intercepted.

Dear F,

The One I warned you about last time has declared themselves temporary leader since the V is ill. We fear how temporary it will be. No one has seen the V in a while. Some believe the V has already passed, but my aunts don't believe this is the case. But they do worry that the V 's health is deteriorating rapidly and that the One will make their leadership permanent. Regardless, things do not look good over here. The One is still pushing their agenda against your people.

If they do become the new V, then war will be upon you. I will do my best to keep you informed of this situation. For now, I recommend keeping it to yourself so as not to cause panic. My aunts doing their best to mitigate the problem, as not all of us want this.

I have told my aunts about the Secret, though we are careful not to speak of it around anyone, not even those we trust. If the Secret were to reach the One, all our efforts to prevent a war would be in vain.

Hopefully, my next missive brings happier news.
- A

Fae flopped into a chair, head in his hand, and let the gravity of Ash's message sink in. The vorais was ill, and the korais wanted to start another war between their people. He couldn't fathom that. Though centuries had passed, Sylandris was still recovering from the last war. Their population remained low, and they had never rebuilt any infrastructure outside of the Sylandrian wards.

The elves weren't the only ones who would be affected by a war. Fae thought of Urka and her mother living on the Manwan Plains. If the dragons came again, the dwarves would never agree to move back above ground, which is what Urka's mother had spent most of her life striving for. Then there were the humans. Their population had exploded since the war, going from a few small fishing villages off the Greenstone River to settlements all across the land. Settlements that didn't have the same magical protection Sylandris had. They'd be slaughtered.

And Ash wanted him to keep this a secret? Despite his misgivings, Fae understood why. If this got out, the kingdom would panic. And that was the last thing they needed right now, with faith in the royal family so shaken up.

Fae leaned back in his chair and stared at the ceiling. Three leaders were ill—what did it mean? It couldn't be a coincidence.

He couldn't keep this all to himself. He had to tell Alysion. Yet...the prince was already so stressed out. Fae didn't want to dump this on him, either. *Maybe I'll wait to hear from Ash again.* If things got worse, then he'd tell his prince.

He reread the letter. What secret was Ash referring to? Did it have something to do with Tarathiel? Fae didn't have a clue. Whatever it was, it was severe enough that his brother feared it would start a war. He wanted to ask Alysion about it, but he wasn't sure how he could do that without bringing up the topic of a potential war with the dragons. *Ugh.* What a mess.

He let out a long breath, imagining his building stress leaving his body along with it. He hid the letter and reluctantly dragged himself off to his next lesson.

· · ● ● ● ● ·

Fae met with Mellith in the library that evening once all his lessons were done. It had been a frustrating day. He swore his tutors were purposely trying to get a rise out of him, and it was becoming increasingly difficult not to snap back at their remarks about his relationship with Alysion. It was almost pathetic. They were grown-ass elves. Did they really have to stoop to the same level as the younger nobles?

"Is something wrong?" asked Mellith, taking their usual seat across from him at the table. They were reading a book about Ancestor worship from before the Syl-Raanian war. "You seem troubled."

Fae didn't want to bother them with his problems, but between Ash's letter and his tutors' behaviour, he couldn't keep it all in.

"I swear everyone here is trying to run me out of the city. I can sort of understand why the younger nobles hate me. Many of them want to court the prince, and now they can't. But the older elves? They're adults! Why are they behaving like their thelim?"

"Not that it helps, but the younger nobles learned that behaviour from their parents. Is it really that surprising?"

Fae crossed his arms and leaned back in his chair. "I suppose not. I just had higher expectations for them."

"The lunaberry doesn't fall far from the bush," they said with a shrug.

"Tell me about it. They're all blaming the queen's illness on me. As if I have anything to do with it!" *She likely contracted something while fighting Tarathiel.*

"Nobles will use anything as an excuse to get what they want. They're terrible."

Fae raised a brow. "You speak as if you aren't one."

"I wouldn't be here if I weren't a noble," Mellith shrugged. "Since I spend all my time with them, I watch them. Learn their habits. It's really helpful for dealing with them."

"How so?" Fae asked.

"Hmm, think of it like sword practice. You have to study your opponent to learn how they fight. Once you do that, you can figure out how to read and counter them."

Fae nodded. Even with all his lessons, court politics were still such a foreign language to him. "I don't see what I can do to get them to stop pinning all of Sylandris' current problems on me." Fae wasn't asking for accolades, but it would be nice if the nobles remembered he'd helped Alysion find the crystals and stop Tarathiel's plot. He'd even scaled down the crater of an active volcano to retrieve one of the magical rocks! It was beyond frustrating.

"I just want them to leave me alone," he finished.

"I hate to say it, but I don't think that will happen any time soon."

Fae sighed.

"Have you talked to the prince about this?" asked Mellith.

"I don't want to bother him with it. He's busy enough trying to run the kingdom." Besdies, Alysion telling them to stop would only make things worse for the both of them. He would surely lose what little remained of the nobles' fickle respect. And even if he wanted to say something, Fae hadn't seen Alysion in forever. The prince was still at the temple.

Mellith frowned. "All right." They clearly disagreed with him, which Fae found oddly touching. It was nice to know that someone here seemed to care for him.

"I can only hope the queen starts feeling better soon."

"Yes, I've heard that the eranyl still doesn't know what's wrong with her."

"Which is why the nobles blame my presence. Sometimes I'm tempted to return to Odenia to see if that has any effect on her health..."

"I don't think so," said Mellith. They leaned in close so that no one would overhear. "Remember, there are those who don't believe in the Ancestors, and nothing bad has happened to them. Trust me, you're not the cause."

Fae desperately wanted to believe Mellith's words, but with everyone constantly telling him he was the problem...

They straightened up. "Look, both moons will be full during the Eburnas. I suspect the eranyl will take full advantage of our heightened magical power to cure her or, at the very least, to find the cause."

"Only if she lasts that long," Fae muttered darkly. No one knew precisely what state Queen Lymsia was in, only that it was bad enough that she'd had to pass off all her duties to Alysion and his father. And what if, even with the power of the Luuya, they still didn't find any answers? Or what if he *did* turn out to be the cause? Fae's chest tightened.

"Hey," Mellith said, suddenly standing beside him. They put a hand on his shoulder. "Easy there."

Fae nodded and took a few deep breaths.

"It'll be all right. How about we get into that scroll?"

His mind slowly calmed.

"Right, so I finished reading it, but it left me with more questions than answers. If you're willing, I'd like you to try coaxing more information out of it," said Fae.

"I don't know if I can do that." But Mellith was already touching the aged paper, eyes closed in concentration.

Come on, Fae silently urged. He needed to know more about this strange prince who bore a strange family name and wielded strange magic.

"I feel something," Mellith muttered.

Fae perked up.

Their face scrunched up as they dug around in the scroll's aura. The old text began to emit a faint pink light as the scroll grew longer, a new section of text appearing before Fae's eyes.

Mellith cut their connection to it and slumped in their chair, sweat beading up on their forehead.

"Are you all right?" Fae asked.

"Just need a moment." Their voice was a touch strained.

They spent the rest of the evening pouring over the scroll. Fae filled them in on what he'd read previously about the Calandriel as a young thelim. Even now and then, Mellith had to coax more secrets out of it. It made reading very slow, but hopefully, it would pay off.

"What are you looking at?" Fae asked, noticing Mellith watching the central aisle. It was the first time either of them had spoken since they'd started reading.

"I thought I felt a strong aura approaching," they said, head cocked in thought. "But it's gone now."

Fae resisted the urge to get up and check, worried some noble would come and harass them. So far, no one had bothered him in the library besides the librarians who only scowled at him.

Mellith, who'd returned their attention to the scroll, frowned.

"What?" asked Fae.

"Well, this certainly proves that this individual is the cursed heir," they said, passing it over.

Fae read the section, heart beating faster at every line. The heir had accidentally knocked out their mother, the Queen of Sylandris, using a strange form of magic.

"Yeah, it sure does," he said. He'd never heard of anyone using a bone to summon a beast. What was this magic? The closest he could compare it to was shadow magic, but that wasn't quite right. During their hunt for the crystals, Gale had mentioned that some magic wasn't bound by the elements. Certain spells were a combination of a few, or in this instance, existed outside the six elements. He now wished he had asked Gale more about it, but since he couldn't use magic, he hadn't bothered.

The scroll ended with the heir escaping by jumping out a window.

"That can't be all of it," said Fae.

"There may be more, but I don't have the energy to pull up anything else today." Mellith didn't sound hopeful.

"That's fine," Fae said with a nod. If that's all there was, then so be it. Already, they'd made some huge discoveries. *My parents were the ones who warned me about this heir.* But why? What did they know? His parents had come to him from the other side, and the heir apparently could use death magic.

Maybe it's time to visit my family home...

He'd been putting it off ever since they'd returned to Sylandris. It wasn't just his family home—it was the place of his parents' murder. Just the thought of returning there made his stomach twist unpleasantly. He hoped to go there with Ash once his twin returned from Fiiraania. But if his parents had left any clues...

I'll ask Alysion to come with me. As much as he didn't want to put any more strain on the prince, Fae needed to tell him about this.

When Fae passed by Alysion's door on the way back to his room, he noticed light seeping out around the frame. His heart skipped. Was Alysion back from the temple? Fae raised a hand and knocked, not wanting to get his hopes up. *It could just be the servants airing it out.*

The door opened, and he was met with a sea of gold. His heart leapt. His beloved prince was home! He stepped forward to hug Alysion, but Alysion stepped aside to let him into the room. The prince closed the door behind him.

"When did you get back?"

"Earlier today," he replied, taking a seat on the bed. His stiff tone was like a bucket of cold water, dampening Fae's excitement. He didn't sound pleased to see him at all.

He must be tired, he told himself, needing to believe it.

"How did it go at the temple?" Fae asked. He followed Alysion to the bed but remained standing.

"It wasn't a great time," said Alysion, staring at the floor.

Fae couldn't help but feel like Alysion was purposely avoiding his eye. "No, I suppose not. Was it...productive?"

"Sort of."

There was a strange tension in the air that set Fae on edge. Even when tired, Alysion was normally very talkative.

"Well, you rest up. I'll come see you in the morning," he said awkwardly.

"We don't have time in the morning. We have lessons," Alysion replied flatly.

He'll grow bored of a damisri like you soon enough. The words rose unbidden from the depths of his mind. Alysion would never grow bored of him, right?

He's just tired, Fae told himself again. Dealing with the traitors would exhaust anyone.

"I'll make time to come see you, even if it's just for a bit." He leaned in to kiss Alysion on the forehead but the prince suddenly lay down.

Something icy gripped his chest as he pulled back. *You're not fit to be in his presence.*

"I *will* see you in the morning," he said, more to reassure himself. He'd tell Alysion about his discovery another time.

Alysion, staring up at the canopy over his bed, just nodded.

Fifteen

Hall of Nobility

When Fae went to greet Alysion in his room early the next morning, the prince was already gone. Reasoning that he'd been summoned by his parents again in order to calm his rising panic, Fae headed down to his morning torture session on the sparring field. But throughout practice, he could not shake off the uneasy feeling settling in his chest.

Alysion isn't avoiding you. He's just busy because his mother's unwell, and Tarathiel's actions have left Sylandris in a spiritual mess. Fae repeated this to himself, but his sparring partners' taunts did little to ease his growing doubt. Focusing on the rest of his lessons was incredibly difficult.

Once free for the day, he began hunting for the prince. He knew where most of Alysion's tutoring took place and searched each area just in case he'd been asked to stay longer. No luck. He checked the local temple where Alysion had his isidyll training, but the prince wasn't there either.

Perhaps he's in the library? He rarely saw Alysion there, but it was worth a shot. Instead of heading to the lower levels where Fae and Mellith met, he searched the upper ones where more recent texts about magic and society were kept. Still nothing.

Frowning, Fae wandered the halls. Where else could he be? If he'd been summoned by Queen Lymsia again, then Fae had no hope of reaching him. He had no idea where the queen was resting and had no desire to be around her for several reasons.

He neared the hall of statues again when he heard voices approaching him from behind. He grimaced when he recognized Ornthalas Goldbark's. *Great, just what I need.* It was bad enough that he had to spend his mornings with their abuse. He wasn't in the mood to deal with it now.

He ducked into the hall of statues just as a handful of young nobles came around a corner.

"Oi, damisri!"

Damn, he hadn't been quick enough.

Fae stood tall and waited. At the very least he would make them come to him.

Ornthalas entered the hall, flanked by Glendarion and two others. He looked at Fae, then the statues. "This must be the first time a damisri has ever set foot in here. You should consider yourself lucky. Show some respect by kissing the feet of every noble here."

Fae didn't miss that Ornthalas included his group in that statement. What a ridiculous notion; he could almost laugh. "You think they want to be kissed by a damisri?" Fae asked, tilting his head towards a statue.

Ornthalas narrowed his eyes. "You shouldn't be here. Your presence is an insult to our entire people." He nodded to the elves on either side of him.

Great. Were these idiots really going to start a fight here? The nobles flanking Ornthalas spread out, encircling Fae.

I guess so.

Fae didn't have a weapon on him since didn't expect to get attacked *inside* the palace. He hadn't even used his longsword since coming to Lyrellis, having left it on the wall in his room.

Ornthalas and his cronies weren't carrying any steel that he could see, but they didn't need to. They could use magic. That was a much bigger problem.

"You're not worthy of living amongst us," said Ornthalas, taking a step closer.

Oh, how Fae wished he could sense auras, if only so that he could determine what these idiots were going to do.

"You should be sent back to Odenia where you belong," hissed the noble of the Mistdawn family.

Fae ducked as something bright whooshed towards him. A few strands of his hair fluttered to the floor as the fireball hit the wall and disappeared.

Ornthalas held a hand up, an unpleasant smirk on his face. "That was lucky."

Something green streaked at him. Fae sprang closer to Ornthalas to avoid it, which was just what the young Goldbark wanted.

He lobbed a sphere of ice-cold water at Fae, thoroughly soaking him.

Eyes full of water, Fae heard the next spell before he saw it. A crackling ball of lightning slammed into his chest. He let out a cry and fell hard onto his back, body spasming. An acrid smell filled his nose, and he gasped for air. Laughter echoed from somewhere in the distance.

Once his head stopped reeling, Fae grit his teeth and tried to stand, shaking all over.

"Hah, look at him. He looks like a newborn foal!"

Before he could get his feet properly back under him, a rush of air knocked him back down. He groaned in pain.

"This is why a damisri can never be with our prince," Glendarion sneered. "You're weak and pathetic."

Fae tried to get up again. Orthnalas' foot came down on his chest, pinning him in place. He looked up at the Goldbark heir through bleary eyes.

"We will rid Sylandris of you."

That sounded oddly familiar. Something red-hot shot through him. With a surge of strength, Fae grabbed Ornthalas' ankle and pushed the noble off him, rising to his feet.

"No you don't," Ornthalas hissed. "You belong down there."

More spells came Fae's way.

He dropped to the floor, too weak from the lighting to do much more. A burst of air struck the wall behind him. Fire streaked towards a statue and fizzled out when it hit the wards protecting it.

"Better. That's—"

"What's going on here?"

The nobles froze, spells dissipating in their hands.

Fae looked up to see Alysion striding purposefully towards them from the far end of the hall. Even from the floor Fae could see that the prince blazed with uncharacteristic fury, accentuated by his red tunic.

The nobles fled at the sight. Not even Ornthalas spared a second glance back.

Cowards, thought Fae, rising to his feet. He brushed himself off. "Thank—"

"How long has this been going on?" Alysion cut in, his tone stiff with anger. It was clear the prince was restraining himself from chasing after them and tearing them to shreds. He wouldn't meet Fae's eye.

As much as Fae wanted to, he couldn't beat around the bush with this one. Alysion had seen firsthand how the others treated him. The prince wouldn't be satisfied with anything less than the whole truth.

"Since we first arrived in Sylandris," Fae said quietly.

Alysion's emerald eyes flashed. "Why didn't you tell me?"

Because you don't need any more stress. "It wasn't a big deal. I didn't see why I needed to bother you with it."

"It *is* a big deal," Alysion hissed, his composure crumbling away. "They meant to hurt you!"

"You have enough to worry about," Fae said, keeping his tone even and calm, hoping it would help calm his prince. "I can take care of myself."

That was the wrong thing to say.

Alysion stuck his face right in Fae's. "No, you can't. You don't have any magic to defend yourself with! Had I not come along, they would have beaten you to a pulp."

Fae knew he was right, but Alysion's words stung. "No, they wouldn't—"

"Yes, they would!" snapped the prince. "I've heard the whispers. They think you're the cause of my mother's illness. It's the perfect excuse for them to have you removed from Sylandris. You should know better than to walk around on your own!"

"Well, if you would spare two moments for me I wouldn't have to be alone!" Fae shot back, volume rising. "Aside from you, I only have one other friend here!"

The prince's face darkened at the mention of Mellith. "Don't bring them up around me."

"And why not? Unlike you, they make time for me." He was being unfair, but Fae no longer cared. He never got to see Alysion anymore, and recently, it felt like the prince was giving him the cold shoulder.

Alysion took a step back. He schooled his features, face turning into a blank mask like Captain Anaril's. "I've told you why I can't always meet."

"Always? I'm asking for the bare minimum! You pretty much kicked me out of your room last night when I came to greet you. You didn't even let me know you'd returned!" Fear shot through him. It was like Alysion really was growing tired of him. "And then this morning, you were nowhere to be found even after I told you I would come see you!"

"I can't help it that my schedule doesn't perfectly match yours," said the prince, mask cracking. "If you need attention that badly, go find your new *friend*."

Alysion may as well have buried a knife in his heart. Mellith was nothing but a friend but obviously Alysion didn't care.

"Fine. *Fine*." He pushed past the prince, needing to put as much distance between them as possible.

Sixteen

The Past

*B*one-headed prince.

Alysion always seemed to know just what to say to set him off. First, it had been the jab at his parents on the Manwan Plains that had earned Alysion a punch to the face, and now this.

Why do I put up with him?

Because you love him.

But do I?

It wouldn't hurt so much if you didn't.

Mellith found him staring vacantly out a window in the library. The sky was a dull grey, hinting at the coming snow.

"Are you all right?" they asked, concerned plastered all over their face.

Even though Mellith was his friend, Fae wasn't emotionally ready to discuss what had just happened. "Just having issues with the nobles," he said.

Mellith gave him a look but thankfully didn't pursue it.

"Do…"

"We—"

"You first," said Mellith.

Fae was silent for a moment, wrestling with his thoughts and emotions. "Do you want to come with me to investigate something?"

"Does it have something to do with the scroll?"

Fae nodded. "I think so. It's a bit of a long shot but…" he took a steadying breath and told Mellith about his parents coming to him during the Aubrillias. It felt odd revealing this to them. He rarely spoke of his parents and when he did it was only to Alysion. "They *might* have left something at my family home. I want to take a look around." Guilt washed over him for not inviting Alysion, but clearly, Alysion wanted nothing to do with him. The guilt immediately twisted into something unpleasant that settled in his stomach.

"And you're fine with me coming with you?" Mellith asked softly.

"Yes," he said, sounding more sure than he felt. "Let's go now." He stood up.

Mellith blinked at the suddenness. "Right now? Are you sure?"

"There's no point in waiting." He needed a change of scenery. Hopefully, the ride there would help clear his mind.

Unfortunately, the journey did not have the desired effect. While he was able to push aside his swirling emotions about Alysion, others rose to take their place. Anxiety gnawed at him. What would they find when they got there? Would his home, nestled high up in the tree's canopy, be just the way they'd left it all those decades ago? Had someone come along and cleared it out. Or—his heart jolted—was someone else living there now?

Sy-Sy picked up on his strange mood as they trotted through the forest; his gait gentler and smoother than normal.

"So, you said your family is from Illerias?" Fae asked, unable to bear the silence.

"That's right," Mellith replied. "We're nobles, though not as high ranking as the lord that watches over the city."

"And your family questions the Ancestors' existence," he said, grasping for the only thing he knew about his companion.

"Yes, but please don't tell anyone."

"Trust me, I won't." He wouldn't wish the nobles' ire upon anyone, least of all someone he considered a friend.

"No, I suppose you, of all people, wouldn't. I'm sorry."

"Don't worry about it," said Fae lightly. "But if you don't mind, what is your family name? You don't wear your crest like everyone else does."

"You don't wear your crest either."

Fae blinked. He'd never considered it.

"It's Jadestream. I don't wear it just in case anyone is familiar with my family's beliefs. Or lack of, I suppose. You should wear yours if you're proud of your family."

"It would only cause more problems," Fae replied. He could easily imagine being belittled for daring to wear a crest, never mind one that belonged to a high-standing family. Still, he held onto the idea. He owned nothing with the Silvermoon insignia, but maybe they would find something at his old home.

They rode in silence for a bit. Then he caught Mellith looking at him. "What is it?"

"I was just thinking about how we're both outsiders to the city, you from Odenia and myself from Illerias. "

"And how we both have to watch our step around the others."

"Yes, that too," said Mellith thoughtfully.

By the gods, it was nice to have someone he could relate to. Someone who wasn't trying to beat him down simply for existing. "Thank you for coming with me."

"You're welcome."

It took them longer than expected to find the correct tree. Fae had hardly left their home as a thelim, so he'd had Alysion mark it on a map not long after they'd returned to Lyrellis. Trying to navigate the massive, unfamiliar forest that was Sylandris was difficult. Mellith also had issues keeping them on track since they were from another region. Eventually they reached an area that triggered something in the back of Fae's mind.

"We're getting close," he said.

"Good, we're going to lose the sun soon."

Finding their way back wouldn't be hard; Mellith could just follow the mass of aura that was the city. The issue was all the wild creatures that lived out here. Being on the ground put them at risk.

The scent of lunaberries hit them as they passed through a small clearing, and a wave of nostalgia washed over Fae. He remembered playing with Ash in the garden below their tree. He chased his twin around, outstretched hands covered in sticky berry juice. Ash was squealing, not wanting to get his new outfit all dirty. It was the outfit he'd wear to his spellcasting lesson in Lyrellis. A lesson that Fae would never be able to attend. A mix of emotions swirled inside him at the memory. *And look at me now, taking lessons in Lyrellis.* He nearly snorted.

"Hold up," he said, slowing Sy-Sy. He stopped before a massive tree. Though his dada's forest floor garden was now completely overgrown, there was no mistaking where they were.

"This one?" Mellith asked, peering up at the leafy branches far above their heads. They couldn't see the house from the ground.

He nodded and slowly dismounted Sy-Sy.

"I feel a really stale aura here," they said, dismounting beside him. "Sort of like...light magic?"

"Yes." The portal his dada had opened to save Fae's life—at the cost of his own. His heart hurt.

He started for the tree, looking for the woven rope ladder he and Ash had used to climb up to their home. Older elves would use magic to hop up from branch to branch, but even now, Fae didn't have that luxury. After a bit of searching, he found it, covered in plant life. He gave it a good pull.

"There's magic on that to keep it from breaking," said Mellith.

"Smart, since it's for thelim." He began to climb.

"I'll look around down here for a bit," they said.

"Thank you." Fae appreciated the gesture.

Much sooner than he remembered, he was pulling himself onto the small platform that stuck out before the door. He stood and silently stared at his old home, throat tightening as he took a slow step forward. It wasn't until he grabbed the metal door handle that he realized he was trembling. He took a breath, trying to calm himself. It didn't work.

He pulled the door open.

Fae's knees went weak, and he let out a choked sob. Memories bombarded him: memories of what they'd had, memories of what he'd lost. It hurt more than he imagined.

Slowly, he went from room to room. Everything had been left the way it was the day Tarathiel had come. Small clothes were still strewn about the bedroom floor he and Ash had shared. A pot of something that had long since decayed away into nothingness sat on the stove. Dada's favourite sky-blue outer robe was slung over a chair. Fae picked it up and shook the dust out of it. The only thing missing was his ama's sword, which she'd grabbed when she'd leaped down to fight for her family. Fae would have to ask Alysion what had become of it later. His heart twisted when he remembered that Alysion didn't want to see him.

It was all too much.

Fae leaned against a wall and slid down to the floor. With knees pulled up and dada's robe wrapped around him, he let his emotions flow freely. Tears streamed down his face as sobs wracked his body.

He cried for his lost family and his failing relationship with Alysion. He wished the prince and his brother were there, but instead Ash was beyond his reach and Alysion was slipping away. And the catalyst to all this was Tarathiel.

Fae would never forgive him for it, yet he sort of understood why the older elf had done it. Tarathiel had loved the king more than anything, just as Fae loved Alysion. Tarathiel's relationship had been ruined by the court, just as Fae's was being torn apart now. Tarathiel and Illuven couldn't have been together because Illuven had been promised to the one person he couldn't deny. Fae and Alysion believed they could break free of this system, but it was just as intent on beating them down as it had Tarathiel and the king. And so far the court was winning.

He could tolerate the harassment from the nobles; they could break his bones for all he cared. It was Alysion's actions that hurt most.

Eventually, his crying quieted. With the release of emotion, his head cleared.

Hopefully, the prince's actions were the result of Alysion being overworked. Once the solstice had passed, things would settle down. If only the queen would get better. It would ease Alysion's load and take the blame for her illness off Fae. Well, at the very least, he could do what he came here to do: figure out why his parents were warning him about the heir.

He slowly got to his feet, the robe still wrapped around him like a blanket. He pulled it off and packed it away to take back to the palace. He was grateful to Mellith for giving him time alone, but he now needed their help. If there was anything hiding in here, he needed their ability to sense auras to find it. They hurried up the ladder at his call, politely ignoring his red eyes.

They began to search the house. Neither one of them found anything about the heir in the main living space or in the bedrooms, though Fae found a scarf with his family's crest on it: a silver crescent moon surrounded by stars. Lastly, they searched the small study, leafing through books and documents.

"There are quite a few rare books in here," said Mellith, breaking the silence. "But nothing that relates to our mystery heir or his magic."

"And you don't feel any strange auras?"

"Not so far." They'd been checking every book after Fae finished flipping through it. "There are some stale auras in here. From your parents."

Fae's hope wavered. Mellith said they'd tried again to get the scroll to reveal more about Calandriel, but it seemed they'd reached the end. There had to be something here—something pertaining to their warning.

Giving up on the books, he checked the shelves to see if they had any mechanisms that would open a secret compartment. Removing books hadn't triggered anything, and he couldn't find any seams suggesting the shelves had ever moved. *If they are hiding anything, it would be concealed by magic.* His parents had been mighty sorcerers, and his father had been one of the rare few with an affinity for light magic.

Wait, light.

"Hey Mellith, hold up. I think we're looking for the wrong aura."

The aelim paused what they were doing and gave him a questioning look.

"Check for traces of light magic. And as weird as it sounds, check the windows, especially the skylights in the ceiling." The skylights only provided light during the winter, but the tree's leafed-out canopy blocked them the rest of the year. Right now, thinning foliage covered them.

Mellith nodded and positioned themself below one of the skylights. They held up a hand, feeling for aura. After a moment, they moved to the next one. "Ah, there's something!" they exclaimed. "It's incredibly faint. You would never notice if you weren't looking for it." They hooked their hand as if grabbing onto something. Face scrunched up in concentration, they pulled their arm slowly down, as if dragging a great weight.

Fae watched in fascination as something materialized in Mellith's hand.

It was another old scroll.

Seventeen

Painful Truths

The sky was a dull grey, reminding all that the Eburnas was less than a moon away. The weather did little to improve Alysion's concentration. He stared blankly at the pages before him, not taking anything in despite the fact they were documents he had found in Tarathiel's secret study. His mind kept drifting back to Fae and the incident in the hall. Why hadn't Fae told him the nobles were harassing him? He could have put a stop to it.

You have enough to worry about.

There was nothing more important than making sure Fae was safe! How could he focus when his love was being targeted by those blasted elves? Ugh. How he hated them. They'd been a nuisance before he'd run away from home, and now that Fae was around, they were a hundred times worse. Hopefully, the Goldbark wouldn't try a stunt like that again, but Alysion had his reservations.

I can take care of myself.

No, Fae couldn't. He didn't understand how the minds of the elite worked. They were tenacious and would do whatever it took to get what they wanted.

Now, he had a better understanding of why the Eburnas needed to go off without a hitch. If anything were amiss, they would blame it on Fae and use it as an excuse to drive him from Sylandris. If they didn't try to do so sooner. His mother's condition wasn't improving, and more and more were claiming it was due to Fae's presence.

And that was assuming Fae hadn't already left. The way he'd stormed off after their fight...Alysion's heart twisted. No, Fae wouldn't leave, not like that. But he was right. They never spent any time together. Yet that didn't mean Fae could go around clinging to the arm of that strange elf in the library!

Alysion had seen them together the day he'd returned. He'd sought out Fae as soon as he'd gotten back, only to find him with the aelim he didn't recognize. Who were they? When did Fae start meeting up with them? A chill had swept through him, and he'd quickly fled to his chamber. Was Fae losing interest in him? Alysion couldn't bear the thought of losing Fae, but that seemed to be the route their relationship was going.

Ugh, why was this happening? He rested his head on his arms on top of the desk. *I shouldn't have snapped at him.* But fear had taken hold of him seeing Fae literally beneath the feet of the nobles—he never should have experienced anything like that. Alysion knew he needed to apologize, but he was afraid. Afraid he'd find Fae in the arms of the elf from the library. But if he didn't do anything, he was guaranteed to lose Fae.

He was never going to get these documents sorted at this rate.

Steeling himself, he pushed back his chair and got up.

A knock sounded at the door.

Alysion groaned. Now what?

"Pardon me, My Prince," said Layniir, his attendant, "but the king is requesting your presence in the queen's chamber."

His stomach plummeted. That didn't bode well.

Alysion tried not to cringe as he entered his mother's chamber. The air inside was clean and fresh, but the mood was dark and sombre. The queen lay in bed, her eyes closed. Her skin was pale and her golden hair was lank and dull. Alysion had never seen his mother like this. She'd always been the picture of vibrant health. He didn't need the eranyl, the kingdom's top healer, to tell him that his mother was close to death.

"Nothing is working, My King," said the eranyl. "Every day, she slips further away from us. We've tried everything, brought in healers from across the kingdom. We even reached out to Odenia—not stating who was unwell of course—but they've been dealing with a similar situation."

Alysion had completely forgotten that Fae had told him that the Odenian monarch was unwell.

King Illuven closed his eyes. "I see. Please, go take a break."

The eranyl bowed and left the chamber.

Alysion stared at his mother. He'd never imagined that she might actually die. It was impossible.

"Alysion, there's something important I need to tell you."

His emerald gaze shot to his father, watching as he went into the attached reading room. Alysion followed.

The king looked exhausted. There were circles that rivalled his mother's under his eyes and lines on his face that no elf should have at his age. He took a seat on the edge of a sofa and patted it for Alysion to join him.

Alysion did so, mouth dry.

His father stared out a window, clearly struggling with something. "Given everything that's happening, it's time you learned the truth. It's not something I can bear to keep buried any longer, and there is a chance this information could get out. It's very likely that Faeranduil's brother, Ashmyr knows this already. If for whatever reason he tells anyone, I want you to be prepared. You've heard the tale about Tarathiel and the copper dragon..."

Alysion nodded, wondering and fearing, where this was going.

"The account we gave the dragons wasn't entirely truthful." Illuven's tired gaze drifted to the sickly queen. Alysion frowned.

"Tarathiel was the one to kill the dragon, and there is no denying that he used shadow magic to do it. But..." his father took a breath, steeling himself. "He wasn't the one who brought them through the Sky Peak wards."

Alysion fidgeted with a lock of his hair, bracing himself for whatever his father was about to unleash.

"Now, please understand that we had let the dragons believe it was Tarathiel who had done it in order to protect our people." The king's voice wavered. "But the one who brought the dragon across was your mother."

The room jolted. *What?* Alysion closed his eyes and leaned back on the sofa, letting the revelation sink in. Somewhere deep inside, he wasn't surprised. "Why?" he asked. Why would she do something that would put their entire kingdom at risk?

The king looked back towards the bedroom. "She was afraid that Tarathiel would take me away, so she devised a plot to get rid of him."

The pain in his father's voice pierced Alysion's heart. Anger flared in his chest. "And you stayed with her. Knowing this?" He stood up and turned to face his father.

Illuven met his son's gaze. "I didn't figure it out right away. I was told Tarathiel died during the failed Silias. Wrapped up in my grief over his loss, it was a decade or two before I realized she must have been the one to bring the dragon across. No one else save for the royal family would be able to do such a thing."

Alysion opened his mouth but his father held out a hand.

"By then, it was too late. We'd already had our joining ceremony and her mother had abdicated the throne. I couldn't leave without tarnishing both our families and risking the truth getting out. Could you imagine what would happen if the people found out their own queen had violated the treaties? What would happen if the dragons got word?"

Alysion understood, but he hated it. Tarathiel had been nothing but a scapegoat for his mother's own selfish plot. No wonder his parents were so miserable in each other's presence! If he'd been in his father's place, he wouldn't have been able to stand it.

He stood and strode back into the bedroom. He looked down at his sickly mother on the bed. Alysion didn't know what to feel. Part of him was worried about her illness, and another part was hurt. Hurt by everything she had put him and his father through simply because they loved someone who didn't fit her ideals. And on top of that, those ideals were born from blind devotion to deities that Alysion wasn't convinced existed. Especially after what had happened with Ash.

Icy fear suddenly gripped his heart. Ash. Did he know the truth? He must.

His father, coming up beside him, must have seen his panic. "What's wrong?"

"You sent Ash to the dragons." Only suncycles of being at court kept his voice steady.

The king suddenly looked very tired. "Yes, we did. And I question that decision every day. It didn't occur to your mother at the time. By the time she realized it, the dragons had already left. Not to mention it would look suspicious if she suddenly changed her sentence. We can only hope that Fae's brother doesn't know or reveal the truth."

Fae's brother. His panic subsided. He didn't believe Ash would do anything to endanger Fae. He'd seen how much they cared for each other even after being apart for so long. Ash had believed Fae dead for many long decades, his actions driven by his hurt. And as isidyll, albeit a fake one, he understood how politics worked.

"No, Ash wouldn't risk Fae like that."

Unlike his mother, who risked the entire kingdom to fulfill her own desires. Did *she* even believe in the Ancestors?

His fingers trailed over the sheets.

His father watched him. "I'm sorry, Alysion."

Alysion looked up at him.

"For placing his heavy burden upon you." He placed a comforting hand on the prince's shoulder. "You deserved better than this. Than us," he nodded towards the queen. "I've seen how you are around Faeranduil, how happy he makes you. Don't ever let that go."

Alysion's heart dropped. Fae did make him happy. Meeting him was the best thing that had come of all this. Yet he'd blown it. He'd pushed him away.

"He doesn't want to be around me anymore," he said, shoulders drooping.

His father's face tightened up. He removed his hand. "I'm sure you can work through it. Love powered by choice is incredibly resilient."

"Perhaps..." He sincerely hoped his father was right. The thought of continuing without Fae was too much.

The king wrapped his arms around him.

Alysion stiffened up. He couldn't recall either of his parents hugging him before. Awkwardly, he returned it, feeling his father relax.

"Please, my son," the king said quietly, "go find him."

Alysion would do just that. But finding Fae, who had no aura to track, was tricky.

He checked the library first, heart racing at the thought of seeing him with that noble aelim again, but he wasn't there. A jolt of panic shot through him, and he quickly tamped it down. No, Fae hadn't left for good. There were many other places he could be.

But he wasn't in his room or on the training field. Panic rising again, he checked the smithy in case Fae had gone there to let off steam. Nothing. Where was he? There was one other place he could look, but the thought of what he might find made his stomach churn. He spoke with Fae's tutors instead, but none of them had seen him since their last lesson. Which meant Alysion had to check the stable.

With leaden legs, he made his way down to the forest floor, nearly tripping down the spiral staircase. What a sight that would be.

Heart racing, he approached the royal stable contained within the exposed roots of a massive, dead tree. *Oh, please let Sy-Sy be there.* He hardly noticed the earthy smell of feed and animals as he entered. He stopped dead when his worst fear was realized.

Sy-Sy's stall was empty.

He whipped his head around. All the stalls were empty. Alysion closed his eyes and put a hand on his chest. *They're just out in the pasture.* Once his heart settled, he checked the patch of forest where the uhaan were free to roam, a special ward around the area to keep out predators.

Alysion wove between the uhaan, looking for Sy-Sy's familiar coat. "Sy-Sy!" he called. He heard hooves behind and turned, heart leaping. But it was his own uhaan, Zen-Zen. He tried not to let his disappointment show as she bumped him with her muzzle, wanting attention.

"Where's Sy-Sy?" he mumbled, eyes prickling. He still couldn't see Sy-Sy anywhere.

Zen-Zen nosed him again.

"He has to be h-here." His throat tightened up. Fae couldn't have left. He couldn't have. But Sy-Sy was always with Zen-Zen. They were inseparable. A sob choked him, and he buried his face in Zen-Zen's neck. She rumbled deeply as his tears stained her coat.

Fae was gone.

EIGHTEEN

BETRAYAL

Normally, Ranath loved flying. Once his flight muscles had gotten stronger, he spent as much time as he could in the air, exploring the mountain range the dragons called home. A few times he and Xyrros had even ventured into the Twinthorn forest, though they made sure to keep away from the humans' logging towns.

"Don't stir 'em up," Sevarak had warned him. "Only Vyrmyris' hooligans do that. It's a pain to deal with every time."

Ranath had no desire to upset the humans, and knowing some dragons took pleasure in it displeased him.

But today, other things bogged down his mind. He'd finally told Sevarak and Nyrvrin the truth surrounding Hammanth's death. While sharing this knowledge had been a weight off his scaley shoulders, he worried if he'd done the right thing. The fewer dragons that knew the truth the better, especially with Vyrmyris' followers becoming bolder with their anti-elf agenda. Now that Vyrmyris was standing in for Korvran while the vorais recovered from his illness, the mood of the thunder was shifting. From what Ranath overheard, it seemed like more dragons were starting to consider Vyrmyris' words about going to war with the elves.

It made him and his cave-mates uneasy. Hopefully, Korvran would recover soon and knock the ambitious korais down a few pegs.

The last thing they needed was for Vyrmyris to learn the truth about who had brought Hammanth through the wards. What the elf queen had done was beyond forgivable, and nothing would stop the sapphire dragon if that happened. He'd quickly whip the others into a frenzy where dragons that didn't support Vyrmyris could be swayed under the influence of high emotions and the promise to act upon them.

Ranath flew absentmindedly, following the mountains west. Unlike the Sky Peaks which more or less ran north to south, the mountain range split three ways. The main range stretched north to south, and a second chain branched off to the west. Ranath rarely ever flew that way; there was no need to. And he didn't want to get farther from his brother than he had to. But maybe some exploration would do his busy mind some good.

He winged his way west a bit longer before something caught his attention: the scent of a dragon. Normally, he wouldn't have cared, but something caused his scales to prickle. Whoever had come through here was trying to hide their presence. He could tell by the way other scents were mixed in with it. Ranath frowned. He opened his mouth to taste the smell, trying to identify it. Though he'd been with the dragons for well over a moon now, he was by no means familiar with everyone, and he often ran into dragons he'd never seen before. They came and went as they pleased, and though most called the mountains home, some preferred the forest or the lands to the far west.

But this scent itched at the back of his mind. Like it belonged to a neighbour one rarely saw.

Ranath angled his wings and followed the trail, suspicion pushing aside his worries about the thunder's politics.

If dragons relied more on auras for identification, he'd probably be able to figure out who it was. However, the region where they lived had become so saturated with their auras over time that it was difficult to distinguish one from the rest.

The weak scent dropped into the trees, where the sweet pines helped hide it. The trick may have fooled someone else, but Ranath wasn't about to let his quarry get away. When it came to aural tracking, Tarathiel had taught him well. It had been his job to locate the crystals scattered all over Odenia, after all. The basic concept between tracking aura and tracking scents was the same.

Ranath winged his way between the trees, moving as quietly as possible. His snout led him on a serpentine path up a mountain, the scent slowly becoming stronger. *They must be close.* He stayed in the air as long as he could, his white scales blending with the grey clouds. But eventually, he had to land on the needle-covered ground. Walking was a lot more cumbersome than flying, but he didn't want to risk losing the trail. The trees soon thinned out, leaving him exposed on bare rock. Hopefully, whoever was around wouldn't see him.

The scent led him a bit further up the mountain. Just before the slope became too steep to climb, the scent turned and cut across instead of continuing up. Ranath came around a bend and saw a dark gash tucked away in the rock. A cave.

He kept his distance. The strength of the smell suggested that whoever he was tracking was still in there. He looked around and spotted a ledge far above the cave. Quietly, he flew up to it and made himself comfortable. He could no longer see the cave from his perch, but that didn't matter. He wasn't here to watch whoever was in there; he was here to listen, providing that his dragon magic didn't give him away.

Ranath closed his eyes and reached into his damis. First, he checked the cave for any wards, but didn't sense any. After waiting a moment to see if the occupant had noticed his presence, he wove a tricky spell to carry voices up to the ledge. Had he still been in his original body with his elven aura, the task would have been a breeze. His dragon magic wasn't as cooperative. After a few moments of struggling, he finally got the volume right while keeping his aural output low.

"There's more to it than that," said a voice he couldn't quite place.

"Of course there is," replied another.

Ranath suppressed a growl. Vyrmyris. He narrowed his eyes but didn't move from the ledge. He didn't want to get caught eavesdropping on the korais.

"I was told that parts of it are true, mainly about the one who killed them. But..." the voice trailed off.

"Get on with it," Vyrmyris snapped.

"The killer wasn't the one who brought them through the wards. It was the queen."

Ranath's blood went cold. *By the Ancestors!* How did they know? He'd never told anyone save for the two he lived with. Neither ziiras was foolish enough to share it with anyone else.

He dug his talons into the rock, muscles quivering. He wanted nothing more than to leap off the ledge and rush into the cave. But he couldn't take both of them on alone.

Vyrmyris was quiet for a moment. Ranath could almost hear his mind working, figuring out the best way to use this information.

It doesn't matter how he uses it. The fact that Queen Lymsia was the culprit was enough to justify an act of retaliation. *I have to tell the others.* But instead of taking off, he forced himself to wait.

"Don't tell anyone else about this," said the korais.

"I wo—"

The other dragon's words were cut off by a horrible screeching that echoed throughout the cave. A loud crunch came through his spell, followed by the strong scent of blood.

Ranath snapped open his wings and took off, putting as much distance between himself and the murderous korais. He had to tell Sevarak and Nyrvrin immediately. But first, he had another stop to make. The dragon Vyrmyris killed hadn't been the one to overhear the conversation. Someone else had told them.

It wasn't hard to find the amethyst dragon. When Ranath returned, he found them hanging out outside the ziiras' cave. His heart twisted. It took everything he had to resist sinking his talons into Xyrros' scales.

Xyrros had to have been the one to tell Vyrmyris' followers. No other dragon routinely came to the cave. And no dragon would have looked twice if Xyrros had been snooping around, figuring out a way to bypass the wards the Sevarak and Nyrvrin had cast upon it to stop eavesdroppers.

He should have known better.

Xyrros had shown up not long after he and the ziiras had come to Fiiraania. In hindsight, it was glaringly obvious they were Vyrmyris' spy. Ranath had been right to be wary of them, and should have kept his guard up. But instead he'd decided to trust and had once again been burned.

Teeth bared, he landed before them. "Inside, now," he snarled, barely able to contain his maelstrom of emotions. They'd been easier to handle when he was an elf, but as a dragon they wanted to rage. He chalked it up to draconic instinct.

Xyrros gave him a confused look but went into the cave.

Once inside, Ranath cautiously threw up a ward of his own and whirled upon them. "I trusted you," he growled.

"What?" Xyrros blinked. "I don't under—"

"Don't lie to me!" Ranath snapped his wings, the sound emphasizing his words. "You're one of his, working to start another war with the elves!"

To his irritation, Xyrros didn't drop their innocent act.

"Ranath, I really have no idea what you're talking about," they said, voice wavering.

He snorted a puff of smoke. "You're the only one who could have told."

They blinked. "Told who? Told *what*?"

Ranath clawed the rocky floor, wishing he could use them to rip the truth from Xyrros. Just like how their words were ripping into his heart. Never again. He'd never trust anyone again.

"Ranath, what's going on?"

"Silence!" he roared.

The amethyst dragon shrunk in on themself and took a step back. Ranath saw their eyes dart towards the cave entrance, but he blocked the way out. He didn't want them running off until they confessed.

"I should have known better than to trust you. No dragon in their right mind would take to a stranger so quickly! It's obvious you were sent to spy on us," he hissed, pacing back and forth in front of the cave entrance. "That damned korais is crafty." Just like Tarathiel.

"You...you think I'm in league with the korais?" Hurt flashed across their face.

Ranath didn't let it get to him. "I don't think. I know."

Xyrros was quiet for a moment. Then their expression shifted, becoming cold and hard. They'd put on a mask. "You know, do you?"

A confession wouldn't lessen the hurt of their betrayal, but it would vindicate his emotions.

"I don't know what you think is going on, but I assure you I have nothing to do with it. And if this is how things are going to be, then from now on, I will have nothing to do with you. Let me out."

"No," he snarled, opening his wings to block the entrance. "Not until you confess."

"I have nothing to confess to," they replied, frustration slipping through their mask.

"Admit you spied on us. And then—"

"And then what?" the ziirar snapped, eyes flashing. "Then you'll let me go? I doubt that."

Truth be told, Ranath hadn't thought about what he would do with Xyrros once they'd confessed. It was rather unlike him.

"Just admit it!" He hated having to deal with their act. He was tired of it. His entire life so far had been nothing but an act. It was only since he'd become a dragon that he'd really been able to be himself, as backwards as that seemed. And now that was crashing down around him.

"Let me go," they growled, getting into a low crouch.

"No."

Xyrros sprang at him like a lyngrax, snarling.

He snapped his wings shut and reared up. His front talons came down hard on the other dragon as they barrelled into him. Both of them crashed to the rocky floor in a tangled mess of limbs.

Ranath scrambled to his feet, his shoulder stinging where one of Xyrros' claws had grazed it.

"Is this how you treat all your friends down south?" Xyrros growled as they got up. They had some shallow scratches on their neck.

"I don't have any friends," he said before he could stop himself.

"That," they said, smoke trailing from their nostrils, "is obvious."

Their words stung more than Ranath would have liked. With a loud roar, he snapped at the ziirar, fangs going for their throat. But before he made contact, a swirling gale filled the cave, forcing them apart.

"What are you two boneheads doing?" someone said. The wind died down, revealing Sevarak and Nyrvrin. "If you're going to play like that," said the red dragon, "do it outside."

Both young dragons looked up at her. Was she not able to read the mood? But then Ranath caught the look in her golden eyes. No, she was fully aware that something was going on.

"Vyrmyris knows," Ranath hissed, "and they're the one that told him."

Despite being covered in gemstone-like scales, both ziiras went pale. But before anyone could say a word, a voice sounded from outside.

"Come quickly. The korais has called an emergency gathering!"

Ranath's stomach dropped.

They were out of time.

Nineteen

Vorais

Nearly every dragon was present outside of the vorais' cave. Vyrmyris stood on the ledge with Korvran nowhere in sight. A strange aura issued from the mouth of the cave, incredibly faint. A quick look around showed Ranath that none of the other dragons had noticed it. Their attention was all on the korais.

Vyrmyris waited until the final dragon settled into place before speaking. Ranath and the ziiras exchanged worried looks.

"As many of you know, one of our own went missing some decades ago. Our dear Hammanth crossed the Sky Peaks Mountains into Odenia, passing through the wards. How did he do this, you may be wondering? I certainly have been. Aside from the few selected to investigate the incident, no other dragon should be able to cross the mountains." He paused amidst a rumble of agreement.

Ranath narrowed his eyes. Vyrmyris was drawing this out on purpose, building up the tension. Ranath was familiar with this tactic, for he'd employed it himself as isidyll. Now that it was being used against him, he fully understood and appreciated its power. It made Vyrmyris all the more dangerous.

"It is clear that Hammanth had help, which is why Korvran ordered that we send our own spies into Odenia to investigate." He gestured towards Sevarak and Nyrvrin with his sapphire snout.

The two ziiras were still as stone. Ranath mentally applauded them for keeping their expressions neutral. Even with all his isidyll training, he found himself struggling to do the same.

"They've recently returned from their mission and have confirmed our suspicions. Hammanth wasn't let through the wards. He was *lured*. Lured by none other than an elf."

Shocked muttering and growls broke out. Some snarled and beat their wings in anger. Ranath recognized them as Vyrmyris' followers. They were strategically planted to stir up emotions. He dug his claws into the ground. This wasn't good.

"Now, our *loyal* spies reported that Hammanth met his end at the hands of this elf. And that this elf has been dealt with for his actions."

Beside him, both his companions were as taught as drawn bowstrings. Ranath's heart pounded in his chest.

"But..." Vyrmyris let the word hang, all eyes back on him. "This is not the truth."

Ranath's instincts screamed at him to act, to silence the korais. But doing so would only bring about disaster.

"It is not the whole truth. Yes, Hammanth was lured across the mountains, and yes, the elf that killed him is dead. But, the one who killed him is not the one who brought him to Odenia."

This was it. It took everything Ranath had not to leap up at the korais and rip out his throat.

"The one who lured dear Hammanth through the Sky Peak wards was none other than Queen Lymsia of Sylandris."

Shocked silence.

For a brief moment, Ranath hoped that the crowd wouldn't believe Vyrmyris. That the claim was too outlandish. A chorus of deafening roars dashed that hope—Vyrmyris' lackeys. More voices joined them, whipped into a frenzy by raging emotions.

"What does Korvran have to say about this?" Xyrros had pushed themselves to the front of the congregation and stood beside Ranath. Ranath's lip curled, but they didn't notice. Their eyes were locked on the korais.

The korais must have given some silent signal, for his followers ceased their cries. He waited until the congregation was back under control. "This brings us to the other topic of today's gathering. With a heavy heart, I must inform you that our beloved Korvran has succumbed to his illness."

Ranath blinked. No. Korvran couldn't be dead! He was the one thing stopping Vyrmyris from running amok. Fear wrapped itself around his heart.

A low keening filled the air.

"Korvran has passed on. Tradition dictates that the next vorais is determined via combat, but in light of recent news..."

Ranath could see exactly where this was going. First Vyrmyris won over the crowd by shocking them with the truth about Hammanth and the queen. Then, he preyed on their vulnerable emotions to set himself up as vorais. It was just the sort of plot Tarathiel would have developed.

"I accept Vyrmyris as vorais," growled one of his followers over the rising din. Braemyrin.

"As do I," said another.

"And I."

Many dragons exchanged looks, unsure about the development but not willing to go against it.

"No!" Sevarak snarled, gold eyes flashing. "This is not how we do things."

"Quiet!" someone hissed.

A smug look flashed across Vyrmyris' face so quickly that Ranath almost thought he'd imagined it. "Sevarak, you Nyrvrin are the ones who journeyed to Odenia. Why did you not tell us it was the dreadful queen who killed Hammanth? Were you trying to protect the elves? Did you spend so much time over there that you grew attached to those nasty thaliir?"

A buzz filled the air. Ranath looked at Sevarak and Nyrvrin.

Neither of them responded.

"Your silence can only be taken as an admission. You know withholding the truth is an act of treason."

"The treasonous one here is you, Vyrmyris," said Nyrvrin calmly. But no one was listening. The hostility in the air was palpable. They needed to get out of there.

"I think not," the korais said just loud enough for her and Sevarak to hear. "Let's put it to a vote," he announced to the crowd.

"All those in favour of Vyrmyris taking over as vorais?" someone shouted.

A few dragons roared their approval, but not the majority. Ranath scanned the crowd, hope flickering in his chest.

"Come now, haven't I proven myself to be a capable leader?" said Vyrmyris. "Not only have I been watching over this thunder while Korvran was ill, but I managed to uncover the truth about Hammanth. And unlike Korvran, I will do something about the elves' horrific actions."

Ranath let out a low growl. He was playing on their emotions again. More voices joined those. Soon, most of the crowd bellowed their approval.

Ranath looked at Sevarak. "Get ready to fly," she said, eyes darting around as she planned their escape route.

Braemyrin landed on the ledge next to Vyrmyris. "It has been decided," she announced, "Vyrmyris is the new vorais!"

Ranath was ready for more deafening noise but instead the crowd went silent. Each dragon raised a wing in a salute.

"Thank you for your support," said the new vorais.

Support? You corralled them into this. A few dragons looked around uneasily, the ones who hadn't wanted him as vorais.

"And while it may seem soon," said Vyrmyris, "we must begin our preparations. Going after the Queen of Sylandris will be no easy feat. And before we can consider that, we must rid ourselves of the traitors in our midst. The ones who hid the truth of the queen's treachery from us."

An unsettling buzzing sound filled the area again. Ranath and both ziiras tensed up, ready to fly. Even Xyrros beside him, who he'd forgotten about, seemed prepared to go. *Ready to stop us.* Ranath didn't want to fight them, but he would if Xyrros got in his way. If the situation weren't so dire, he'd tear them apart now for their betrayal. *Later.* One thing Tarathiel had taught him was to be patient and how to bide his time until the right opportunity to strike arose.

The buzz turned into snarls. Talons and wings flexed.

"Traitors!"

"Siding with the thaliir, disgusting!"

The crowd began to close in on them. If they didn't leave now, they would be ripped to shreds.

They shot into the air. He, Sevarak, Nyrvrin, and a small handful of others took off as fast as they could. There wasn't time to look back, but judging by the sound of wingbeats, most of the crowd had thankfully stayed behind. But that didn't mean they were in the clear.

Angry roars followed as they headed west. They drew on their magic, calling on the wind to help them fly faster.

"If we can put a few mountains between us, we'll throw 'em off," Sevarak called. Ranath could hardly hear her over the rush of air.

It wasn't long before they flew around the mountain where Ranath had overheard Vyrmyris learning about Queen Lymsia. Was the body still in there? If it was, they could use that to knock the new vorais off his perch, dragons didn't condone murder within the thunder. But they couldn't do anything about it now. Not with their pursuers on their tails. They were still stirred up by Vyrmyris' antics, and he doubted they would listen to anything they said.

They flew as fast and as hard as possible to keep ahead of their pursuers. Their group contained roughly twenty dragons, a fraction of those who had stayed behind. Vyrmyris' original circle of supporters was double that, and then there was the rest of the thunder. Their odds weren't good.

A loud snarl behind him pulled him from his thoughts. He looked back to see a hostile dragon shooting towards him like an arrow, their body limned in blue light. Ranath angled his wings and swooped down. The dragon shot over him. He silently thanked his small, agile size. He could out manoeuver many of the older dragons.

The attacker let out a pained cry as Nyrvrin dropped onto their back, biting at their neck. Their blue magic dimmed.

More cries rent the air. Ranath glanced back and almost wished he hadn't. The rest of their pursuers had caught up. He swerved as a burst of flame came at him, so close that he could feel its heat. Normal fire wouldn't hurt him, but dragonfire could.

The darkening sky lit up as more dragons loosed their flames. He ducked and rolled in the air. It took all his concentration to avoid the blazing streams—and other dragons. The sky was chaos. From what he could see, they were evenly numbered. A small relief. But the rest were with Vyrmyris preparing for war.

He rolled to avoid a burst of white-hot fire. Ranath swung around towards his green attacker and returned the favour, shooting a jet of flame towards their face. The dragon avoided it but that's what he wanted. He reared up and crashed into them talons-first. The dragon snarled as he tore at their chest, ripping through scales. The green tried to right themselves in the air, but their combined weight dragged them down. Ranath only had a moment before they recovered. He snapped at their face, not aiming to kill, as Nyrvrin had instructed, but to scare them off. The dragon let out a pained sound. Ranath let go. His opponent turned tail and fled, blood dripping from their cuts.

A few more dragons turned back. Ranath collided with another. Unlike the green, this gold wasn't so easily scared off. She ignored him as he clawed at her, her jaws coming for his neck. He dropped away. She opened her mouth and loosed a blast of fire. He growled as the flames painfully licked at his wings. Ranath dropped into a steep dive to escape when a red dragon appeared out of the chaos to engage the gold—Sevarak. She soon had her opponent retreating.

"Not bad, she's a tricky one," she called to him.

Ranath nodded. He tried calling on his magic to soothe his wings but it wouldn't cooperate. *Come on!* If he'd still been an elf it wouldn't have been a problem. Not many dragons had the ability to heal.

Irritated by his magic, he winged his way back to the group. They'd managed to chase away all of Vyrmyris' lackeys.

"Let's get going!" Sevarak called. "They'll be back before we know it!"

He wondered if that was true. Would the vorais bother sending more dragons after them when he was preparing to attack the elves? Ranath wasn't about to stick around to find out.

Part Four

Calandriel spent many long moons on the road. Keeping abreast of the Elithar and his parents' rage became much easier once he left the forest. Wanting to put as much distance between himself and his birthplace, he made his way west towards the distant Sky Peak mountains.

The journey was difficult. He'd left with only the clothes on his back, and he'd never ventured outside Lyrellis before. Everything he knew of the outside world came from books, but books and the real world were two very different things. He'd been at a loss as to what to do when he grew tired, he'd always had a roof over his head. Not that the Elithar following him would let him stop for long.

Calandriel quickly learned how to hunt, discovering that his magic allowed him to take life just as easily as it restored it. Unfortunately, his spells left aural signatures that were easy for the warriors to track. Once he figured out how to suppress his aura, their presence receded. Only then did he allow himself to stop in dwarven towns to rest and resupply.

Once he crossed the Bluetail River, he could no longer sense their presence. He even risked reaching out with his aura, but theirs had faded. Still, he wouldn't relax until he'd crossed the Sky Peaks.

The distant mountains soon came into view. They were like nothing he'd ever seen before; drawings in books didn't do them justice. Jagged mounds of stone seemed to pierce the sky, tipped with white tops that merged with the clouds. He was in complete awe. *No one would ever find me in there.*

Their size was deceptive. He figured they were but a half day's journey away, but they were much further than that. His steps never seemed to get any closer, and being completely exposed on the Manwan plains made him anxious. Not only did he have to watch out for the Elithar, but for dragons as well. They liked to prey on the massive nuu that roamed the grassland. Sometimes he heard them out hunting when he rested during the daylight hours and would hide in a veil of shadows until the noise died down.

But after a few nights of travel, dragons became the least of Calandriel's worries. He sensed the Elithar behind him, quickly closing in. Near daybreak, he suddenly felt a familiar presence in front him, one he'd hoped to never encounter again.

His parents.

They'd cut off his escape.

A burning rage filled him at the sight of them. They sat astride grey uhaan, wearing golden armour that shined brightly as the sun's first rays struck them.

His mind raced, trying to devise a way out of this. But he couldn't see a way out. With his parents before him and the Elithar quickly circling behind, he was trapped. The rising sun ate away the darkness of night. All he had to rely on was his own magic.

The Elithar closed in, forcing him towards his parents. Fear gripped his heart. He didn't want to return to Lyrellis, to a life trapped in the palace. *No, they're not here to bring me home. They're here to finish what they started.* He kept his eyes low, their armour too bright to look at. *They're doing it on purpose.*

"Calandriel Goldensky," his mother started, "for crimes against the royal fam—"

"Crimes? What crimes?" he spat, anger boiling up inside him. He met his mother's cold gaze. "The ones in the wrong here are you."

The Elithar moved, ready to attack.

"Silence," his father ordered, his grey mount shifting beneath him.

"No. Neither of you have ever shown me any sort of affection."

"How dare you! We fed and clothed you! We made sure you were safe!" replied the queen, her face twisted in anger.

Calandriel let out a humourless laugh. "Safe? You weren't trying to keep me safe." Smokey tendrils wound themselves around his wrists, comforting him in a way his parents never had. "You kept me hidden away, ashamed of what I am."

"Call off your magic at once," the captain ordered.

Calandriel paid them no heed. "All you did was try to protect your reputation." He took a step forward.

A crackling orb flew at him.

Shadows rose, engulfing the orb. It fizzled out.

"Take him!" the queen shouted.

Chaos erupted as the Elithar attacked.

The rising sun cast long shadows across the grass. Calandriel called on them, forming a murky dome around himself. The warriors' spells struck but did not penetrate. The dome wouldn't last for long. He needed something to anchor its magic to, something that wouldn't run out. More spells struck his barrier. He placed on hand the ground, feeling for any life beyond the swaying grasses. But aside from some burrowing rodents, the only life nearby belonged to the ones attacking him.

That's it.

He touched the swirling dome, flinching as a fiery blast washed over it, trying to consume him. Closing his eyes and praying the barrier wouldn't fail under the onslaught, he called upon his magic. The misty tendrils around his arms turned pink, then deepened to red, slithering like serpents onto the fracturing barrier. They began to split, creating a smokey web-like pattern across the dome.

A razor-sharp piece of ice pierced through, grazing his arm. He bared his teeth at the burning pain but kept going. If he could pull this off...

More spells struck. One hit the web, flaring like the colour of fresh blood. The dome grew stronger. *Perfect.*

The web grew as it absorbed more magic, and soon the dome was completely covered. He served his connection to the barrier, relieved when it didn't disappear. The web flashed again, consuming the aura of another spell. He was safe, but now he had another problem: he couldn't stay in his protective shield forever. There were too many Elithar around for him to wait for them to exhaust themselves.

The hazy shape of a warrior rushed at the dome. They struck it with their sword, but it bounced off like they'd hit a wall. The barrier was unaffected.

"Destroy it!" his mother yelled, voice muffled.

After a few moments of non-stop barrage, the attacks ceased. Not sure what they were planning, Calandriel drew out a bone and called forth a shadowy hawk. The bird took off, passing through the barrier like it was nothing. *Thank the shadows that worked.* He was doing a lot of experimental magic on the fly, and one wrong move would cost him dearly.

He couldn't see the bird through his shield, but he could feel it. He sent it towards his parents, its talons reaching for his mother's face. She drove it aside with a flash of lightning. His father summoned his own fiery bird, bright even through the shadows of the barrier. It collided with the hawk, a repeat of the fight in Lyrellis. Calandriel bared his teeth.

So caught up with the bird, he almost didn't notice the warriors approaching. They attacked the swirling mass of shadows, hoping to break through. To his dark delight, the web immediately began to drain their aura. They retreated a few steps.

If the barrier can sap their aura, then perhaps I can as well. But it meant exposing himself.

A familiar aura hit the barrier. His mother. It too, faded. Not even the might of the Ancestors' blood could reach him. *Because I also carry their blood.* Though the kingdom wanted to deny it.

"Calandriel, come out here this instant," the queen ordered.

A small part of him wanted to obey, the part that had blindly done everything his parents had asked of him over the decades. But that urge was quickly squashed by the unbridled anger blazing inside him. He conjured an orb of shadows and lobbed it towards the queen. Her mount stumbled. But she did not fall.

"Calandriel!" she roared. Shapes surrounded her.

"I'll come out if you tell the Elithar to stand down," he said, voice steadier than he felt.

"My Queen," said the captain, "we cannot—"

"Stand aside. Let me deal with him on my own," she said, dismounting. Her voice was emotionless, but her aura betrayed her intent. Once the barrier dropped, she would kill him.

Something in him snapped. Fire coursed through his veins. On the battle-field, his hawk let out a horrible screech.

Frowning, he flicked his hand, dispelling the swirling dome. It quickly faded in the morning light.

His mother was already on the move.

"Don't interfere!" Queen Illyndria shouted at the warriors. She hurled a powerful blast of light at him.

Calandriel was ready for it. At his command, shadows leapt up to meet the light. The spells spun as they collided, slowly fizzling out. He darted to the side as another beam of light came at him. Then another. His mother wasn't going to allow him to retaliate. She wanted to end this quickly.

Of course she does. She has better things to do back home. Nobles to suck up to.

It took everything he had to avoid her spells, as they quickly became more powerful.

And more varied. A jet of steaming water just missed scalding his arm.

In the heartbeat it took for the steam to clear, he pulled a small bone from his pocket. He'd picked it up somewhere on the prairie, believing it belonged to a small rodent. As his magic returned the creature's shape, he quickly realized that wasn't the case. He stepped back as the spectral shape of an adult nuu formed before him. He smiled. Perfect.

The animal bellowed, a hollow, low sound one could feel in their bones. It lowered its horned head and charged at the queen.

She sent a volley of colourful spells at it, but they had no effect. As she dodged its attack, Calandriel lobbed a buzzing sphere of pitch-black magic at her. It stuck her armour with a loud clang, sending her back a few steps. A faint aura emanated from the polished metal.

He frowned. Annoying, but not surprising. As the queen collected herself, giving him a look of pure disgust, the armour's aura flickered; his spell had weakened it.

The nuu came for her again. She deftly leapt out of its way and shot an arrow made of light towards her son. A dark tendril shot up from the long grass, knocking the arrow aside. Before he could react, a volley of light rained down on him. He flung an arm over his head, darkness following in its wake to shield him. He grunted as they struck. It stung but his shadowy cloak took the brunt of the damage.

The nuu bellowed again, this time in pain.

He dropped his shield to see it stuck full of arrows. Bright light suddenly burst from each one, obliterating the beast's spectral form. He winced as the bone dropped to the ground.

"You're next," his mother spat. Her armoured foot came down on the bone, crushing it to dust. "I will wipe you from our history. You're nothing but a stain."

Calandriel narrowed his eyes. "I am what you made me," he hissed.

His hawk screeched. It wasn't going to last much longer against its' fiery opponent. So he sent it towards his father instead. As much as he wanted to watch it tear at the king's face, the one that had scorned his existence from the start, he had to move.

A wave of fire rushed towards him across the grass, growing wider as it approached. He couldn't dodge it; there was nowhere to go.

Help me.

The shadows answered his plea. Tendrils wrapped around him. He blinked and found himself on charred grass, the burning wave roaring behind him. He met his mother's gaze, which was equally as shocked as his.

"Unclean," she spat before emitting a blinding flash of light.

Calandriel spun to protect his eyesight. A mistake. He gasped as white-hot pain erupted along his arm. His sleeve was on fire. He lost connection with his hawk as he snuffed out the flame.

"He's mine!" his mother bellowed at her partner.

"We don't have time for this," said the king, a flame dancing in the palm of his hand.

"I have—"

"Forget your pride. Let's just kill it and be done with it," he said.

Calandriel's heart iced over. Hearing the words spoken aloud hit in an entirely different way. Whatever remaining feelings he'd had for his parents evaporated.

"It is you who shall perish here today," he said. The dark heir closed his eyes. There were auras all around him from the fighting, but the ones he sought were the brightest: the auras of the living. And he could sense their positions as if he could see them. Inky tendrils veined with red shot out from below his feet towards the queen and king. They ensnared his parents and the warriors closest to them, rendering them immobile.

"Release us!" his father snapped, struggling against his bonds.

His mother shot him a look of pure loathing.

Calandriel ignored them, for the captain and a handful of warriors were coming for him. A wall of dark wriggling tendrils jumped up in front of him, fending off the attacks.

"Stop!" his mother commanded the Elithar. There was a sliver of panic in her voice. Calandriel savoured it.

The tendrils ensnaring her and the others glowed blood-red, sapping their auras like his dome had.

No, not just their auras, Calandriel realized, *their life force.* And that force was being carried straight to him. His head snapped back as a wave of energy hit him. The burn on his arm healed and his fatigue disappeared. Within moments, he felt completely refreshed. And the feed of life didn't stop.

The captain eyed him warily. Calandriel detected a hint of frustration in their stony grey gaze. The warriors were itching to attack, but the queen's command kept them at bay. And they could not safely free those bound by Calandriel's magic.

Calandriel smiled. For once he was in control. For once, his parents had no say.

The tendrils crackled, increasing their draw. The bound Elithar went limp, their life force draining away. One's aura flickered out. The tendrils released them.

"GET HIM!" the queen screeched at the unrestrained warriors. They sprung into action. The captain came at him with their blade drawn.

Really, they thought he could take him on?

He swept them back, like dry leaves in a breeze, with a burst of magic. Only the captain managed to stay on their feet. Calandriel snapped his fingers. More tendrils sprang up, trapping the fallen elves.

"Ancestors damn you!" his mother spat. She wriggled weakly against the tendrils, her golden locks losing their luster. Beside her his father had gone deathly pale. He wasn't long for this world.

The Ancestors? He'd forgotten about them. "The Ancestors blessed me with this magic."

The queen's face turned red. "Do not speak of them with your tainted mouth! They would never bestow such magic upon their people."

Calandriel strode up to her, careful not to let the tendrils break. "Then where did it come from?" More warriors went limp, drained to death.

"I know not." Her eyes flicked towards the king. "But it is their will that you be eliminated!" She suddenly threw her head back. "Ancestors, hear my plea. Grant me strength to remove this blight from our lands. Allow me to purify our soiled bloodline!"

There was a tremendous clap, like thunder. Calandriel's connection to his parents was suddenly severed by a series of jagged rocks bursting through the ground. Each glowed gold.

He felt a flicker of fear. Could it be?

Queen Illyndria drew his attention. Her form was limned in the same gold light as the rocks.

No, it wasn't possible. The Ancestors...?

Then Calandriel remembered something important. A family secret. While his mother preferred light magic, her natural affinity was for another kind: earth.

The blood drained from his face. He gathered everything he had, all the energy he'd absorbed and poured it into one spell. The auras of his remaining captives flickered out. The sky darkened like night, his magic blotting out the sun.

He hurled the darkness towards his mother just as she struck the ground with a golden fist.

The earth split open.

Calandriel fell.

TWENTY

THE WEDGE BETWEEN

Fae was relaxing in his room the evening after the trip to his family home when Alysion burst in.

He jumped at the sight of the prince. Alysion's golden hair was messy, and his outfit was dishevelled. It reminded him of when they'd first met just inside the Sylandrian wards. Alysion had just run away from home and Fae had been looking for Ash. Frankly, Fae was impressed that Alysion had made it that far on his own; the trip from Lyrellis to the border near Redwood wasn't a quick one.

"I would appreciate it if you knocked," he said stiffly.

"You're here," Alysion said, eyes wide and very red.

"Yes?" replied Fae, crossing his arms over his bare chest. "Where else would I be?"

"I thought...I thought..." The prince trailed off into silence, gaze dropping to the floor.

"You thought what?" he urged. What did Alysion want now?

The prince looked up, emerald eyes meeting brown. "I thought you left. I looked everywhere for you. When I saw that Sy-Sy was gone..."

Fae didn't respond right away. Alysion's hands were clenched at his sides, his voice wavering. He wanted to comfort the prince, to tell him that everything would be all right. But after what Alysion had told him, had accused him of back in the hall of statues...he was still too hurt by it.

And deep down, a small part of him was pleased that Alysion had learned what it felt like to be let down.

"Well, I'm still here," he said more sharply than intended. And he was, but without Alysion, it was becoming harder by the day. He dug his fingers into his arms. "With my inability to defend myself."

Alysion blinked. "I—"

Suddenly, all Fae's bottled-up emotions from the past few moons took hold.

"Do you think I enjoy it? Being looked down upon by everyone? Having to take their taunts and abuse because if I react any other way, it gets worse?" He uncrossed his arms, voice rising as he spoke. "I could easily beat my sparring partners with the sword. But I have to hold back because if I don't—well, you saw what happened. I don't dare complain about *anything* they do because it comes back to me tenfold. And even if I wanted to tell you, you're never around! Every single time I've asked to meet, you haven't shown up!"

Alysion had gone still.

"I ask for the bare minimum, and I don't even get that!" snapped Fae.

"We got to go to Ashdale."

"That was already a moon ago, and even then, we hardly had any time together!"

"Look. I'm sorry—"

"Sorry doesn't cut it! I want to see you, Alysion. You're the only thing tying me to this place. If it weren't for you, I really would leave."

"I'm trying Fae, I really am. I can't help that my mother is ill, that the noble families are demanding a new isidyll by the solstice, which might I remind you," his voice started to rise, "is less than a half-moon away! I wish I could spend time with you, but every time I try, something comes up. Even today, I thought I had an evening free but now I have to entertain the Skyshades and deal with their attempt to force their awful heir upon me! Do you know how many times a day I get accosted by different families? I have to sneak around my own home because they try to corner me at every chance!"

Blinded by his hurt, Fae didn't care. They were all excuses. His clenched hands shook at his sides. "The Skyshades, really? You'll go see them, but not me?"

"By the Ancestors, Fae! I just told you why," snapped the prince, eyes blazing.

"Enough!" His voice suddenly dropped, becoming ice-cold like Captain Anaril's. "Go. Go to them. Since it's what you really want."

Alysion stared at him for a moment longer before spinning on his heel and storming out.

• • • ● • • •

Damnit! This wasn't how things were supposed to go! They were supposed to make up! Why did he tell Fae about his meeting with the Skyshades? Their son had been one of the elves he'd caught attacking him! Ugh, what a mess.

Mind racing like an uhaan, Alysion trudged through the palace.

What had Fae meant by that last part? Alysion wanted nothing to do with any of the noble heirs! Fae was the only one for him. His heart hurt like someone was trying to rip it from his body. He wished someone would; it would hurt less than this.

He clenched and unclenched his hands as he made his way out of the palace to the Skyshade residence, sparks jumping off his fingertips. It was tempting to huck a ball of fire down the walkway, but setting his home ablaze wouldn't solve his relationship problems. Instead, he resorted to rubbing the scarred burn on his wrist.

He eventually reached the Skyshade residence. Being one of the oldest and most prominent families, they had an entire tree to themselves. It wasn't as large as the trees that made up the palace, but it was nonetheless impressive with all the vines that artistically covered it.

With a sigh, he raised a hand to knock. The door opened before his fist struck. A belim in resplendent robes of grey and green greeted him.

"Welcome, My Prince. We've been expecting you." Nelliana Skyshade. She placed a fist over her heart and dipped her head before stepping aside to allow him entry.

Alysion got a whiff of something floral as he entered the hall.

"Please, follow me," said the Skyshade matron. "Glendarion is looking forward to seeing you."

Alysion just politely nodded as she led him up a level to an open sitting room with large windows. Living vines wound around them, giving the impression they were outdoors. They let in a lot of natural light, but the view of the half-naked trees and grey sky did little to boost Alysion's spirits.

A short nelim stood up from one of the plush chairs and came over. "Prince Alysion, welcome to our home." Livion Skyshade wore a tunic and bottoms of the same grey and green as Nelliana. "Glendarion will join us in a moment."

Oh great. So he'd have to entertain the parents first. He wasn't in the mood to deal with their veiled complaints about his family.

Livion gestured towards one of the four chairs setup around a low table. Alysion, hiding his reluctance, took a seat.

"How are preparations for the Eburnas coming along?" asked Nelliana politely. They'd left the chair across from him empty for Glendarion. "Has a new isidyll been selected and trained?"

You know one hasn't, he thought irritably. "No, not yet. We've been working on it, but so far the few candidates haven't shown enough promise."

"Does that mean King Illuven will be assuming that role again?" Livion's tone was conversational, but he wouldn't quite meet Alysion's eyes.

The Skyshades, while perhaps not as noisy about their displeasure as the other families, were just as unhappy with the current state of affairs as the rest. And like the others, they planned on using it for their own gain.

Alysion knew the sole reason they had invited him over was to force Glendarion upon him. They didn't have a daughter, but ever since they'd learned that Alysion liked nelim, they'd been subtly hinting that he should take their heir as his sera. With their current noble status, the only higher they could go was to join with the royal family. Alysion would have declined the invitation to visit today if he could, but the Skyshades would have taken it as an insult.

Getting out of this was going to be difficult.

"No, my father will not be the isidyll. While he is fully capable of the duty, we decided it would be best if someone directly related to the Ancestors did it."

"Well you surely don't mean your mother. Unless she is on the mend?" said Nelliana.

Nosey. "I will be the isidyll for the Eburnas. I've been preparing for it since the equinox."

A servant entered with a wooden tray of pastries and the fixings to make tea. "Glendarion is on his way," they said before retreating.

Alysion wished Glendarion would both take his time and hurry up. He didn't want to deal with the young noble but also wanted out of here as quickly as possible.

Nelliana set about preparing the tea, magically heating the water and preparing the leaves. "Different blends require different temperatures. We don't want to scald the leaves. Do we? It would ruin the delicate flavours."

Was that a veiled jab at him? He mentally shrugged it off and instead watched her with mild interest. She was practiced and precise, moving with perfect efficiency—as expected of someone of her breeding.

"I can assure you, the solstice will go off without a hitch even with myself acting as isidyll. It coincides with the Luuya, after all."

"Indeed it does," said Livion, his expression unreadable. "With both of these events occurring at the same time, we must assure that the Ancestors are appeased."

"Of course," said Alysion. His tone was light, a stark contrast to how he felt inside.

"For you, My Prince," said Nelliana, pouring him a cup of tea and setting it before him.

"Thank you." He picked up the cup and inhaled its' scent. The tea was a blend of herbs and spices well suited for autumn. Even the cup had been selected for the season, painted with brightly coloured leaves.

It was then that Glendarion finally arrived. Alysion tensed but forced himself to relax. Thankfully, none of the Skyshades noticed, as they were occupied with their son's arrival.

"My apologies for being late," he said, placing a fist over his heart and dipping his head. Alysion was pleased to see that he looked on edge. He hadn't forgotten the incident with Fae. *Do his parents know?* He took a sip of his tea, eyes wandering over them. It was hard to say. If they did, he suspected they would sweep it under the rug.

Glendarion took his seat. He reached for a pastry but pulled back at a glance from his father which wasn't as subtle as it should have been.

"Now that we are all here, we can get down to business," said Nelliana, tone becoming more serious. "We are hoping that you are still considering Glendarion as your sera. We don't see why you would refuse. Our families are a perfect match. Undoubtedly, the Ancestors would be wholly satisfied with the decision. We have long worked to cultivate our bloodline and uphold our status."

Alysion took another sip of his tea, pretending to think it over for the sake of propriety.

"Glendarion is skilled with both magic and steel. His tutors sing nothing but praises," added Livion.

Alysion nearly choked on his tea as he suppressed a snort. Fae could beat this guy's ass in a sword fight a in heartbeat. Blood had nothing to do with it. *But Fae is of noble blood,* he reminded himself. He looked at Glendarion, who was looking everywhere but at him.

Good. At least one of them realized where he stood in all this.

"What can we do to convince you to accept him as your sera?" asked Nelliana.

Alysion set down his cup.

"There is more to picking a sera than bloodline," he started, eyes slowing panning up to meet Nelliana's.

Hers narrowed.

Had he not already been accustomed to the captain and his mother, perhaps he would have been intimidated. Instead, all he felt was annoyance. "The one to eventually join me on the throne requires more than a good pedigree."

"As we've said, he does well in all his lessons," said Livion.

"Yet there is still more to consider than that."

"Such as?" asked Nelliana sharply. "What more could you possibly desire?"

Like his own parents, Nelliana and Livion must have been arranged marriage. Perhaps they didn't understand what it was like to fall in love with someone of your own choice. Which meant he had no hope of ending this nicely. What a pain.

"I need someone who is just and kind. Someone who isn't going to judge others for their faults and weaknesses. And most importantly," his eyes flicked to Glendarion, who he was pleased to see was shifting awkwardly in his seat, "someone who isn't going to discriminate against those who are different."

"We can assure you that our son—" started Livion.

"No, you cannot," Alysion said sharply. "Just yesterday I witnessed him and a few of his companions attack Fae unprovoked."

The room went dead silent. Glendarion tried to melt into his chair. Livion looked shocked.

Nelliana blinked, her face a mask. He could practically hear the gears of her mind working to turn this around. What she didn't realize was that while the mask may have hidden her emotions, its' mere existence exposed her nature: she was not bothered by the fact that her heir had attacked another. Because like most of the families, she didn't see Fae as a person.

"This is a serious accusation," she said.

"It's not an accusation. I personally stopped the incident." Alysion's emerald eyes blazed.

Nelliana turned her to her son.

Glendarion stared at the floor, silent.

"I think we should look into the matter," said Livion softly.

Alysion rounded on him. "There is nothing to look into. Glendarion attacked a member of this kingdom without just cause." Alysion stood, glaring down at all of them. "And not only that, the one I have chosen as my sera." He paused to let the implications of that sink in.

It was no secret that Fae held the title of sera. There were simply those, like the elves before him, who wished to have it moved to another.

"You are lucky that I have no desire to see Glendarion stand trial for this."

Glendarion and his father paled. Nelliana turned bright red.

"Have a good evening." Alysion strode from the room, leaving the stunned family behind. He very well may have made new enemies today, but that didn't matter.

His father's words echoed in his head as he hurried back to the palace. *Please, my son, go find him.* Alysion didn't want to end up like his father, living only the shadow of a life with someone he didn't love.

He needed to find Fae and remove the wedge that had grown between them.

Twenty-One

Realization

Fae didn't see Alysion again until the day before the winter solstice, and the time between was torture. Horrible thoughts filled his mind day and night, wearing him down. Was this it? Was their relationship over? Should he leave Lyrellis and hide in the forest until Ash returned? He wouldn't have to deal with anymore harassment if he did. But what if Alysion still cared for him? Leaving could be a huge mistake.

No, Alysion was no longer interested in him. The prince had made that clear.

Fae couldn't focus, and he couldn't sleep. Between his exhaustion and mental state, he no longer had to pretend he was bad at swordplay each day.

So when the prince burst into his room late that morning, panting like he'd run a lap around the city, a maelstrom of emotions threatened to sweep him away. Fae wanted nothing more than to hold him again, but at the same time, he was tempted to snap at him to leave.

Instead, he furrowed his brow and crossed his arms. "You could've knocked." He was shirtless again, in the middle of changing out of sweaty clothes after his session on the training field.

Alysion's ears turned red, but Fae wasn't sure if it was from embarrassment, running, or seeing him topless. But it didn't matter. "What now?" he asked sharply.

"I'm sorry for how I acted," Alysion blurted, standing awkwardly in the doorway. "I know there's no excuse for my actions, but I was scared. Scared that you'd been hurt. Scared by the thought of losing you. I just want you to understand I did it because I love you. I can't bear the thought of losing you."

By the gods, being in a relationship was *trying*.

"Close the door," Fae said, tone softening a smidge.

Alysion wasn't fully to blame for this. Fae had been frustrated and had taken it out on him. The prince couldn't help that he was being pulled in every direction, having to clean up the messes left by others. Plus, his mother was unwell. Fae couldn't imagine what Alysion was going through, which was why he hadn't wanted to trouble the prince with his own problems in the first place. But clearly, bottling them all up hadn't been the right thing to do. The sooner they dealt with whatever was happening between them, the better.

Alysion closed the door, then took a hesitant step forward.

Fae sighed, suddenly exhausted, and took a seat on his bed. "Come here."

Alysion sat stiffly beside him.

Fae twisted to look at him. This close up, he could see streaks down Alysion's face. It was like a punch to the gut. He put a hand on the prince's cheek and gently turned his head so their eyes met, his skin soft and warm beneath his fingertips. Alysion's pointed ears flushed under his touch, sending a jolt through him.

There was no way he could get through life without Alysion. The thought of it was unbearable.

"Both, yet neither of us are at fault for this. We just want to spend time together."

"It's all my fault. I haven't been fair to you," Alysion said. "I shouldn't have said those things."

"I'm also to blame. I should have told you what was going on with the noble families. I thought I could handle it, but as you said, I just can't. Their abuse hasn't solely been physical. They've been trying to convince me you've grown bored of me. And with your busy schedule, it certainly seemed that way."

Alysion opened his mouth to protest, but Fae moved his hand from his cheek to silence him with a finger over his full, soft lips. Lips he had gone far too long without kissing.

"I'm sorry. My pent up emotions took hold of me. Both of us said things we shouldn't have." He dropped his hand. "And I apologize for ever doubting your affections. So many things are happening here outside of our control. It's taking everything we have to stay afloat."

"After the Eburnas tomorrow it should settle down..." Alysion mumbled, scooting closer to him.

Fae caught the familiar scent of lunaberries. Heat pooled in his stomach, and his heart skipped a beat. By the gods, no one else had ever made him feel like this. "It'd better," he said softly.

Alysion leaned in close. "I'll make sure of it," he whispered into his ear. "It won't be a repeat of the equinox."

Fae shivered. Suddenly, his lips were crashing against the prince's. He didn't know who leaned in first, but it didn't matter. Their lips moved frantically against each other, as if the connection was the only thing keeping them alive. Keeping them sane.

Alysion pulled him close. He ran his hands along Fae's bare back like he feared Fae would disappear if he didn't. It set Fae's skin ablaze as he tangled his hands in Alysion's golden locks. The prince made a sound of longing that pierced him to the center of his being.

Fae fell back in the bed, pulling Alysion down with him. Neither broke the kiss, lips locked together even as Fae flipped them over to get on top.

One of his hands found its way up under Alysion's shirt. The prince shuddered beneath him. He broke the kiss to pull off Alysion's top, sending it to the floor in a crumpled heap.

Alysion took one of Fae's hands and brought it to his mouth. Fae nearly melted when the prince began to lick and suck at his fingers. He rubbed his thumb over Alysion's smooth, flushed cheek. Fae wanted more, but he forced himself to be patient. Alysion wasn't making it easy.

"I love you," he murmured, voice husky.

The rest of their clothing joined Alysion's crumpled top on the floor.

Movements eventually stilled, and silence fell over the room. Fae had an arm wrapped around his golden prince, whose face was nestled in the crook of his neck. While the prince dozed, his other hand idly played with a lock of Alysion's silky hair.

He tensed up when he heard voices in the hall, but thankfully, they continued on. Both he and Alysion had skipped out on their tutors to be together.

And I'd do it again.

By the gods, how he'd missed spending time with his prince.

Alysion soon stirred beside him.

"How are you feeling?" Fae asked.

Alysion mumbled something unintelligible into his neck.

"What's that? I don't speak *tahtter*," he said referring to the large burrowing rodents that lived beneath the Manwan Plains.

Alysion unburied his face. "I'm sore," he grumped.

"I'm very sorry to hear that," he said solemnly. He wasn't.

Alysion snorted. "It was worth it."

Fae kissed the top of his head. "We're going to be in so much trouble later."

"Shhh, don't ruin the moment."

They lapsed into silence again.

Fae looked out the window. It was snowing, a reminder that the solstice was nearly upon them. That whatever his parents had warned him about was coming.

Reality came crashing down. He'd never told Alysion about his parents. "I need to tell you something," he started.

Alysion waited.

"During the Aubrillias, I saw my parents."

Curiosity flooded Alysion's face. "And? How did it go?"

"I didn't see them for very long. They had come to warn me about something, about someone. A cursed heir from times past."

"A cursed heir?"

"It's what Mellith and I have been researching in the library. We've been trying to uncover their identity and figure out my parents' warning."

Alysion fidgeted beside him but didn't interrupt.

"Mellith and I found a scroll that Tarathiel magically hid within his family's records. It tells the story of a prince from long before the Syl-Raanian War. The prince is clearly the Crown Prince of Sylandris, but his family name is Goldensky. It's strange."

Alysion sat up, expression serious. "When I was at the Great Temple, I found a study that Tarathiel had magically concealed underground with some papers that contained a bit of lost history regarding my family. We were once called Goldensky, but after some unmentioned incident, we changed our name. Whatever happened must have been serious for my ancestors to go that far."

Thanks to the scroll he and Mellith had found, Fae knew exactly what had happened and why. He filled Alysion in on everything they'd learned from the document Tarathiel had hidden.

"Mellith and I visited my childhood home—that's where I was when you couldn't find me...and we found another scroll. Like the others, it was hidden. My father used his light magic to conceal it."

Alysion nodded, eyes gleaming.

"I have yet to open it." He looked towards his desk where the scroll lay. After the last fight with Alysion he hadn't been able to bring himself to read it.

"Then shall we?" Alysion slipped from the bed.

Fae couldn't look away from the prince's shapely naked body. He was slim but had a healthy layer of muscle from wielding his sword, and his hips were the perfect place for Fae to rest his hands.

Alysion returned with the scroll. Silence fell as they got comfortable under the blanket and unfurled the document.

"By the Ancestors," Alysion whispered once they were done. "That's the aura I was feeling in Tarathiel's study. The aura of the Canyon of Lost Souls."

Fae couldn't believe that the battle between the royals and Calandriel had resulted in the canyon's creation. "The armoured spectres we saw down there are the Elithar warriors that Calandriel killed..."

Alysion shuddered. He'd nearly ridden through one of the fallen warriors. "Tarathiel was studying Calandriel's magic. Learning how to use it himself. My parents said he cast a life-sucking dome during the fight at the temple."

Just like Calandriel had. It was strange how history repeated itself; the same spell being used against the Queen and King of Sylandris, thousands of suncycles apart. "I hate to say it, but if we want to figure out what my parents warned me about, another trip to the canyon might be in order."

Alysion grimaced. "I think you're right. Remember how I said the canyon's aura felt strange on our way back from Ashdale? Something is going on down there. Something I suspect we'll need the power of the crystals to help with."

"But the crystals didn't work last time we were there," said Fae.

"I have a feeling things will be different."

"How so?"

"Because the Luuya is tonight."

Twenty-Two

Heist

There was no way King Illuven would let them take the crystals, or leave Lyrellis. Too much was riding on the success of the Eburnas. They would have to steal the crystals and sneak away before the alarm was raised—a task that was much easier said than done.

"And you're sure we can't wait until after the solstice?" asked Fae.

"If Calandriel or something is stirring down there, then I bet you anything they're relying on the power of the Luuya to facilitate whatever is happening," reasoned the prince.

"Do you really think Calandriel is still alive? It's been millennia!" Fae whispered. Elves had long lives, but not *that* long.

"With his magic, I won't rule it out."

Fae couldn't argue that. Still, taking off right before such an important event didn't sit right with him. It could ruin whatever was left of the Brightstar's dwindling reputation. There was no way they would get the crystals and make it to and from the canyon—not to mention deal with whatever was down there—before the festival tomorrow.

"At least all the crystals are in one place this time," Alysion said, "and we know they're somewhere in the city." Despite all the magic concealing their auras, he could sense their presence due to their existing bond.

Fae looked at his wrist. The circular mark he and Alysion had received when they'd first been tasked with finding the crystals had faded to white like an old scar. He suspected it would never go away, but that was fine. It was a reminder of how he'd met Alysion and everything they had gone through on that crazy journey with Gale.

His heart panged. He missed Gale. And Master Cane. And Ash.

"So how exactly are we going to do this?" he asked, pulling himself back into the present before his thoughts spiralled.

"Finding the crystals won't be difficult, but freeing them will be. I know a handful of powerful elves have put a wards up, and the Elithar must be guarding them."

Fae got up and started dressing. "Let's go take a look, see what we're dealing with." Despite what they were about to do, he felt strangely giddy with excitement. He belted on his sword, glad it had it at his side after so many moons.

Fae thought the crystals would be hidden in the palace, but Alysion assured him they weren't.

"The palace is too busy," the prince whispered as they crept out of Fae's room and down the hall. Before they'd left, Alysion had taken a moment to suppress his aura and alter his appearance. "There are too many nosy nobles poking around. They would inevitably find them, intentional or not. They've been moved to someplace quieter."

Sneaking out of the palace was no easy feat. There were elves everywhere. Fae was too recognizable but they could do little to conceal his appearance, and Alysion wasn't confident his own disguise would hold for long. Fae wished they had some talismans to help hide their presence. A few times they had to wait for halls to clear before proceeding, hiding around corners while nobles idled about. It was both nerve-wracking and frustrating.

Once they made it outside, Fae breathed a massive sigh of relief.

"I never realized how many elves fit in there," he said, patting one of the thick branches that twisted out from the palace tree to become part of the raised walkway.

"Too many," Alysion grumbled.

They hurried down a spiral staircase to the forest floor, where there was less traffic and more foliage to conceal them.

"Should we grab the uhaan?" Fae asked as they neared the stable.

Alysion shook his head. "Not yet. If we do and someone notices, it might raise suspicion." Fae caught a hint of something sharp in Alysion's tone. He felt a twinge of guilt and was glad they had made up.

They had just skirted the stable when someone called out.

"Fae? Is that you?"

Both of them froze. How had they been caught already?

To his relief, it was Mellith who approached. Alysion frowned beside him, but it quickly disappeared.

"What are you doing out here? Don't you have to prepare for tomorrow?" they asked. They eyed the prince curiously but made no sign that they recognized him.

"I could ask the same of you," Fae replied. They needed to end this conversation quickly before someone found them. "We're just running a quick errand."

"You and your...friend?"

Uh oh. Mellith knew he had no other friends beyond them and Alysion. And Alysion didn't look disgusted enough to be in his damisri presence. They *really* needed to leave. "Yeah. And we've got to get going. I'll see you later, Mellith."

"Will you be at the library tonight?"

"No. This errand we're running will take us the rest of the day."

"Oh, all right." Their expression fell.

Guilt immediately filled him. Mellith had only ever been kind to him.

"Do you want to come with us?" Fae offered.

Alysion shot him a dark look. "We don't need their assistance."

"Can you give us a moment?" he asked, dragging Alysion out of earshot.

Mellith nodded, eyes bright with curiosity.

Alysion glared daggers at him. "They can't learn about the crystals," the prince said, his tone reminiscent of his mother's. It was clear there was more he wanted to say.

"Look, I know how you feel about them, but they could be helpful." *And I think you'll like them once you get to know them.* "They're no slouch when it comes to magic, and we don't know what we'll find. At the very least, they could cause a diversion if needed."

The prince was dead silent, but the subtle shifts in his expression gave away his racing thoughts.

"We don't have to bring them to the canyon," continued Fae.

"Fine," Alysion eventually said, his displeasure obvious. "But if they do anything—"

"Mellith won't betray us. And this way, we can keep an eye on them."

"How do you know that?" Alysion huffed.

"Because that's how friendship works." Fae waved the aelim over. "Come on."

Sneaking out of the palace had been stressful, but it paled in comparison to the tension now wafting off the prince. And Fae knew Alysion was doing his best to keep it under wraps in sight of the other noble. While searching for the crystals, he'd learned that Alysion had a jealous streak. It was something they would work through later.

"What exactly are we doing?" Mellith asked quietly as they hurried through the forest.

"We're collecting something important," replied the prince, not looking at them.

"Is it related to the heir?"

Fae glanced at Alysion, wondering how much to tell them.

"Indirectly," grunted Alysion.

With Alysion's approval, he filled Mellith in on what more they'd learned about Calandriel but held back that they were currently after the crystals; their existence was only known by those who had been at the temple. After what Tarathiel had attempted, Fae understood why it was best to keep them a secret. Yet that secret had still gotten out...

"So Calandriel is still alive in the canyon," Mellith surmised.

Fae leapt over a log. "It's possible." Yet last time, he hadn't encountered any living things down there, just the ghostly forms of the fallen warriors...but why would the warriors still be there if they had no charge to guard? He shivered.

"And you think he's planning on using the power of the twin moons to break free," they continued.

"Yes, we believe so."

"Stop," Alysion said, coming to a sudden halt.

"What—" Fae started.

"Their aura got stronger." He started touching the massive trees, much like he had in the Glimmering Forest when they were looking for the Emerald.

"I sense something, but it's very faint," said Mellith, frowning. "What is it?"

Alysion ignored them. Or maybe he couldn't hear them. His eyes were closed, and he was muttering something under his breath.

"You'll see soon enough," Fae said with an apologetic smile.

Thankfully Mellith didn't look bothered by the secrecy, if anything they looked intrigued.

Something flashed brightly, making Fae's eyes water.

"Sorry," said Alysion. "Didn't expect that." The prince stepped away from the tree he'd been speaking with. The trunk, wider than all three of them put together, began to split. The opening grew wider and taller, but it didn't go all the way through the trunk. Once it was large enough to accommodate an elf, the crack stopped growing. Green light filled the space—a gate.

Fae looked at Alysion expectantly. To his dismay, Alysion's disguise had disappeared.

Mellith seemed unsurprised by the revelation of their prince's identity. They were much more fascinated by the gate. "Wow, you did that all on your own? That's impressive magic, even for a member of the royal family."

"All I did was call forth an existing one. I have no idea where it goes," said the prince with a shrug. Without hesitation, he stepped into the light.

Fae followed with Mellith right behind him.

They emerged into a shimmering tunnel made of light.

"My parents made this," Alysion mumbled.

Fae kept close to him, unnerved. To their backs was the gate, still filled with swirling green light. He could see something at the far end of the tunnel ahead, but couldn't make anything out even with his keen elven eyesight.

Mellith tried to touch the wall, but their hand passed right through it. "Fascinating. Yet the floor is solid." They tapped it with their foot to make sure.

Alysion tensed up. "We have company."

The shape at the far end of the tunnel split into two distinct forms as it quickly approached. Elithar.

Fae drew his sword. It would do little to protect him from the elite warriors, but holding it helped to calm his nerves.

Mellith stepped forward with Alysion. If they felt any fear about fighting the elite warriors, it didn't show.

Woosh.

A large orange ball of fire shot towards them. Alysion held out his hands as if to grab it and jerked them to the side. The fireball shot harmlessly through the wall, disappearing into the void.

Fae hoped it hadn't gone somewhere where it would cause harm.

"Don't let yourself get knocked out of the tunnel," Alysion warned, eyes narrowed. "I don't know what'll happen, but it likely won't be good." He retaliated with a fireball of his own, flames bluer than Fae remembered. *He's getting stronger.*

The Elithar doused it with water, which filled the tunnel with scalding steam. Mellith flung out a hand and exhaled deeply. The steam was diverted harmlessly around them, disappearing through the sides and top of the tunnel.

When it cleared, they saw that the Elithar had reached the tunnel's midpoint.

Alysion hit them with a blast of air that would have swept any elf off their feet. But the warriors held their ground, sturdy as boulders, the wind whipping their long hair about. Alysion cut off the spell.

"Throw another fireball at them; I'll help this time," said Mellith.

The prince nodded.

Fae watched, envious of their prowess. Alysion created another ball of fire which Mellith encircled with a current of air. The air cut through the water the Elithar threw at it. The fireball struck true.

When the fire fizzled about, the warriors were prone on the tunnel floor.

"That won't keep them out for long. Let's go," said the prince, already running. They leapt over the fallen warriors as they passed by.

At the far end was another gate, its light a pale pink. As far as Fae could tell, it was already active, but Alysion held out an arm to stop them.

"If we run through it now," he said, "it'll spit us back into the forest. Give me a moment."

Alysion got to work.

Fae turned around to check on the Elithar. The warriors were already halfway to their feet. "Hurry up!"

Mellith stepped between them, making slicing motions with their hands. Bursts of air buffeted the warriors, pushing them back down.

"Almost there," said the prince, face scrunched up and hands glowing.

Fae hoped so, because Mellith could only keep the warriors down for so long.

As they rose to their feet, one of the Elithar managed to create a shield. A tendril snaked down from the tunnel's ceiling and connected with both warriors, limning them in its light.

Mellith grimaced and ceased their onslaught. They assumed a more defensive stance, ready for whatever the Elithar were about to throw their way.

A beam of light shot towards them like an arrow just as another flashed from the gate.

"Got it!" shouted the prince.

Fae defensively jerked up his sword with one hand. He grabbed Mellith with the other, hauling them through just as everything went white.

• • • ● ● • •

Alysion pat Fae's face, trying to wake him up. Relief washed over him when he stirred, mumbling and rubbing at bleary eyes.

"Take it easy," he said, steadying Fae as he rose to his feet.

"Where are we?" Fae asked.

They were...somewhere. Alysion wasn't entirely sure. It looked like they had landed in the night sky. It was dark all around them, but the darkness was dotted with stars stretching in to infinity. It both filled him with awe and made him uneasy. He felt so small.

When he looked down at whatever they were standing on, Alysion saw more pinpricks of light. Hopefully, the ground would stay solid and they wouldn't fall into a sea of stars.

His stomach jolted with unpleasant familiarity at the thought—he'd been in a space like this before. Ash had dragged him there right before he'd been kidnapped and taken to the temple.

"I think we're on the aural plane," said Mellith. "Though I don't know how that's possible.

Alysion tried not to bristle at their words, irritated by the aelim's presence. *Stop it*, he chided himself. Mellith had been nothing but a huge help. He was being unfair. But acknowledging it didn't make it any easier. He focused on Fae instead.

"How are you feeling?" he asked.

"I'm okay." Fae pat his hand reassuringly. "But my sword didn't make it." The Elithars' last spell had destroyed it.

"Thankfully it saved you." Concerned but satisfied that Fae wasn't about to topple over, Alysion let go. He turned about, studying the area. The pull of the crystals was strong, and the mark on his wrist had darkened. They were somewhere in this strange space.

"Do either of you recognize any of those?" he asked, indicating at the stars around them. He avoided looking at his feet.

His companions stared at the stars for a bit, then shook their heads.

"There are powerful auras in here," said Mellith.

Alysion wasn't surprised they could sense the crystals. Their pull was so strong. It was as if he could reach out and touch them, but he couldn't see them anywhere. "Those auras are what we're looking for." He closed his eyes and pushed his own aura outward, reaching for the crystals.

He was instantly met with thousands and thousands of auras. Their magnitude was staggering, but distant; even so, he suspected a lesser sorcerer would be overwhelmed. The auras of the crystals flared before his mind's eye. They were all around him, even the Kunzite, cleverly hidden amongst the stars.

His aura easily mingled with theirs, like reuniting with an old friend. He held up a hand, beckoning them to come.

One by one, the auras enveloped his physical body. Magic rushed through him, filling voids he hadn't realized had formed when the crystals had been taken from him. It was comforting.

"Does he always glow like that?" asked a distant voice.

"Sometimes," another replied. Fae.

Alysion pulled back into himself and opened his eyes. Coloured light flickered across his vision, then faded.

"I'd say that was a success," said Fae. "How do you feel?"

"There was no painful bonding process this time," he said. "I'm fine." He felt better than fine.

Fae smiled softly. Alysion's heart swelled. His smile was brighter than any of the crystals' auras. Alysion would do anything to protect it, even if it meant fighting an elf who had been trapped in a hole for millennia.

Fae's ring flashed. A letter appeared before them. Fae snatched it out of the air and began to read, the colour quickly draining from his face.

"What is it?" asked Alysion. He took the letter and read it.

Dear F,

The V is dead and the one I worried about has taken over. He and his followers have used a strange power to break through the Sky Peak wards. Be prepared.

-A

"By the gods," he whispered, the ground lurching beneath his feet.

"What's wrong?" Mellith asked sharply.

"The dragons are coming," Fae said quietly.

Mellith blinked. "What do you mean?"

"My brother Ash has been sending letters about the situation over there. Their old vorais was overthrown by a dragon who wants to rekindle the war between our peoples," Fae explained quickly.

Alysion handed the letter to Mellith. "Take this to my father, immediately."

Mellith furrowed their brow in annoyance, but did not protest.

"Sorry," said Fae, looking guilty. He clearly wanted Mellith to come with them.

"Don't be. Delivering this is just as important. I wish you both luck with Calandriel. I'll see you on the battlefield," they said before stepping back through the wards and into the fading gate.

Fae and Alysion exchanged a look.

"Your father will take care of it," Fae said.

Alysion wasn't convinced. How were they supposed to fend off any army of dragons? And with his mother in such a state...

A comforting hand touched his cheek. "We have to deal with Calandriel," said Fae, looking less peaky now that the shock had worn off. "We can't take on an army of dragons on our own."

"I suppose..." Alysion wanted nothing more than to abandon this venture and return home. Instead he called on the crystals to revive the closing gate. By the Ancestors, how good it felt to have them back.

They stepped through the gate and found themselves in the forest at the base of the gate-tree. Mellith was nowhere to be seen, but their aura trailed back towards Lyrellis.

Alysion immediately set about opening another gate, worried that if he didn't, he would rush back to the palace. As he worked, the canyon's oppressive, draining energy poured through the widening portal.

That didn't bode well.

Alysion entwined his hand in Fae's as they stepped through.

Twenty-Three

Teeth and Talons

Though they were no longer using magic to speed along, the fleeing dragons didn't stop flying until the twin moons were high in the sky, the mountains around them taking on a silvery sheen from their light.

They're both nearly full. Ranath knew that the Luuya was only a day or two away. Tarathiel had plans for that legendary night. Plans that involved attacking the dragons as retribution for the crimes they'd committed against the elves centuries ago.

Ranath sighed. And now Vyrmyris was doing that very thing. Who was really in the wrong? The dragons or the elves? He would never get over how similar the two males were.

The group took shelter in a series of caves somewhere in the southern stretch of the Jagged Teeth mountains. Ranath had paid little attention to where they were going; his wings ached too much from the fight. It had been nothing like the mock fights he and Xyrros would have. His heart panged at the thought. It was a shame the ziirar sold them out to Vyrmyris.

He curled up on the rocky floor, licking his burns to soothe them. He'd long ago stopped being surprised by the actions his draconic instincts pushed him to. It felt perfectly natural. The licking only temporarily relieved the pain but the act helped settle his mind. He eventually fell asleep.

Ranath woke up with a start. He looked around to see if it was time to leave, but the handful of dragons sharing the cave with him were still fast asleep.

Something was off.

He closed his eyes and pretended to go back to sleep. Almost instantly, he noticed a familiar aura. One that nearly had him leaping to his feet with his fangs bared. Xyrros. What was that traitor doing here?

Instead, he kept up his facade. Xyrros' feet were silent as they made their way closer to him. If they hadn't betrayed him, Ranath would have been impressed by their stealth. Who were they after? Sevarak, Nyrvrin, or himself? Xyrros had to get by him to reach the ziiras, and he had no intention of letting them do that.

He waited until they were nearly upon him before he struck.

Xyrros squealed loudly in surprise as he collided with their side. All around them, dragons leapt to their feet. The scent of fear filled the cave.

Xyrros stumbled, wings flapping awkwardly to maintain their balance. Ranath forced them down.

"What's going on?" someone growled.

"Is it Vyrmyris!?"

"Have we been found?"

Not if I have anything to say about it. He pinned Xyrros' neck with his front talons, eyes gleaming in the dim moonlight. The other dragon stopped thrashing when they realized who he was, going completely limp in submission.

"Who's that? Is that Xyrros?" asked Sevarak, shouldering their way through the nervous dragons. Nyrvrin was right behind her. "It is! Let them up, Ranath."

"No."

There was a pause.

"And why not?" asked Nyrvrin.

Ranath didn't want to have this discussion in front of all the others. But he couldn't exactly ask for everyone to leave.

"Because Xyrros is working for Vyrmyris," he said.

"No, I'm not," Xyrros said quietly.

Ranath bared his teeth.

The ziiras exchanged a look. "That doesn't make any sense," huffed Sevarak.

"That's how betrayal works," snapped Ranath. It never made sense right away.

She shook her head. "As if Xyrros would ever help that blue bastard! Now let them up before I knock you over."

He suppressed a growl and reluctantly removed his talons from Xyrros' neck. He had no doubt that Sevarak would toss him across the cave if he didn't.

Xyrros rolled into a more comfortable position but kept their head down.

"I suppose they never told you about their parents then," Sevarak said, looking at the dragon curled up on the floor. "Might be time you did that."

Told him what about their parents? He'd never met them and Xyrros never spoke of them. Ranath had never thought to ask. Not that it mattered now.

Nyrvrin went around soothing the other dragons, reassuring them that it was safe to go back to sleep.

Xyrros slowly rose to their feet and headed for the mouth of the cave.

He and Sevarak followed.

"Vyrmyris killed my parents," they said quietly.

Ranath blinked but didn't say a word.

"We don't fully know what happened, but Sevarak was the one who found them. Vyrmyris' scent was the only other around."

"They were good friends of ours," said Sevarak. "It was a real shame."

Ranath shuffled his wings awkwardly. This story was familiar. Tarathiel had killed his and Fae's parents and then lied to him for decades about it. He'd pinned their deaths on the Elithar and the royal family in order to manipulate Ash.

His anger began to evaporate. "Why did he kill them?" he asked, already having an idea.

"Because we," Sevarak nodded back towards the dragons, "wanted Korvran to choose a different korais. We understood why he chose Vyrmyris; he thought it would temper him, but we know how that turned out. Xyrros' sire planned on challenging Vyrmyris for the position, but a few days before it was supposed to take place, we found him and his mate dead on a distant mountaintop. Not long after, Nyrvrin and I were chosen to investigate Hammanth's disappearance. Too much of a coincidence if you ask me."

"We were always good candidates to go," said Nyrvrin, joining them. "It wouldn't have taken much for Vyrmyris to persuade Korvran to select us."

How old is Xyrros? Ranath thought the young dragon was his age, but Hammanth had been killed at least a century before his birth. Just how long did dragons live for?

"Then if Xyrros wasn't the one who sold us out, who did?" he asked. Had it been the dragon he saw Vyrmyris murder? But how had they found out? His gaze swept over Xyrros as his mind worked. Something clawed at his stomach at the sight of them. It wasn't anger, nor was it sadness. It felt like a heavy weight had dropped over him.

"Braemyrin is my guess," said Sevarak. "She's always snooping around our cave."

Ranath recalled the dragon they'd first encountered on this side of the mountains, who had seen him in his native body and quickly sped off to tell Vyrmyris of their arrival. He'd noticed a scent frequently at the entrance to the cave but never inside. He'd figure it was one of their neighbours, but it might have been hers.

Still, how had anyone found out? When he'd told the ziiras about the queen, they had put up extra wards to ensure no one could listen in. *Yet someone still overheard that.* Unfortunately, it was a mystery for a time when they weren't being persuaded by hostile dragons.

He turned his attention to Xyrros. The amethyst dragon was a sorry sight. They hung their head, their wings drooping so low they nearly touched the ground. Their tail was a limp lump behind them.

Guilt.

That's what Ranath was feeling.

Guilt for accusing Xyrros of betrayal was compounded by what he'd learned about their relationship with Vyrmyris. But he couldn't help it; Tarathiel's betrayal ran deep. He only trusted Sevarak and Nyrvrin because they had looked after Fae. He'd never taken time to learn about Xyrros because he'd been too busy watching for their betrayal. Watching for something that was never going to happen.

"I'm sorry," he said quietly.

Xyrros looked up with sad eyes that sent a painful twinge across his chest.

"I'm sorry for accusing you of allying with Vyrmyris," he said a bit louder.

Xyrros perked up at that. They studied him for a moment before speaking. "I forgive you."

He blinked. How could they forgive him so easily? Ranath felt no relief. Instead another wave of guilt was over him. His entire relationship with this dragon was built on a lie. He didn't deserve Xyrros' forgiveness, and he doubted they would give it if they knew the truth: that he was an elf in disguise. If they ever found out...his heart twisted with another emotion he didn't quite understand. Ugh, were these strange feelings the result of being a dragon? Or the result of being free of Tarathiel?

Ranath was drawn from his confusing thoughts by a triumphant roar. The four of them looked up. Beneath the twin moons, dark shapes moved through the sky, coming right for them.

They'd been found.

"Up, up!" Sevarak roared, tearing into the cave to rouse everyone.

Ranath and Xyrros took off. They flew so close together that their wingtips nearly brushed. Nyrvrin swooped up in front of them, leading the way. The rest of their group soon filled the moon-lit sky around them.

But try as they might, they couldn't outpace their pursuers; they were still too tired from their earlier flight.

How were Vyrmyris' dragons holding up so well? Ranath reached out with his aura and immediately felt something around the approaching group, not the usual dragon magic. *Figures. They must be using some sort of magical artifact.*

Another screech rent the air, followed by a loud *whump* and frantic wing-beats. He looked over his shoulder to see Sevarak tearing into one of the lead dragons. Immediately, the strange aura dimmed.

"Don't look back!" Xyrros urged him.

He tore his gaze away. Something dark shot up towards him from below. He gave Xyrros' wing a hard whack with his own, knocking them aside. He rolled just as a hostile dragon appeared between them, jaws snapping at nothing.

Too close.

Ranath spun in the air, swinging his spiked tail. It ripped through the dragon's leathery wing. The dragon slid sideways in the air, beating their wings furiously, trying—and failing—to regain their balance.

Xyrros returned to his side, nodding their thanks. Ranath didn't have time to acknowledge it before another dragon came for them.

Xyrros blasted them in the face with their bright orange fire. The dragon yelped and winged past them. Ranath caught sight of ruined eyes. They wouldn't be a problem anymore.

A large yellow dragon nipped at his tail. Ranath growled and dove. The dragon followed after him. Ranath turned his dive into a roll, passing belly-up underneath them.

Xyrros snapped at their tail.

The yellow dragon pulled out of their dive and whirled on Xyrros, unleashing a stream of flame that Xyrros avoided. Still, the dragon gave chase.

Ranath tried to follow, but a small (yet still much larger than him) ziiras got in his way. He tried to swerve around her, but she nimbly moved in front of him. He tried diving, but again, she matched his movement. Ranath's scaly lips curled in frustration as all his attempts to get past her were thwarted.

Xyrros roared somewhere nearby, making his heart race.

He shot at the ziiras and struck like a serpent, fangs sinking into her shoulder. She let out a surprised squeal but didn't back down.

Damn it, move!

They became locked together, claws tearing, fangs ripping. Blood poured from their wounds, but neither backed down.

A pained cry reached them above the sound of fighting dragons. His heart seized.

Xyrros.

The ziiras bit at his face but he ignored her. Calling on his magic, he opened his mouth and unleashed a devastating blast of bright fire. She screamed, the scales melting off her face. She let go and dropped away from him. Ranath didn't stay to see the results of his attack. He took off towards his friend and their large opponent. They had disappeared in the crowd but Ranath could follow the smell of Xyrros' blood. His stomach churned. When he finally found them, his heart nearly stopped.

The yellow dragon had Xyrros' neck in their bloody mouth. And Xyrros wasn't moving.

No.

The yellow met his eyes and opened their mouth.

The limp form of Xyrros fell.

Twenty-Four

Truth

Ranath tucked in his wings and streaked after Xyrros, unable to hear the rush of air over the pounding of his frantic heart. *Go, go, go!*

He manipulated the air around him, increasing his speed. He tried to slow Xyrros' fall but couldn't concentrate on moving that much air at once. Tch, he knew he should have practiced his draconic magic more!

He was slowly gaining on Xyrros, but the ground was rising just as quickly. He tucked his body in as tightly as he could, resembling a speeding dart of ice.

But he still wasn't going to make it. Ranath growled. He was just too tired from being chased all day and night.

A familiar aura touched his. His speed suddenly increased enough to make his eyes water. He didn't need to be able to see to know that Xyrros was now within his grasp.

Almost there—

He sunk his claws into his falling companion and snapped open his wings. The leathery appendages screamed in protest as he struggled to redirect their fall. There was no hope of slowing it with the dead weight of Xyrros dragging him down.

They careened through the air, parallel to the side of the uncomfortably close mountain. The familiar aura grew stronger, and they started to slow. Ranath was grateful for the assistance; his wings felt like they were going to snap off.

But it wasn't enough; Ranath lost his hold on his precious cargo as they hit the ground and skidded down the rocky slope. He lay stunned, gasping for air.

Get up!

Tarathiel's voice sounded in his head, snapping him to alertness. He growled at the memory and slowly rose to his feet. The shale-covered ground was unsteady beneath him, but he approached Xyrros' unmoving form with tense determination.

Ignoring the fighting above, he nosed his friend. Relief washed over him like a tidal wave when he saw the rise and fall of their chest. But it was shallow and weak. Blood still seeped from the wounds on their neck—if he didn't do something now, they would bleed out.

A dragon landed nearby. He whirled around, teeth bared, talons scraping at the ground.

"Easy, it's just me," said Sevarak, swiftly beginning to assess Xyrros' wounds.

Ranath watched her with a strange intensity as she nosed the fallen dragon. He didn't know what to do. If he had access to his native magic, he could stabilize Xyrros. But like this, he was utterly helpless. It was a horrible feeling. He was reminded of when he'd been kidnapped from his home, his family all supposedly slain. Back then, he'd been powerless to save them.

Sevarak growled.

Ranath didn't like the frustrated tone it carried.

"They're losing blood too quickly," she said. "We need moss or something to stop the bleeding."

But the only thing around them was an endless sea of shale. Useless.

"Can't you cast a spell or something?" he asked, not daring to hope.

She shook her head. "Our magic doesn't work like that. It's very rare for a dragon to have that ability."

It took many suncycles for an elf to become a proficient healer, and they had access to more of the magical elements than dragons. As isidyll, he'd had to master it.

His eyes flicked to the sky. The fighting had quieted. It appeared that all the Vyrmyris' followers had been driven off. Their dragons began to land on the barren slope. If he was going to do this, he had to do it now.

"Try to cover for me," he said, shouldering her aside.

"What're you—" She stopped when she saw the burning look in his eye, then nodded and stepped aside. She spread her massive wings, shielding him from view. A strong aura came from her, swallowing his own.

Ranath closed his eyes and searched inside himself, for the magic that had been hidden away. He dug into it and let it flow through him. A soft glow limned him as his wings and tail retracted and disappeared. His body shrank, and long white hair flowed from his head. His scales softened and turned back into clothes.

Ranath pressed his glowing hands to Xyrros' neck, not caring one bit about the blood. His light took on a blue hue as he tapped into his healing magic. Using it was like meeting an old friend after time apart.

He carefully released his magic, not wanting the dragons to detect it over Sevarak's aural shield. Slowly, the flow of blood ceased. It was a start, but it wasn't enough. He needed to seal the wounds.

This proved to be a much more difficult task, as Xyrros' dragonhide resisted his magic. He could either use more magic and risk being detected, or he lose Xyrros. It wasn't a difficult choice.

He furrowed his brow and poured everything he had into his magic. Soft tissue began to knit itself back together, the damaged scales fell off as new ones, slightly lighter in colour, grew in their place. Would they darken with time? It didn't matter.

Exhaustion hit him like a galloping uhaan. He collapsed on top of Xyrros, darkness creeping into the edge of his vision, his head dense with fog. He pressed an ear to their chest.

Good, their breathing is normal, he thought as the world faded.

Ranath awoke to a red sky. He stared at it, trying to put together what he saw, gaze wandering over the strange lines that spiderwebbed through it. He'd never seen clouds like this before. Or were they shadows? He couldn't wrap his mind around it.

The sky suddenly shifted, and with it came the rumbling of thunder. Was he in a tent? That wasn't the best place to be during a storm. He reached up to touch it. It was leathery. The sensation helped to pull him from the murky depths of his mind. That wasn't thunder, and he wasn't in a tent. He was under a wing—Sevarak's wing.

The memory of the past few days came back to him. Vyrmyris. Their flight. Xyrros falling from the sky. Ice gripped his chest.

Xyrros. Right, he'd taken on his native form to save them with his Elven magic. Were they all right?

He rolled over onto his stomach and lifted the edge of Sevarak's wing to peek outside. The sun was up, but he couldn't tell how late into the day it was. They were still on the rocky mountain slope with no other dragons in sight.

Cautiously, he crawled out from under his dragonwing tent. His legs trembled as he stood up. Between transforming and healing Xyrros, his magic had taken a lot out of him. It was a miracle he was functional.

He strode around Sevarak's massive form—she was still dozing—and found Xyrros. The amethyst ziirar was laying where Ranath had left them. Nyrvrin was keeping watch. She looked up as he approached.

"I'm glad to see you up," she said in Illithen.

"How are they?" Ignoring how the shale dug into him, he sat near Xyrros' head, twice as large as an uhaan's, and lay a hand on their cheek.

"Your magic saved their life. I'm impressed. I haven't seen such a powerful display in one as young as you."

"That's because I have Fae's damis."

"Yes, I suppose that's true," Nyrvrin said softly, a hint of something like sadness in her voice. She was the one who'd raised Fae back in Odenia. When she found him, she'd been disguised as a human blacksmith living in Redwood near the Sylandrian border. Ranath owed his brother's survival to her.

He wished he'd had a parent growing up. Instead he'd gotten Tarathiel. Ranath had never once thought of the deceptive elf as a father figure. A mentor certainly, but not a parent. Yet his betrayal had still cut deeper than any knife.

Ranath eyed Xyrros' side as he continued to stroke their crystal-like cheek. The newly grown scales stood out, lilac flecks amongst an amethyst sea. Like scar tissue, he suspected they would remain discoloured for a while. Possibly forever. He hoped Xyrros wouldn't mind.

The dragon moved and Ranath froze, heart hammering, but thankfully they didn't wake. He didn't want Xyrros to see him like this, but he didn't have the strength to turn himself back into a dragon. And it was possible he never would. When they'd first come to Fiiraania, he'd had residual aura from the crystals. That initial transformation had burned through it.

If Xyrros saw what he was, it would be the end of everything.

The thought of losing them tore him up. That he'd accused Xyrros of betraying him while being the deceptive one made him feel all that much worse.

Ranath sighed and laid his head on their neck, brushing his aura against theirs. It felt normal, which was a relief. Its familiarity brought him comfort.

"I'm going to catch some food and check on the others," said Nyrvrin, startling him. He'd nearly forgotten she was there. "You keep an eye on them. Wake Sevarak if you need anything."

Ranath nodded as she took off down the slope. He hardly felt his hunger. He settled against Xyrros' side and closed his eyes, wondering what he was going to do.

He must have dozed off because he woke to the sound of Xyrros groaning. The dragon twisted and stretched. Ranath quickly got to his feet. In this body, he could easily get knocked around by Xyrros' many appendages.

The amethyst dragon blinked open bleary eyes. Ranath stood out of sight. His pulse quickened. This was it. In a few moments, his truth would be out, and their relationship would be changed forever.

Xyrros looked around in front of them and slowly rose to their feet. They shook, wings rustling.

Ranath waited with bated breath.

It took an eternity for Xyrros to notice him. Slowly they turned. Confusion clouded their face when they caught sight of him.

"An elf?"

Their question could be interpreted in a few ways. *You're an elf*, or, *why is there an elf here?* Ranath wasn't sure if they recognized him. His aura was different, but there had to be some level of familiarity to it.

"Yes?" he said. The draconic tongue felt strange in his mouth.

Xyrros stared at him momentarily, trying to piece together what was happening.

"It's me, Xyrros." Only many suncycles of isidyll training kept his voice steady because he felt like he was going to fall about.

They scrunched up their face. "Why are you an elf?"

Ranath wanted to disappear.

Xyrros swayed.

"You need to lay back down," he said, "You're still recovering."

Xyrros did so and examined the injuries they could see. "Did you heal me?"

He nodded, fighting the urge to curl up beside them. "One of Vyrmyris' dragons got you. They nearly snapped your neck. I was able to close your wounds."

"As an elf," they said without emotion.

Yes, as an elf.

Ranath rubbed a hand over his face. By the Ancestors. This had to be one of the hardest moments of his life, topped only by losing his family and Tarathiel's betrayal. No. This was worse than the betrayal because now, *he* was the betrayer.

He realized Xyrros was waiting for him to explain himself.

He sat on a rock and fidgeted with the hem of his shirt. Taking a moment to gather his thoughts, he launched into the tale of why he was here.

"I'm an elf from Sylandris. I was sent here as punishment for committing treason against the court."

"The court whose queen supposedly killed one of us."

"Yes…I was sent here to oversee Sevarak and Nyrvrin's report about Hammanth to the vorais, and to carry back any messages from Korvran."

Xyrros' expression was unreadable—a first since the dragon was usually so expressive. "Is what Vyrmyris said about your queen true?" they asked quietly. "That she's the one who killed Hammanth?"

He nodded.

"And you knew this the whole time?"

His heart seized. "Yes…"

"Were you going to tell Korvran the truth? I see why you wouldn't tell Vyrmyris."

Ranath blinked. This question felt like a test. A test he wished he wasn't taking but needed to pass. "I didn't want to start another conflict between our people."

Xyrros growled, not appreciating that he avoided the question.

"No." He had never planned on telling anyone, not even the ziiras. And he wished he never had.

They made a sound in their throat.

"It was to protect my nest-mate," he said quickly.

"Your Elven nest-mate."

What else would Fae be? "Ye—"

"I'd like to meet them."

Ranath blinked. What? Wasn't Xyrros furious with him for lying? For concealing his identity? "You...you want to meet him?"

"Mhmm," rumbled Xyrros.

Why weren't they yelling at him? "I don't—"

"Don't get me wrong, I'm hurt by what you've done, but I don't blame you. Well, not fully." They picked at a piece of shale with a talon. "It's a complicated feeling. You didn't do it out of malice or to cause us harm. You did it out of duty."

"Part of me wishes I could have done it looking like this, but that wouldn't have worked."

"Only part of you?"

The question struck him and he had to think for a moment. "As odd as it sounds, this is the first time I've been able to be myself. Back home I had a role to fulfill that had been determined by others. Coming here and living as a dragon has allowed me to be free. No one here knows me or my past. It was a fresh start." He stood and walked up to Xyrros, laying a hand on their snout. It was warm. A sense of comfort started to push away his worries.

Xyrros closed their eyes.

"Being back in this form has allowed me to access parts of my magic that were closed off." But it felt weird. He didn't have enough appendages and felt oddly rooted to the ground. His dragon body was much more comfortable.

"So you like being a dragon." It wasn't a question.

"Yes, I do. If I could change back right now, I would—and not just to hide my identity." He pressed his forehead to theirs.

Xyrros made a low rumbling sound that travelled throughout his entire body. "You saved me. You put yourself at risk by changing back to save my life. I can't be mad at you for that."

Ranath's eyes stung. "Thank you."

"Sorry to interrupt your moment," said Sevarak, not looking sorry at all. There was a gleam in her eye that had Ranath wondering if she'd actually been asleep. "But we gotta go. We've been here too long."

"What about Nyrvrin?" asked Xyrros, rising to their feet. They still looked tired.

"She'll catch up." Sevarak dipped her shoulders. "On my back, quick."

"I can carry him," said Xyrros.

She snorted. "You can barely carry yourself, never mind his elfie butt."

Ranath shrugged and climbed up her red shoulder.

Xyrros' look of disappointment made his heart swell. It was nice that someone genuinely cared for him.

The *thump* of frantic wingbeats cut through the air. Ranath tensed up. To his relief, Nyrvrin soon came into view, but it didn't last long. "Bad news," she said, sides heaving as she landed. "We think Vyrmyris is getting ready to make his move."

"Already?" said Xyrros.

"He's planning on using the power of the full moons to break through the barrier," said Ranath.

"But dragons aren't affected by the moons," said Nyrvrin, frowning. "And the elves will be at their most powerful. It's an odd time to attack."

"But they won't be expecting the attack. They're too busy with the Eburnas. As far as I know, no one keeps watch in the mountains anymore," said Ranath. "Besides, it will take time to reach Sylandris. They'll arrive after the Luuya has passed." Which meant he had to get a message to Sylandris immediately. If the elves had enough warning and could meet the dragons early on while the moons were still full...

"I need someone to fly me to the border right now." He didn't have his ring on him. It was in its usual hiding spot in the cave, and he didn't have the strength to send a message through two sets of wards. He needed to get through the Sky Peak wards.

"I'll go," said Sevarak.

"No, you're needed here," he said, sliding from her back. He locked eyes with Xyrros, their expression blazing with determination. He climbed onto their shoulders.

"You sure you can do it?" asked Sevarak, doubtful.

"Let them be," said Nyrvrin. "They'll be fine." She pressed her snout to Xyrros'. Xyrros perked up as her aura flowed into them, exhaustion melting from their features. They unfurled their wings and sprang into the air.

"May the winds be at your back," said Sevarak.

Part Five

There was nothing but barren rock around him. When he ventured out of his lair—a cave nestled within the canyon's wall—he could not see the sky. Swirling magic obscured it, blotting out the sun, the moons, and the stars. Even on a bright midsummer afternoon, the sun's rays barely reached the canyon floor. Not that the dark or cold bothered him. Not anymore.

Calandriel had spent some time trying to figure out how to escape his new prison, but his early attempts had not gone well. Each time he left his cave, the vengeful spirits of the Elithar were there waiting for him. Their spectral swords had a nasty bite that left him feeling unwell for days. He quickly learned that his magic did not affect them. It was sucked away every time he tried to use it, turning into a strange misty stream that cut along the canyon floor.

The stream eventually widened into a river, separating him from the Elithar. For some reason, the warriors wouldn't cross the dark water, perhaps because it was born of his magic.

But he still couldn't venture far from his cave. The strange aura that filled the canyon weakened him even when he wasn't using his magic—a side effect of his mother's spell colliding with his.

Or the Ancestors' power. He still wasn't sure if the Ancestors had come to his mother's aid that day. He'd felt a strange aura when their magic had collided, but it was hard to say if that was the Ancestors' intervention or simply the product of their spells. Not that it mattered. The Ancestors had never done anything for him but cause him pain. What mattered now was finding a way out and making his mother pay.

But that wasn't easy when he was the only living being around. Aside from himself and the ghostly warriors, nothing else lived down here, no plants, no animals, not even cave moss. It was frustrating. If he had even a bone, he could summon something to scout the canyon for an exit. And maybe to see what his parents were up to now that he was out of the way. And if the creature couldn't leave the canyon, then at least he would have a companion. Though he was used to being alone, the canyon didn't have the same underlying hustle and bustle of the palace.

Then, one day, it happened. A bird fell from the sky. Deep within his cave, he sensed its life leave as it hit the canyon floor, the impact snapping its small neck.

Unfortunately, the songbird wasn't as helpful as he'd hoped. It was only able to regain life within the confines of his cave. As soon as it left the tunnel, it returned to its lifeless state. He would have to come up with another way to free himself.

Sometime later, be it days or centuries, he knew not, something bright pulsed through the haze. Life.

Shrouded in shadows, he slipped from his cave. Someone stood on the far side of the river, unbothered by the Elithar floating mindlessly around them.

They don't touch intruders? Interesting...

The elf was staring intently at his side of the river. Something flickered in his chest, something he hadn't felt in a long time. If that elf crossed the river, they could be his way out of here.

The stranger bent down and stuck their hand in the swirling river, and immediately the river began to rise, overflowing its banks. The elf yanked their hand out and ran back the way they'd come.

Calandriel retreated into his lair. To his relief, the strange river had not entered his cave. Inside, he followed the progress of the elf's bright life force. It was suddenly extinguished, swallowed up by the river. He knew he wouldn't find their bones.

Disappointment weighed down his shoulders. The canyon was set on preventing anyone from leaving, wasn't it?

When he next ventured out, he was pleased to see that the river had returned to its usual depth. Clearly, it only responded when bothered, and that response only lasted until the intruder was dealt with. But if he could create safe passage for visitors...

Loud screeching far above caught his attention. Something was happening on the surface. Through the layers of mist, he could see flashes lighting up the sky and sometimes felt the faintest caress of aura.

What was going on up there?

He soon got an answer. The burned corpse of a dragon crashed onto the canyon floor. Calandriel stared at it, hardly daring to believe his eyes. A dragon? As much as he wanted to try reviving it, he could not drag its immense bulk back to the safety of his cave where he could access the full force of his magic. Calandriel left it for now.

More corpses fell into the canyon. Some belonged to dragons, while others belonged to elves. There were even a few dwarves and rounded-eared folk who resembled elves.

Was this some dirty trick his parents were playing on him? There were more corpses here than he'd ever seen before. And yet, there was nothing he could do with them. He tried reviving the elves, but the bodies wouldn't respond, even in his cave; another one of the canyon's effects, he suspected.

Yet it seemed like such a waste to let them rot. As he stared at the decaying pile, an idea came to him. He may be unable to give them new life, but he could use their bones for something else...

· · ● ● ● · ·

The bone bridge was one of his greatest accomplishments. Creating it had used up much of his magic. He'd gone into hiding deep within his lair in order to recover. But not long after (or perhaps it was centuries later, who was to say?), an elf reached his cave for the first time. He hovered in the shadows, observing them silently as they wandered the cavern at the head of the tunnel that led deep into the wall of the canyon.

The aelim carried something of great power on them, something that tasted of shadow magic, but not *his* sort of shadow magic. This was the kind that touched the realm of dreams.

"Who's there?" they asked, eyes darting around.

He remained concealed but spoke, his voice raspy from disuse. "What do you carry?"

The elf spun around, one of their hands glowing orange as they looked for the source of his voice. They wouldn't find him until he chose to reveal himself. "Who's there?" they repeated. "Show yourself!" They were afraid.

"I am the one who calls this place home." No he didn't, and he never would. But the elf didn't need to know that. They didn't need to know his motivations—yet.

"What are you called?" they asked.

His voice came from all around. "I do not have a name." It had slowly slipped from his mind over time, unneeded in this prison.

The elf mumbled something under their breath.

Demon? Is that what he was? Perhaps. He'd never met one before. Gold flashed before his mind's eye. Or...maybe he had. Only a demon would have trapped him down here. Yes, that made sense. She was a demon. A demon carrying out the Ancestors' will. Which made them not gods but demons as well.

Something clicked. It all finally made sense. They were jealous of his power and had banished him to this pit to prevent him from usurping their rule! Well, he would show them!

But first, he had to escape.

The elf moved, drawing his attention. Their steel grey eyes settled on the tunnel leading to his lair.

"Why are you here?" he asked them.

They didn't reply right away, fidgeting with something at their waist—a silk drawstring bag embroidered with the moons and stars.

That's where the aura was coming from.

"It's none of your concern," the elf said.

Bold. He didn't get the sense that the elf was here for him. This meeting was unplanned.

"Then I ask again, what do you carry?" A tendril of shadow rose from the floor and caressed the pouch. Hmm, he wasn't sure if he would be able to use its power.

The elf leapt away, a hand covering the pouch.

"You did not come down here bearing such a treasure for nothing," he said softly.

"I will not reveal myself to you, dark one," they said.

The dark one was beginning to tire of this. He sent out a pulse of aura, snuffing out the glow on their hand. Shadows rose to cover the cavern's entrance, plunging them into pitch darkness that not even elven eyes could pierce.

To their credit, the elf didn't shout, but he could tell they were nearly at their wit's end.

"You don't have a choice." His voice was a whisper in their ear. "You're in my domain."

The elf tried to cast a spell, but his shadows immediately consumed it. "Leave me what you have, and I will let you go."

They hesitated, torn between their sense of duty and their desire to leave this place. "You're confined to this canyon, correct?"

"Yes."

The elf gathered themself. "I'm here to hide this artifact. If I leave it in your possession, will you stop it from falling into the hands of others?"

"Do many seek it out?"

"Yes."

Interesting. While he didn't think its power would resonate with his, letting it go would be very foolish. "I will watch over it." He recalled his shadows, giving the elf back their magic and their sight. A wispy tendril rose up in front of them.

The elf took their time untying the pouch, questioning whether or not they were making the right decision. They passed it to the tendril. It receded into the floor and disappeared.

The elf left without another word.

There were more visitors as time passed, all of them human. Most touched the river and were swept away by its rising current. A few managed to anger the spectral Elithar and were promptly slain. Only a small handful ever made it to his cave, and even fewer escaped with their lives.

It was a long time before another elf appeared. And this pale elf brought exactly what he was looking for—the potential for escaping this prison.

As soon as the elf set foot on his bridge, he knew they were different. And it shook him. This elf was touched by the shadows. But not the sort of dreams. No. The shadows of death clung to this stranger.

Impossible. There was another out there like him?

The elf had come for the stone the other had given him, but they wanted something else as well. Something that no one else had ever asked of him before.

The pale one wanted to learn how to wield the magic of death.

And in exchange, for the elf—Drath—wasn't so rude as to offer nothing in return, he would help free him of his prison.

Their deal was made. Drath visited once a moon, bringing him documents and telling him of the outside world. He claimed the queen had perished millennia ago but that didn't matter to the dark one. All would pay for what had been done to him.

He taught Drath the basics of reviving the dead and creating necrotic barriers.

Eventually, he gave Drath a hint as to where the stone he sought had been hidden, but said that the elf must retrieve it on his own. He didn't expect the outsider to survive the ordeal. Yet Drath surprised him, emerging from shadows with the Amethyst in hand.

Not long after this, the visits ceased. He didn't know why; Drath simply stopped coming. But it was of no concern, for during the last visit, Drath had brought him the key to his freedom; a scroll containing an ancient ritual that would magnify his power. And if he combined it with the power of the Luuya, happening in only a few decades, he could break free. He was missing just one component: the divine blood of an Ancestor.

But that, too, came to him in time.

Twenty-Five

The Canyon

The Canyon of Lost Souls was horribly unsettling at night. It had been daylight when they'd gone down with Gale, meaning there had been some light at the bottom. Now, it would be pitch black, even with the full moons shining overhead.

Great. Fae almost wished they were taking on the dragons instead. His last experience in the canyon hadn't been great; the strange murky river at the bottom had nearly swallowed him up. It had caused him to remember the day his parents died—the day Tarathiel had stolen Ash. Its foul aura had also spurred him to lash out at Gale, wrongfully calling her the traitor that the crystals were meant to defend against. Though in the end, there had been some truth to his suspicions. She hadn't been the traitor. That was Tarathiel. Instead, she'd been a dragon in disguise.

And Alysion had had a strange vision down there, too, something about his mother calling him a failure and then receiving a cut on his neck that had carried over into the real world. There was no sign of the cut now; the only marks Alysion bore from their adventure were the mark that bonded him to the crystals that matched Fae's and the burn scar from trying to remove an aura-suppressing cuff the captain had slapped on him near the end of their quest.

"Let's go." He didn't let go of Alysion's hand as they began their descent. As soon as they entered the cloud of magic-nullifying mist that hovered near the top, the light of the moons disappeared. They had to climb down in the dark.

Thankfully, Alysion had dropped them on the side of the canyon with a straight shot down. The path on the other side zigzagged, which neither wanted to deal with while essentially blind.

Nevertheless, the descent was hair-raising. The path was wide enough for them to walk side by side, but it was incredibly unnerving not to be able to see their feet.

Fae couldn't even make out Alysion beside him. Tense hand holding was the only thing stopping them from completely losing themselves to fear. After far too long, they reached the bottom.

"Where do you think we need to go?" he asked, breaking the silence. There was no echo.

"The bone bri—" Alysion stopped in his tracks. "No, I feel something."

Fae only felt the suffocating, depressing aura of the canyon. And he hated it. Why was this the only aura he could sense? Perhaps because it affected more than just aura—it was draining away their very life force.

Alysion guided them through the inky blackness. Fae was glad the lost souls of the Elithar weren't on this side of the dark river. He'd probably lose his mind if they had to deal with the spectral warriors. Alysion had nearly ridden through one last time; Zen-Zen's quick footwork had saved them.

They eventually reached the rickety bridge that Fae had nearly fallen through, the incident that had caused the dark river to rise. He trembled with every step, chest tight.

"You're all right," Alysion said from beside him, squeezing his hand.

He didn't breathe until they were back on solid ground. But it was laboured from the canyon's influence.

"We're almost there," murmured Alysion.

By the gods, he hoped so.

The prince turned, walking towards the canyon wall. "We've arrived," he said after what felt like an eternity.

Fae's head spun as they passed through a barrier. Dim light flickered to life. He squinted as his eyes adjusted. To his relief, Alysion who was the source, a small ball of light in his hand.

"My aura is no longer blocked," he said.

Fae still felt the canyon sapping his strength, but it wasn't as bad as before. Head clearing, he let go of Alysion's hand and looked around.

They were in a small cave, and at the far end was a crack large enough for them to fit through.

"We're going in there, aren't we?" Fae asked.

Alysion nodded.

The prince kept his light going as they squeezed through the crack. Fae's hand went to his side, grasping for his sword. Belatedly, he remembered the Elithar had blasted it to bits. He dropped his hand. *A sword likely won't be of any use down here.*

The tunnel widened out just enough for them to walk side by side. The walls and ceiling were roughly hewn, almost appearing naturally formed. Thankfully, the floor was smooth.

The light in Alysion's hand went out. The prince frowned.

"What's wrong?" Fae asked.

"Something is messing with my aura."

Fae hadn't felt the usual sensation of passing through a barrier while coming through the crack. "They canyon...?"

Alysion shook his head. "No, it's something else."

A torch on the wall suddenly lit up beside them, its flame an unsettling shade of pink.

Alysion squinted at it.

Fae looked between them, trying not to get distracted by how the pink light reflected off Alysion's golden locks. "Is the torch sapping your aura?"

"Yes," the prince grumped. He took a few steps down the tunnel. Another torch flared to life.

"At least we don't have to worry about providing our own light," Fae said.

More torches lit up as they made their way down the tunnel. The ones behind them remained lit.

"I wish they would go out," grumbled Alysion.

Fae wished so as well. Clearly, this was meant to drain visitors of their auras—and likely their lives.

A fork appeared before them. They both groaned.

"Of course it couldn't be easy," said Fae.

There were no signs marking the paths, just two dark holes. Judging by Alysion's pinched expression, he couldn't sense where Calandriel was. "The torches' auras are messing me up."

Fae frowned. With the torches constantly feeding off Alysion's aura, they couldn't afford to go the wrong way. "Are the crystals of any help? You used the Sapphire to navigate the Glimmering Forest."

"This place is worse than the forest. Even with the Sapphire, I can't pinpoint a specific direction. In the forest, I found an aura trail that grew stronger the closer we got to the Emerald. Here, it's just a massive swirl of aura. Some of it may be the canyon's influence despite the wards in the cave."

Or it was all Calandriel's doing. The fact that the lost heir was strong enough to confuse even a crystal was impressive—and alarming.

They needed to get moving. Fae took Alysion's soft hand. "This way, then," he said, leading his prince to the left-hand tunnel.

Alysion followed without protest.

Fae cursed himself when they reached a dead end.

"It's fine," said Alysion as they turned back.

No, it wasn't. Every step took a toll on the prince.

They followed the right-hand tunnel as it twisted and turned. Occasionally, other tunnels would branch off, but Alysion was confident they could ignore those. "I'm becoming familiar with different auras here," he explained. "There's a faint one underlying the rest. Someone who didn't have magical crystals helping them would never notice."

But the crystals couldn't help them when they ended up at a three-way split.

Alysion's hand tensed in his grasp. The prince closed his eyes, concentrating. A faint rainbow glow emanated from the pouch around his neck.

Fae stood silently beside him, wishing he could do more to help. He rubbed the back of Alysion's hand with his thumb, marveling at its smoothness. His own hands were covered in calluses from when he'd worked in Master Cane's forge.

Alysion eventually opened his eyes. "This way," he said, leading Fae to a tunnel that gently sloped down.

The tunnel didn't immediately take them to a dead end, but Fae wasn't sure if that was a good sign. It would be awful if they wound up in a winding tunnel that led to nowhere.

A current of air ruffled his hair.

Hmm. They weren't anywhere near the surface, and the tunnel continued to slope down. Where was the air coming from?

"There's something I need to tell you," said Alysion.

Fae's stomach clenched.

"It's not about us," the prince quickly said. "Well, not our relationship. My father told me a secret that, given your brother's latest message, may not be a secret for much longer."

Oh?

Alysion played with a strand of his hair. "You know that Gale and Cane were here to look for a dragon who'd gone missing and that Tarathiel was the one who killed that dragon."

Fae nodded. He clearly remembered the meeting after the fight at the Great Temple.

"While Tarathiel is undoubtedly the one who killed their companion, he wasn't the one who brought them through the barrier."

He didn't like where Alysion was going with this.

"It was my mother."

Despite their rush, Fae stopped in his tracks. Alysion's hand pulled from his grasp. "Your *mother*?" The queen? He stared wide-eyed at the prince. "Why would she do that?"

Alysion stopped and turned to face him. "To get rid of Tarathiel. There was some...tension between her, my father, and Tarathiel."

"But, but—"

"I know. She put the entire kingdom at risk. That's got to be why the dragons are coming."

The blood drained from his face. "How would they have found out?"

"I don't know. Only my parents and I know. And now you." Alysion took his hand again and led him along the tunnel. Fae walked in a daze.

Ash was the only one who might know the truth, and he didn't believe for a moment that his brother would betray them. "Ash didn't do it," he said out loud, praying it was true. Yet he recalled one of Ash's earlier letters mentioning a secret. This must have been it.

"I don't think it was your brother," said Alysion. "He likely knows the truth; I don't see why Tarathiel would have held that from him, especially since he wanted Ash to hate my family. But in the short time you had together, I saw how much he cared for you."

Fae nodded.

"But how they found out isn't important right now. What *is* is that Sylandris is in danger, and my mother is likely to blame. If we survive all this, I may have to take the throne."

Fae nearly tripped. "T-take the throne?"

"My mother has committed a terrible crime. Between that and the incident at the temple, the nobles will demand her removal. I have no choice but to step up."

He knew that Alysion would eventually claim the throne one day, but he hadn't expected it to be so soon. They hadn't even had the Striiya yet to receive the tattoos that would mark them as adults.

"But my ascension won't make all the problems magically disappear. I will still have to prove myself to the nobles. As will you."

"M-me?"

"Well, you're with me, so you'll eventually become king, too—once we have our joining ceremony."

Fae thought the floor was going to drop out beneath him. He stopped and held his face in his free hand, head spinning. By the gods, he wasn't ready to be king! Not yet. Not when the nobles hated him.

"I know it's a lot, and I'm sorry for dumping all of this on you," said Alysion, gently squeezing his hand. "But with how things are going, I want you to know and be prepared."

It was too much. First Calandriel, then the dragons, and now becoming king? Fae just wanted to lie down and pretend everything was fine.

Alysion kissed his forehead. The prince's lips were chilled.

Right, the torches. They needed to get out of this canyon before it sucked Alysion dry. And to do that, they needed to find Calandriel.

One problem at a time.

Twenty-Six

The Lost Heir

The current of air remained constant, neither getting stronger nor dying. It wasn't a natural breeze, but one caused by the ominous magic filling the labyrinth.

The tunnel eventually opened into a dark cavern, discernible by the echo of their footfalls and the whooshing of air. Alysion looked up but couldn't see the ceiling through the darkness. He got the feeling that the cavern was massive.

Oh, please let this be the end.

Their hands were clammy, the magic of the canyon taking its toll.

A red torch came to life at their feet, then another, and another, creating a path that gently curved forward.

Exchanging a wary look, they ventured onwards. A dark shape lingered in the middle of the space. More torches flared up, leading them towards it: a tall stone mound. The path slowly wound up it, similar to the stairs that spiralled around the trees in Lyrellis.

Fae's pulse quickened in Alysion's hand, matching his own. What they sought was at the top. It had to be. But just what would they find?

The climb took ages. Around and around they went. It drove Alysion mad. They didn't have time for this! He was weakening with each step, and they still had to get back to help with the dragons! Ugh. How had things gotten so messy so quickly? *Perhaps we should have brought Mellith with us.* Then the canyon would have another elf to feed from. But no, they'd needed Mellith to warn his father about the dragons.

Eventually, they reached the top.

The flames flitting around the chamber suddenly closed in, encircling the platform they were on, and lighting up the area with their unsettling red glow. The stone platform had strange runes carved around the edge that Alysion didn't recognize.

"Welcome, My Prince," a voice rasped.

A figure blinked into existence in the center of the platform. Both of them jumped at the sudden appearance. The figure wore long dark robes and a fringe of leather that covered the upper portion of their face, leaving only their mouth visible. Their teeth gleamed in the low light. They wore their hood up, covering the top of their head, but locks of dark hair spilled forth from it.

"Prince Calandriel," Alysion said, stepping forward and putting a respectful fist over his chest.

"It has been a long time since I've heard that name. I had forgotten..." said Calandriel. "I would ask why you are here, but I suspect I know the reason. I will tell you that you are too late."

"If you're still down here, then we aren't too late," said Alysion.

"I was referring to the queen."

The blood drained from his face. "What about her?"

Calandriel swept a sleeved arm over the runes. They began to glow with an eerie pink light. "I borrowed her power to facilitate my escape from this place. It appears she has finally run out."

Alysion blinked as the cavern swayed. No, it couldn't be. She couldn't have—

A hand squeezed his.

Fae.

Gritting his teeth and blinking back tears, Alysion squashed the rising storm of emotions threatening to carry him away. He couldn't afford that now.

The glow of the runes grew brighter until it coalesced into a beam of light shooting towards the ceiling. A current of air kicked up in its wake, as the beam pierced through the rock, obliterating it.

Alysion staggered as its aura washed over him. Fae clung to his hand.

The beam faded. Through the hole far above, they could see the sky. The silver light of the full moons shone down through it.

Calandriel stepped into the faint moonlight. He raised his arms, basking in the moons' glow. "Finally, I will be free. Thank you, Prince Alysion, for it is your blood that allowed me to perform this ritual. Without it, I would never have been able to leave this place."

His blood? What was—it hit him like a slap in the face. The strange vision of his mother that he'd had on the bone bridge when they'd been searching for the crystals! Right before the apparition had disappeared, she'd cut his neck and turned into a dark shape. When he'd come to, he'd been bleeding.

"That was you?" he spluttered.

"I needed the blood of the *Ancestors*," Calandriel nearly spat the word, "to start the ritual. "It allowed me to tap into the auras of the leaders of the living realm and collect their power for myself."

His mother, the vorais, and now mostly likely the Queen of Odenia, too. All of them were dead because of Calandriel. Because of him. Alysion simultaneously wanted to break down in tears and tear Calandriel apart. He trembled.

"Easy," Fae said softly beside him.

His love's presence anchored him. He took a few steady breaths. They could still stop this—Calandriel wasn't free yet. He seemed to be waiting for something...no, not waiting. Gathering power. The runes may have blasted through his physical prison, but there were still wards in place that could stop him from escaping. Alysion could feel them.

Alysion summoned a ball of fire and lobbed it at the dark prince, but a shadow leapt from the ground and consumed it.

Damn.

"Stand back," he murmured to Fae, who backed away.

Drawing on the Ruby's power, he shot a stream of blue flame towards Calandriel.

The shadow leapt up to meet it, but the endless flames passed through, and the shadow dissipated. The bright flames struck their mark. Calandriel disappeared in the conflagration.

"Did you get him?" Fae asked.

"No." That would have been too easy. Calandriel's aura felt as strong as ever.

Alysion ended his spell, and as expected, Calandriel reappeared as the flames died down. He looked unhurt. Not even his robes were singed.

Fire was Alysion's strongest element, but perhaps he needed to fight darkness with light. He fished the Topaz out of his pouch; the yellow crystal was warm in his hand. He held it up. The crystal flared brightly, its light piercing the darkness of the cavern.

Calandriel waved an arm. Shadows seeped in from the cracks in the stone, devouring the light.

Alysion furrowed his brow and poured more aura into the spell. The light pulsed, fighting to push back the encroaching darkness.

"You're wasting your time," said Calandriel. "You cannot stop me." His pale, long-nailed fingers curled as he called forth the shadows.

A bead of sweat rolled down Alysion's face. If light wasn't enough to stop Calandriel, he only had one other option. He had to combine the power of all the crystals and amplify them with the Kunzite. The thought of harnessing so much magic made him pause. So many things could go wrong. When Ash had tried, it had nearly consumed him.

Alysion looked at the mark on his wrist. It had darkened when they'd taken the crystals from Lyrellis. He wouldn't lose control; they had a proper bond.

A wave of nauseating aura washed over him as the Topaz's light dimmed until it glowed faintly in his hand. Calandriel covered the platform with a dark dome, save for an opening where the moonlight shone through. Red veins spiderwebbed across it.

He glanced back at Fae. He was trapped in the dome with them. Damn. "Don't touch it," he warned. "It'll sap your life force!"

Fae shouted something, but Alysion couldn't hear it. He darted to the side to avoid a projectile of inky darkness.

He had to get Calandriel away from the moonlight.

But Calandriel wasn't about to let that happen. He hurled more dark spells at Alysion.

The prince threw up a wall of light. A shadow shattered it like a pane of glass and struck him in the chest. Alysion grunted as he was flung into the barrier, barely hanging on to the Topaz. Instantly, it drained his strength. At this rate, he wouldn't have enough energy to use the crystals! He was already tired from the blasted torches.

"Alysion! Are you all right?" came Fae's voice.

Alysion blinked to clear his vision and staggered to his feet. "I'm fine. Keep away from him." Calandriel seemed to be ignoring Fae for now—a small blessing.

A strange aura rippled through the dome, punctuated by a loud screech. A shape shot towards him. Alysion rolled to avoid it. The shape swooped around, passing in and out of the barrier, and came at him again.

It was an eagle. Fae had told him about this magic. The bird's curved talons came for his face, and he threw a ball of fire at it.

The eagle avoided it, zipping past so close that his hair fluttered.

Irritated, Alysion threw another fireball. This time the bird let out another piercing screech as it connected.

Yes!

But the eagle didn't disappear as he'd hoped. It winged around and came for him again. His spell didn't seem to have affected it.

"Break the bone!" Fae hollered.

Right.

He avoided its reaching talons and shot a stream of blue fire at it. *I'll burn this stupid bird away!* The eagle's cry echoed throughout the cavern as the fire engulfed it.

Fae crouched nearby, hands over his ears.

Alysion swore his head was going to explode from the sound, but he didn't dare ease up on the spell.

Calandriel, not wanting to lose his precious bird, sent a wave of shadows his way.

Cursing, Alysion threw up a barrier to protect himself, the flames dying.

The eagle thrashed about on the ground, blue flames mixing oddly with its shadowy form.

Fae dashed up to the flailing creature and stomped on it. *Crack.* The bird's form dissolved, leaving only a broken bone.

"No!" Calandriel hissed, sending a shiver down Alysion's spine.

The dark prince raised a hand and dark tendrils burst from the ground at Alysion's feet.

He jumped out of their reach, his barrier fading. Shards of ice formed in the air around him, sharp as blades, and flew at Calandriel.

Calandriel flicked his hand. More tendrils appeared, snatching the ice out of the air. "You're an interesting one," he said, his attention on Fae. "I sense no aura coming from you, yet you're clearly one of us."

To Alysion']'s horror, tendrils erupted from of the ground and wrapped themselves around Fae. He choked and quickly grew pale as the tendrils sucked away his life.

Don't you dare! He was not about to let Calandriel take Fae away from him. He closed his eyes and called on all the crystals. The Kunzite flashed as he pulled it out of the pouch. Connecting with it, he let the building auras flow through it. An iridescent ball of magic rapidly grew before him.

That caught Calandriel's attention. He cloaked himself in shadows just as Alysion loosed his spell.

It passed harmlessly through the dark mass.

Alysion's stomach lurched. It had had no effect. How? Why? What had he done wrong? Nothing should be able to beat the crystals! They'd been used to end the Syl-Raanian War!

"Magic like that cannot harm me," came Calandriel's voice. "Not anymore."

Alysion set his jaw and clenched his fists. Behind him, Fae's face turned white.

Twenty-Seven

Iridescent Blade

Despite everything he'd done, Fae couldn't help but feel sorry for Calandriel. He'd only become this because of the environment he'd grown up in. Fae could relate. The way the nobles treated him was no different from what Calandriel had endured. Given his parents, Calandriel had had much worse. As his consciousness faded, Fae wished there was something he could say to comfort the lost heir. But no words could undo the emotional harm that had been left to stew for millennia.

I'm sorry. His eyes slowly shut as Calandriel's shadows drained his life away. The last thing he saw was a flash of gold. *Alysion?*

Pain burst across his shoulder, the constricting sensation of the tendrils suddenly disappearing. Fae sucked in a breath of stale cavern air. He wasn't dead. He forced his leaden eyes open. Dust floated in the air, looking spectral where it passed under the hole in the ceiling. He couldn't see either of the princes from where he lay. Gritting his teeth, he pushed himself upright.

Calandriel was nowhere to be found. Had Alysion gotten him?

His heart lurched when he spotted his prince. Alysion lay on the ground, the Kunzite beside him. He wasn't moving.

Please be all right, please be all right.

Drawing on his final dregs of strength, Fae crawled over to him.

His chest loosened when he saw that the prince was still breathing. There was no sign of blood, yet the prince didn't wake when Fae shook his shoulder. He caught sight of the bond mark on his wrist. It was still dark. He picked up the Kunzite. He may not be able to use magic, but the crystal might do something. He was bound to it just like Alysion was. He pressed it to the prince's chest.

Nothing happened.

Fae's throat tightened up.

He looked around fruitlessly for something that would help. If only Gale or Master Cane were here. They would know what to do.

The pouch around Alysion's neck caught his eye. Right, the Kunzite couldn't do much on its own. *Here goes nothing.*

He dumped the rest of the crystals into his hand.

The back of his neck prickled. He looked up to see a mass of shadow forming under the moonlight.

Calandriel was back.

And he was out of time.

Or was he? The moons had nearly moved past the opening. If he could stall Calandriel long enough to let their light pass...but how would he manage that? Calandriel didn't view him, a damisri, as a threat. In fact, he was paying Fae very little attention. The lost heir knew his chance to escape was dwindling with each passing moment, and he wasn't about to waste it.

Fae closed his eyes and pressed the crystals to his chest, praying to whatever gods were listening. *Please, help me save the prince—both of them.*

The bond mark on his wrist began to burn. Fae bit back a cry, not wanting to alert Calandriel. The crystals began to glow in his hands. He tried to hide it but they were too bright. Thankfully, Calandriel was occupied with his escape. But it didn't bode well that the prince had become incorporeal again.

Fae pulled his hands away from his chest. The seven crystals floated up and began to twist and stretch, assuming a shape Fae would recognize anywhere.

The lights became solid, forming a longsword. It was simple in design, but there was no mistaking the rainbow hue of the metal. A gentle pink light emanated from it. The mark on his arm stopped burning when he plucked it out of the air and swung it. It was as if it had been crafted just for him. Which he supposed it was.

"What is that?" a voice hissed.

A sphere of pulsing darkness shot towards him.

He wanted to escape its path, but something told him to stay. Fae readied himself for pain and slashed at the magic. It felt like he had cut through nothing, yet the sphere dissipated before his eyes.

More shadows came for him, detaching from the smoky wisps that rolled off Calandriel.

Fae assumed a readied stance and cut at each one as they came for him. The sword did not let him down. Each time it connected, the dark magic disappeared.

Despite the situation, a faint thrill bubbled in his chest. The first time in his life, Fae could defend himself against magic. And he now had a chance of stopping Calandriel. He just had to get close.

The blasts soon took on the forms of small dark birds. They were fast, streaking towards him like arrows. It took all his concentration to fend them off while slowly advancing on their master. To his relief, the birds left Alyison's fallen form alone. He couldn't afford to worry about his dear prince at a time like this.

Another bird disappeared in a puff of misty feathers. Calandriel wasn't far off from him now.

But the prince had sensed his approach. The shadows whirling around his incorporeal form took the shape of a massive feathered serpent. Dark jaws opened wide, revealing razor-sharp teeth. Inside, Fae just caught the flash of something white.

The blood drained from his face. Where had Calandriel gotten that bone?

"You will *not* stop my revenge," Calandriel rasped.

Fae didn't get the chance to respond. The serpent struck faster than he could track. Only instinct and the sword's magic had him bringing the blade up fast enough to meet the beast head-on. The sword connected with something solid.

The bone?

As the massive serpent drew back, he saw that one of its large spectral fangs had disappeared. Good, he could injure it.

It struck again, meeting him head-on, and Fae swung the rainbow sword across its face. He hardly heard the serpent's piercing cry as he dropped to a knee, hand grasping his upper arm as pain exploded through the limb. It had managed to sink its other fang into him. The pain radiated up and down his arm. His vision swam and the ground lurched. Was its bite poisonous? It wasn't alive...but it was made of necrotic magic.

The sword's light pulsed a warning. He lifted it with his good arm. The serpent stuck the blade with an angry hiss, knocking him back. Fae groaned as he slammed into the ground. The sword's magic must have kept it in his hand because there was no way he was hanging on to it by his own merit.

The serpent loomed above him, shaking its plumed head. He scrambled to his feet, body moving too slow for his liking. He couldn't hope to win like this. He had to shake off whatever was in the bite.

The sword's pink glow turned red. Fae's brow furrowed. Had the sword been affected by the bite? No, the glow looked familiar. The sword resembled a raw blade he'd just pulled out of the forge. It had even begun to heat up like one.

I see. He touched the flat of the blade to his injured arm. Fae hissed as the Ruby's heat sought out Calandriel's magic and burned it away. As the blade returned to its normal colour, he caught sight of the serpent's reflection. It thought he was an easy target.

Well, he would prove it wrong. Cleansed by the Ruby, he grabbed the sword with both hands and swung it at the massive head. He called to the Ruby as he did, praying his idea would work. The blade flickered red again as it slashed through the serpent's neck.

For a moment nothing happened. Then fire erupted from the cut.

The serpent let out an ear-splitting screech, flailing about wildly. Fae dove towards Alysion, fearing it would strike the unconscious prince.

Fire quickly consumed the serpent. Soon nothing remained but a charred bone that crumbled to ash. He'd done it!

Now to deal with Calandriel. His stomach jolted. The mass of shadows that was the prince was still floating in the moonlight. A giant ball of crackling dark energy was forming above him—a spell to break the invisible barrier trapping him down here.

Sword out, Fae ran towards him.

He swung the blade back as it flashed every colour. Still well out of range, he cut towards Calandriel. A rainbow crescent flew towards his target, cutting through Calandriel's shadowy form.

"Damn you!" the prince screeched, but he didn't stop his spell.

Fae threw another crescent of magic at him. This time, when it cut, wisps of darkness dragged after it before dissipating into nothing.

Calandriel shifted, his upper half reforming within the swirling shadows. The leather fringe still concealed his face. He raised a hand, and shards of black crystal shot towards Fae.

He twirled his sword, shattering the shards. The bits that got through sliced his skin, burning like bug bites. Blood welled up on his cheek from a deep cut.

But he ignored them and slung another iridescent sickle at Calandriel.

Shadows leapt out and consumed it before it got close to the forgotten heir. "That's not going to work anymore," said Calandriel.

Fae clenched his jaw and asked the Ruby to help. Flames flashed from the tip of the sword. They hissed loudly as they whipped through the shadow. Unlike the serpent, the shadows didn't catch fire. But Calandriel let out a cry of pain.

The sound shook Fae. It wasn't the cry of a crazed sorcerer. It could have belonged to Alysion. Or to anyone he knew. And that made fighting the tragic prince that much harder.

He felt eyes on him. Calandriel's fringe had burned away. A soul-piercing stare, both foreign and familiar, met his. Despite how gaunt he looked, there was no doubt that Calandriel was related to Alysion. He could see it in the shape of his pale eyes, the curve of his nose.

Fae glanced up at the moons. They had nearly cleared the opening. In a few more moments, Calandriel's window would pass. But he would simply try again next time, no matter how long he had to wait.

Fae had to end this tonight. And to do that, he would take advantage of the moons' power.

He dashed into a patch of moonlight, holding the sword up high. Its pink glow flared the light nearly blinding.

"What is that?" Calandriel hissed from somewhere above him. "Such magic will not work against me."

Squinting against the light, Fae drew the sword back. Relying on the magic to guide him, he swung up at Calandriel. A burst of pink light flew from the blade and crashed into him. The prince was ripped from his mass of shadows and knocked to the ground, the rest of his physical body appearing. Before he could become incorporeal again, Fae grit his teeth and charged at him. Calandriel rolled to his feet and leapt out of the way.

Right into a blast of magic.

Fae chance a glance over his shoulder. Alysion was lying on his stomach with one hand raised.

"You're too late to stop me!" Calandriel snarled.

"No, we're not," Alysion snapped.

Fae raised his sword again. "I'm sorry."

The forgotten prince's eyes went wide as Fae plunged the iridescent blade into his chest.

The sword flashed. The prince's mouth opened, but instead of a scream, dark vapour poured forth. Fae flinched as it washed over him, chilling his bones like an icy winter gale. A hair-raising howl filled the cavern.

Fae pulled the sword out and leapt back. Alysion staggered to his feet and stood beside him.

"What's happening?" Fae shouted.

Alysion, his gaze on Calandriel, didn't reply.

The lost heir's form turned dark and translucent, becoming one with the shadows he'd once commanded. The necrotic dome around them flickered then disappeared as the magic died. The wispy darkness slowly dissipated until no sign of him remained.

Fae collapsed to his knees, shaken. The sword clattered to the ground beside him.

"It's over," Alysion said solemnly. He knelt beside Fae and put a hand on his shoulder.

"I-I..." The shock of having killed someone hit like a kick to the head. Tears rolled down his cheeks.

"Fae. It's okay. You did what had to be done." said Alysion, wrapping his arms around him. Fae tightly hugged him back.

"He..." Fae trailed off when he remembered that Calandriel had caused the death of the queen. Of Alysion's mother. Alysion didn't need to know his thoughts—how Fae saw bits of himself in the lost heir.

"He's now free," Alysion whispered gently in his ear, running a hand soothingly down the back of his head.

"I should be comforting you," said Fae shakily, loosening his death grip on Alysion.

"We'll—"

Fae's ring flashed. Instead of a letter, a familiar female voice issued from it. Mitchy.

"The dragons have left the mountains. They're on their way."

Panic surged through him. His eyes met Alysion's.

"We need to go now," said Alysion as they rose to their feet. "Where are the crystals?"

Fae picked up the sword and held it out to him.

Alysion cocked his head but accepted it.

"How do we get out?" asked Fae. They were so far underground.

Alysion raised the sword and pointed it at the ceiling. Silvery moonlight still filtered in through the hole. "The same way Calandriel was going to escape."

Twenty-Eight

The Plains

Once they were out of the canyon, Alysion opened a gate that spat them out in the middle of the Manwan Plains. It was a ridiculously complex and dangerous bit of magic since the gate wasn't connected to a specific location. Instead, it sought out the largest concentration of draconic aura and sent them there. Or close to it.

Fae was impressed.

The vast plains opened up before them, covered by a dusting of snow. It was nearly as bright as day under the light of the full moons. Yet dawn was still a ways away. Cold winds whipped across the land, rustling the dead stalks of grass, kicking up the dusting of snow.

Fae shivered, wishing he'd brought warmer clothes. Well, soon, he'd have bigger issues. Another sound joined the swishing grass, one that was unfamiliar yet unmistakable: the low thumping of many large wings. With their keen eyes, they could just make out a dark mass flying from the west.

The dragons were coming.

Alysion held out the sword. "You'll need this more than I will."

Fae looked at it. "Are you sure?"

"You no longer have a sword of your own, and I have my magic."

He accepted it with a nod. The sword still fit his hands like a pair of perfectly tailored gloves.

A gate opened nearby. Captain Anaril stepped out of it.

Alysion approached them while Fae hung back, not thrilled about seeing the captain.

He swung the sword around, getting a better feel for it and trying to distract himself from what was coming. He practiced different forms, pleased by the sword's performance after each set. If not for the impending battle, he would have tested out more of its magic.

Elithar poured from the gate, fanning out across the snowy grass. He paused and watched them with mild interest.

A loud roar suddenly split the sky.

All eyes turned upwards.

Fae's stomach dropped. Nothing, not even seeing Gale and Cane in their native forms could have prepared him for the sight of dozens of dragons coming straight for them. It was terrifying. Every bone is his body screamed at him to turn tail and run. He'd seen what Gale could do on her own. Did they really stand a chance against such raw power and brute strength?

Ah, but the elves have magic. And that was a force to be reckoned with. He even had the rainbow sword—which they needed to give a nicer name to if they made it out of this. Still, it was hard to believe they stood a chance.

He straightened up and clenched his jaw.

The roaring didn't stop, becoming louder as the hoard drew nearer. The Elithar spread out, taking up positions all over the prairie.

"What did Anaril say?" Fae asked as the prince returned to him.

"We're calling in all our forces, save for a few to guard the remaining prisoners at the temple," Alysion explained quickly. "Civilians are also being asked to fight, though there is some hesitation. Most don't want to believe the wards have been breached."

Fae nodded. It was a terrifying thought. The elven population was still recovering after the last war had decimated their numbers. Elves didn't have thelim at the same rate as humans did.

"You're staying with me," said Alysion.

"I wouldn't go anywhere else," he replied.

A single roar, louder than the rest, sounded across the plains. Fae squinted against the sudden blinding light that filled the western sky.

A jolt of fear shot through him. Dragonfire.

"We need to move!" Alysion hollered as warriors formed up around them. "We're falling back for now!" The prince grabbed his arm and dragged him away from the approaching dragons.

Alysion didn't release the death grip on his arm until they were well behind the ranks of the Elithar, near the gate. The elite warriors started casting all sorts of protective wards.

"So we're just going to sit back here and watch?" Fae said more sharply than he intended. All this waiting had him on edge. The dragons hadn't reached them yet.

"Yes. The captain wants me—us to return the Lyrellis. It was difficult to persuade them otherwise."

As the sole remaining descendant of the Ancestors, and heir to the throne, Alysion couldn't be on the front lines. Fae was surprised the captain hadn't physically thrown him through the gate that was still letting through elves. These had to be the civilian fighters, for their armour varied in colour and design. Instead of the royal crest the Elithar wore, they wore the one belonging to their own bloodlines.

Cries went up as dragonfire reached the Elithar's ranks. It suddenly struck a barrier and swirled harmlessly around it. All the snow in its' path melted instantly.

The first row of warriors, carrying spears that glowed orange in the light of fire, stepped forward. They drew back their weapons back in unison, then threw them. A hundred spears shot off almost faster than the eye could see.

It was pure pandemonium. The dragons scattered, looping and diving through the night sky to avoid the volley. Some tried to burn them up and let out pained cries as the magical projectiles pierced their wings.

"Glad we made more of those," Alysion muttered.

Fae rocked back and forth on his heels. He hated waiting and watching, it was almost worse than being part of the fight. At least when he was fighting he could lose himself in the heat of the battle. *This is better than being burned to a crisp,* he chided himself. Well, he could entertain himself by trying to find their leader.

Alysion's burrow furrowed. "What are you looking for?"

"The one leading them, Vyrmyris."

"How can you pick him out?" asked Alysion. "There's too many of them, and they all feel—er, look the same."

Even in the light of the fire and the moons, it was hard to make out individuals.

"Fae!" A muffled voice hollered. Fae turned towards the gate.

He hardly recognized the elf that stepped through, Mellith. Gone were the loose robes they wore in the library, replaced by scaled armour. They bore their family crest.

Mellith approached the Elithar guarding him and the prince.

"Ask them to let Mellith through," he said to Alysion.

Alysion's expression tightened but he nodded and turned to one of the warriors. The wards rippled as the aelim passed through them.

Cries broke out before they could speak. Dragons swooped into the crowds of elves, spewing mouthfuls of fire. One stream struck the dome around them.

Fae squeezed his eyes shut against the blinding light. The wards protected them from the heat, but not the intensity of the blaze.

When he opened them, he saw that Alysion's jaw was set. The prince wanted to be part of the fight, but the Elithar would never let them out. Fae rubbed his thumb over the pink crystal embedded in the sword's pommel, anxious.

"Where's King Illuven?" Mellith asked.

Alysion met their gaze. "Organizing Lyrellis' defense."

They frowned. "Shouldn't he be here?"

"Not with my moth—no."

"I suppose the queen is too ill to take part," they said, frowning.

Fae shot a look at Alysion, who gave an almost imperceptible shake of his head. His mother's death wasn't known yet? Then, they would keep it that way for now. The news of her passing could demoralize their troops. And that was the last thing they needed.

The wards around them rippled as more fire struck them. The first blast hardly died down before the next came, then the next. The dragons must have realized someone important was there. When the onslaught died down, more Elithar gathered outside of the wards.

The fire came again, but their new line of defense was ready. Jets of water shot towards the flames, turning them into a cloud of steam that blanketed the area.

They couldn't see a thing from within the wards. A loud cry suddenly rent the air, shaking them to the marrow of their bones.

"What was that?" he asked.

"A dragon with a strong aura," said Mellith.

"Vyrmyris? Their leader?" Alysion pressed.

"Might be," replied Mellith.

Fae gripped his sword handle and stepped closer to Alysion, nearly touching him. Fire engulfed their bubble, brighter and more encompassing than before.

"This isn't going to last. The wards are failing!" Alysion shouted. He grabbed Fae by the arm. When the fire died down, Alysion pulled him away.

They were instantly bombarded by deafening sound; Fae hadn't realized the wards had muted the noise. Dragons roared, elves shouted, and magic exploded all over. Fae's chest tightened. It was like the day his parents had been killed.

"Fae, move!" Alysion yelled, suddenly shoving him.

He ran, narrowly avoiding being squashed by a falling dragon. The ground shook from the impact. The dragon lay in a mess of broken limbs, their green scales discoloured where spells had struck, neck bent at a strange angle. Fae felt sick, picturing Gale or Master Cane.

He scanned the sky, looking for flashes of red or silver, but picking out any individuals in the fray was difficult. He wouldn't recognize their dragon forms from a distance anyways.

"We need to find Vyrmyris stop this," said the prince. They started running, avoiding spells and blasts of fire. Their guards shouted at them to stop, but they ignored their cries.

A few dragons had landed and were fighting with tooth and claw. Groups of elves crowded them, slashing with swords and blasting with magic. Fae and Alysion stayed clear.

Fae nearly jumped out of his skin when a shape suddenly materialized before them.

"It's me," said a rather pale-looking Mellith. Some of the tension left his body at the sight of them. "Don't leave me behind again," they said.

Over all the chaos, a horn sounded.

"Must be the nobles," shouted Alysion.

"Is it wise to announce themselves like that?" Fae hollered.

The prince shrugged and then threw out a hand. A wall of water appeared before them, protecting them from a wayward puff of fire.

"We need to keep moving," Alysion replied.

A dragon roared overhead and dove straight for them.

Alysion called a gust of wind to knock them off their path. The dragon wavered but held their line. Mellith stepped up to help. They threw a crackling ball at them, striking one of their wings. The dragon veered widely off to the side.

Their progress was excruciatingly slow. Dragons dove at them from the sky, and wayward spells flew through the air. It was far worse than the fight at the temple.

If only Gale and Master Cane were here. But as far as he knew, they were still in Fiiraania, far from the fight. Ash too. By the gods, the last thing he needed was for Ash to get caught up in this.

Fae tore after Alysion.

"I think I've found his aura. He's keeping to one spot," said the prince. "Easier to track."

"Easier for him to think and give orders," said Mellith. "He's likely tucked away somewhere cozy."

Meaning somewhere at the back of the hoard. Great.

Another dragon shot toward them out of the sky. This one was smaller than the rest and had purple scales like amethyst. Alysion was just about to launch a spell when Fae suddenly threw himself between them.

"Wait! Ash is up there!"

Twenty-Nine

Reunion

Ranath remembered little of their flight to the border, only that it felt agonizingly slow. Xyrros flew as fast as they could, wings straining. They made it there in record time, aided by the magic Sevarak had given them, and by the few spells Ranath dared to cast. Even with the Luuya, he needed to save his magic for later.

There was no one around when they reached the Sky Peak mountains. If not for Ranath's ability to sense aura and Xyrros' nose, they would never have believed that the thunder of dragons had passed through here. But the magic around the wards was chaos.

Ranath detected strange magic as they approached, similar to the aura he'd sensed coming off their pursuers. Vyrmyris' army had used something to warp the wards, twisting their magic. Part of him wished he could stay and examine how they'd broken through. But time was of the essence.

They had no hope of stopping Vyrmyris' army; the best they could do was get a message to the elves and eliminate the devastating element of surprise. Ranath stepped through the barrier and beckoned to Xyrros. Hesitantly, they pressed their snout to the invisible ward. It rippled but didn't repel them.

"Come on," Ranath said.

Xyrros huffed and stepped through the ward, movements stiff as if expecting to be burned to a crisp. It wasn't an unreasonable fear.

Ranath gave them a moment to get their bearings once through.

"It looks the same as home," they said as Ranath climbed onto their back. They spread their wings and lifted off.

"It'll change once we leave the mountains. We'll be flying over Odenia while I restore my aura," He wasn't sure exactly where they were but he suspected they were somewhere around Tyrrell.

Ranath immediately sent a message to Mitchy. Using his native magic felt strange. He felt much more at home in his dragon body, able to fly wherever he pleased.

He basked in the moonlight as they flew, drawing in as much of the moons' power as he could. Once he felt recharged, he opened a gate. A bright portal appeared ahead of them.

"In there!" he shouted.

Xyrros pumped their wings without hesitation, and they shot through it.

It spat them out near the Sylandrian border.

"Does Vyrmyris have the ability to open gates?" he asked Xyrros as they landed. He slid from their back.

"I don't think so," they said, tucking in their wings and picking at the ground. "But he's probably using that weird magic to fly fast." Xyrros started for the wards.

"Hold on," he threw out his arm as if it could stop a dragon. "You won't be able to pass through that one."

They stopped.

"Once you touch that barrier, it will trigger an alarm. I expect the Elithar to appear shortly afterwards."

"The Elithar?" Xyrros asked.

"The elite warriors that protect our realm. They won't take kindly to your presence, especially if they've already received my earlier warning." Which he had no idea if they had. He didn't know how long it took for his message to get to Mitchy, then to Fae. He hoped it was instant, but it was hard to say since he hadn't used the ring. "They know who I am so I hope they will listen before they attack." But he didn't have a good reputation with the realm. He prayed his position as messenger would be enough. "If you don't want to do this, I understand. You can wait here, and I will deal with them on my own." His heart clenched. Despite it all, he wanted Xyrros by his side.

"I'll go with you," they replied without any hesitation.

Ranath's heart lifted. "Then touch the barrier."

Xyrros pressed their amethyst muzzle to the ward. As expected, they couldn't pass through it. It was as if a wall of glass was stopping them. They stepped back and waited.

It didn't take long for the Elithar to arrive.

Through the wards, Ranath saw a gate open up and a hoard of warriors pour through, quickly surrounding them with weapons raised.

One he didn't recognize stepped forward. "Be still and state your business," they barked.

"I am Ashmyr, the one whom Queen Lymsia sent to Fiiraania to accompany Se—Gale and Cane. I have returned bearing grave news. Some dragons have broken through the Sky Peak wards and are on their way here."

"We are aware the wards have been tampered with."

He would have been shocked if they weren't. "Then you understand the gravity of the situation." He stepped forward and was met by the tip of a sword.

"You have brought a strange dragon here," the warrior said.

Ranath stiffened up. They didn't have time for this. "Yes, Xyrros brought me here. They are under my protection."

He could practically feel the eyerolls. The Queen may have been ordered by the queen to go to Fiiraania, but it had been a punishment, not a reward. These elves didn't trust him, and he couldn't blame them. He'd done some horrible things. "The queen can confirm my identity and my mission."

"The queen is dead," they said flatly.

He blinked. Lymsia was dead? How? When? Had Vyrmyris gotten to her already? No, that was impossible.

Xyrros shuffled uncomfortably beside him. The Elithar were closing in.

"That is unfortunate, but many more will die if the approaching dragons are not stopped," Ranath said firmly.

The warrior narrowed their eyes. Ranath held their gaze. He couldn't afford to back down; they would tear Xyrros to shreds.

At some imperceptible signal, elves lowered their weapons. "We are on our way to the battle," they said. "You will come with us."

"Very well," Ranath nodded.

Xyrros, not understanding Illithen, dipped their head.

A gate was opened, and they stepped into chaos.

A wave of sound crashed over them. Bright moons shone overhead, illuminating the battle. Dragons roared and elves screamed. Colourful spells exploded everywhere. Ranath could barely process what he was seeing. Xyrros' tail twitched, and he put a hand on their side. "I won't let anything happen to you."

Xyrros rumbled nervously.

"Let's find my brother, Fae, all right? We'll avoid the fighting as best we can." He climbed onto Xyrros' back. With no aura, Fae would be near impossible to find, but the prince would be easy. There were many powerful auras around but a small handful stood out—especially the ones that felt like the crystals.

Drawing on the moons' power, Ranath cast a barrier around them. "To stop arrows and smaller spells," he explained.

Xyrros, wings tucked tight to their sides, began walking. They kept their head low, trying not to draw attention.

But an elf on the back of a dragon wasn't inconspicuous.

Armoured elves charged Xyrros, screaming all sorts of things that Ranath was grateful the dragon couldn't understand. Fending them off was no easy task. Spells blasted the ground around Xyrros' feet, and many more streaked toward their head. Elves kept trying to pull Ranath from their back to "save" him.

"Let go of me," he hissed, blinding one with a burst of light. They wouldn't listen to a word he said, so magic had to speak for him. But even that had its limits.

"Fly, Xyrros!" he cried after fending off what seemed like the hundredth elf.

Xyrros' wings snapped open, and they took off. Deflecting arrows and spells was much easier than dealing with the crowd. They flew high, escaping the fight.

"Are you all right?" he hollered.

Xyrros nodded.

He frowned. They were trembling beneath him. "Let's stay up here while I look for aura."

Xyrros started a slow lap of the battlefield, keeping well above the fighting. It was much colder up there, but their scales and inner fire staved it off.

Ranath cast a quick spell to keep himself warm, then set to work.

He honed in on the crystals' auras. Though they were surrounded by other auras (wards, he surmised), there was no denying they belonged to the magical stones. But they felt different from before, as if they had fused into one. That would have made sense if the prince were wielding them, but he wasn't. Alysion's aura was present, but wasn't part of the aural rainbow.

Ranath tilted his head. Who was wielding the crystals? The prince was the only one who could properly bond with them. He'd learned that the hard way. Regardless, they had to get down there.

"I'm sorry Xyrros, but we need to land."

"It's fine."

If Ranath had a way of getting down there himself, he would. But turning into a dragon now would be suicide, and not solely because he was lacking the magic. He was better off as an elf, as much as he wished otherwise.

Xyrros angled their wings and dove down. Ranath threw up more wards, protecting them from all but the strongest spells. Those Xyrros would just have to avoid, unless they wanted him to run out of magic. Even with the Luuya infusing him with power, there was still a limit to what he could do.

He held on tight as Xyrros dipped and rolled through the air. Spells whizzed past, many bouncing off his wards and disappearing into the distance. Volleys of enchanted arrows flew at them as they got lower. Many of the dragons had landed but some still soared through the sky. Ranath ducked low on Xyrros' neck, fearing he would be seen by one of them. But thankfully, the elves on the ground held their attention. No one cared about a small purple dragon.

The volley of arrows and spells increased as they flew lower. It took everything Ranath had to repel the elves' valiant efforts and keep Xyrros on track.

"There!" he shouted over the noise, hoping Xyrros would hear him.

Their clawed feet hit the ground just as Fae threw himself in front of them. Behind him, the prince was carefully nullifying a spell.

"Ash!" Fae cried.

Ranath's heart twanged. He couldn't believe how good it felt to see his twin. Even in a place like this.

Thirty

The Scorched Earth

It took everything Fae had not to climb up the strange dragon and crush Ash in a hug.

Ash slid from the dragon's back. "Xyrros," he said quickly, patting their neck. "And I go by Ranath now."

Fae blinked at the new name, then nodded. Hopefully, Ranath had chosen it himself. "Nice to meet you," he said to the dragon. Xyrros rumbled a response he didn't understand.

Elithar warriors advanced around them.

"Stand down, this one is with us," barked Alysion. "They are under my protection. Spread the word." He immediately whirled around and threw up a wall of earth to catch a stream of dragon fire.

"We'll talk later," Fae said. He was relieved that his brother was fine. Same with his dragon friend. But what were they doing here? They were supposed to be in Fiiraania!

"Help is coming," Ranath said. "Sev—Gale and Cane are bringing reinforcements, but they're far behind."

Fae and Alysion exchanged a look. Captain Anaril had informed them that messages had been sent to Odenia and even the dwarves, but they wouldn't arrive in time.

"We're trying to find Vyrmyris," explained Alysion. "We know he's hiding somewhere safe nearby." The prince began to forge ahead. Fae and Mellith followed.

"We'll go with you," said Ranath.

Fae nodded gratefully. They'd need all the help they could get.

They pressed on through the chaos, Alysion, Ranath, and Mellith blocking spells left and right. Xyrros hunkered down, trying—and failing—not to draw attention to themself. Alysion's orders to leave them alone hadn't reached everyone yet.

Fae did his best with the sword, fending off stray attacks the others missed. Soon, the density of the fighting lessened; they were getting closer to the edge.

"He's close," Alysion called out.

A loud roar sounded, echoing across the plains. A cacophony of snarls answered.

Fae's hands tightened around the sword.

"It's him," said Ranath.

Xyrros bared their teeth and growled.

"What's that?" Mellith asked, eyes narrowed. They whirled around and deflected a stray arrow heading straight for Alysion. The prince nodded in thanks.

"Vyrmyris is rallying his followers," said Ranath.

A bright spell lit up the plains before them, illuminating a cluster of large rocks.

"There!" Fae shouted.

A dragon swooped towards them, fire spilling from their jaws.

Alysion grumbled and threw up a wall of water. Mellith joined him. The dragon flew by with a roar. They angled their wings and swung back around faster than Fae expected.

But the sorcerers were ready. Alysion flicked a hand, and a pillar of rock shot out of the ground. It clipped the dragon's wing, sending them spinning downward.

The group ran full-tilt towards the rocks. As they got closer as dark shape emerged.

Xyrros growled.

That's him, thought Fae.

Vyrmyris stepped into the moonlight and roared again, opening his wings and taking to the sky.

By the gods, he was huge!

Behind him, Ranath made an odd growling sound. It took Fae a moment to realize he was talking to Xyrros. Their wings snapped open, and they lifted off.

"A-Ranath!" Fae hollered. While Ranath was powerful, he didn't want his twin taking on Vyrmyris alone. "Ranath, Xyrros, come back!"

But the pair did not turn around.

Fae tore after them.

The pounding of feet told him the rest of the group was behind him.

"What are you thinking?" Alysion hissed, coming up beside him.

Fae didn't respond; his eyes were on Vyrmyris and the spell streaking towards him.

Ranath.

The spell struck the massive sapphire dragon. He let out an ear-splitting roar.

• • ● ● ● • •

Ranath barely heard Fae's cries over the sound of rushing air. It pained him but he didn't look back. He couldn't afford distractions.

His spell hit its mark.

The corners of his mouth twitched as Vyrmyris careened through the air, knocked off balance. The giant blue dragon whirled around, eyes narrowing at the sight of them.

"Is that an elf riding you?" he roared, hovering in place.

"Not just any elf," Ranath shot back. Wisely, Xyrros didn't get any closer.

Confusion fell over Vyrmyris' face, but it was quickly replaced by recognition. "I always knew there was something strange about you," he snarled. "Trust those elf-loving ziiras to bring one into our lands!"

He fought the urge to roll his eyes. Vyrmyris was just like Tarathiel. Instead, Ranath threw another spell at him.

Vyrmyris dropped below it. He opened his mouth and spat blue flames up at them. Xyrros rolled out of their path. Ranath felt the heat on his cheek and frowned. He wasn't fire-resistant in this body—another point against it.

More blue fire roared towards them. He tapped the side of Xyrros' neck, urging them to move that way. They angled their wings and slid sideways, lining them up perfectly for Ranath's next spell. But before he could cast it, a shape darted out of the night. Braemyrin.

Xyrros dove to avoid her, nearly dropping them right into Vyrmyris' next stream of fire.

Damn it, they couldn't take on both of them.

But something drew Vyrmyris' attention. He turned and flew towards the thickest part of the battle. That didn't bode well.

"I knew it!" Braemyrin snarled at him. "I knew Sevarak was lying!" Her bright orange fire came at him.

Ranath clung to Xyrros as they barrel rolled out of its path.

"I won't let them get you," they said. Ranath's heart skipped a beat.

Braemyrin flew at them faster than either of them expected, crashing into Xyrros. Her claws ripped into scales, and her jaws snapped at Ranath's head. He ducked down, narrowly avoiding being decapitated.

Xyrros screeched as her talons tore at their sides; the sound had Ranath seeing red. They frantically flapped their wings, trying to break away from her.

Ranath blasted her in the face with an orb of bright light. As he did, he caught a faint whiff of something that tickled the back of his mind.

Blinded and hissing loudly, she loosened her grasp on Xyrros. They wriggled free.

"Blasted thaliir, I'll tear you apart for that!" she snarled.

It was *her* scent around the cave. She was the one who had overheard him talking about the queen. His cave-mates had been right to suspect her.

Ranath snapped his fingers, sending another ball of light zipping at her. It struck her side while she floundered about in the air, knocking her over.

Braemyrin snarled all sorts of obscenities as she wildly beat her wings, trying to roll over and catch the air. Ash watched with satisfaction as she began to fall belly-up.

Xyrros, riled up by her attempt to kill Ranath, dove after her, jaws open. Fire poured from their mouth, chasing after the falling dragon.

She screamed as it licked at the underside of her wings.

Ranath clung tightly to Xyrros as they shot towards her. They clamped their jaws around one of her flailing wings. He heard the cracking of bone over the sound of rushing air.

Braemyrin screamed again.

Xyrros let go and let her fall. With her ruined wing, there was no hope of saving herself. They both watched as she struck the ground, kicking up a flurry of snow. She didn't move.

"Is she dead?" Xyrros asked quietly. Their breathing was laboured, and they struggled to stay in the air.

"If she isn't, she will be soon. Her aura is fading quickly. Land, you need a break." Crimson blood rolled down their sides, dripping onto the snow far below and soaking into Ranath's pant leg. He healed the injuries he could reach, but they needed to be on the ground for him to deal with the larger ones he couldn't reach; trying to crawl across Xyrros' back while flying wasn't wise.

"We can't land now. We need to go after Vyrmyris." They started flying in the direction the large blue dragon had gone.

"He'll tear you apart in this condition! I need to heal you. I'll put you down there myself if it comes to it," he warned. It didn't help that Xyrros was still tired from their flight across the mountains and the earlier fight with Vyrmyris' lackeys.

Xyrros wavered in the air.

"I want to go after him too, but we can't. The sooner you land, the sooner we can get back into the air."

They rumbled something unintelligible in their throat but angled their wings towards the ground. As they descended, Ranath caught sight of Fae and his crew racing towards where Vyrmyris had gone. His heart clenched. *Stay safe.*

He hopped off Xyrros' back as soon as they reached the ground. Calling on his magic (and grateful for the twin moons), he walked around his violet dragon, running a glowing hand over the worst of the cuts. It was slow going, and he feared that they would be attacked. But it seemed that the prince's word had gotten around; the elves left them alone. Mostly.

Someone approached. Ranath tensed, recognizing their aura. Elithar. Xyrros growled.

"Do you require assistance?" they asked, stopping a respectful distance away. "The prince sent me."

He didn't know the particular warrior, but he couldn't detect any malicious intent in their expression or their aura. *If Alysion truly sent them...*

"Close the larger wounds," he said, returning to what he was doing. He murmured a few words of reassurance to Xyrros.

With the warrior's help, they quickly stopped the bleeding.

"How do you feel?" he asked.

"Fine," Xyrros replied. They dipped their head in thanks to the Elithar. The warrior turned and returned to the fight.

"Get on," they said.

Ash didn't argue. They soon returned to the air and flew toward Vyrmyris' aura.

THIRTY-ONE

VYRMYRIS

Fae and his companions raced across the melting plains after Vyrmyris. Dragons swooped out of the air, but his entourage fended them off. Alysion practically glowed with aura under the full moons.

The Elithar they passed clued in that something was happening and did their best to clear the way. Some joined their ranks, determined to protect their prince.

Another horn sounded, echoing above the chaos.

Alysion grimaced but didn't slow. "My father has arrived."

The horn was answered by an ear-splitting roar—Vyrmyris. He hovered above the fighting, looking for something. Or *someone*.

Alysion threw a crackling ball of lightning at him, sending it streaking across the plains like a shooting star.

But Vyrmyris opened his massive jaws and burned it up.

"Again!" Mellith called over the noise, powering up something of their own. "I'll distract him." They lobbed a sphere of green at him as Alysion shot off another.

Both spells hit their target and exploded, creating a cloud of smoke.

"He's still up!" cried Fae.

"I'd be shocked if that had been enough," muttered Alysion.

The smoke soon cleared, revealing the furious blue dragon. He swooped down at them, mouth open. Fire spewed forth, vapourizing what remained of the snow and charring the earth. Alysion and Mellith threw up a shield of water. It took everything they had to maintain it as the fire turned it to steam.

Beyond the dissipating vapour, the flame died, and Vyrmyris' form began to recede. Clearly he had bigger things to worry about. Like the king.

Alysion dropped the wall. "I'm the crown prince!" he shouted.

The large dragon slowed.

Did he understand Illithen? Fae hoped not.

Vyrmyris whirled around and landed before them, lips drawn back in a snarl.

Fae fought the urge to shrink back. He'd forgotten how big dragons were. Xyrros, who was at least twice the size of an uhaan, was absolutely tiny in comparison. Vyrmyris' teeth were longer than daggers and wickedly sharp; each beat of his massive wings buffeted them like a gale. How were they going to stop him?

He glanced at Alysion. If the prince was intimidated, he didn't show it. His jaw was set and his emerald eyes blazed. "You're here for me."

How could he sound so strong and confident? Fae's entire being screamed at him to flee. How had their people ever waged war against them?

"You? You're nothing but a whelp," said Vyrmyris, his voice rumbling like distant thunder. "But you will draw out the ones I seek."

Alysion's parents. He didn't know the queen had already passed.

Fae was suddenly shoved to the side. He landed on the ground, the melting snow instantly soaking his back. *I really need to get some armour.*

Alysion stood over him, blond hair whipping around as blinding fire lit up the plains. He scrambled to his feet. The prince was holding up another wall of water, and it was evaporating faster than he could maintain it.

Come on, Alysion. The bright fire died down just as the last of Alysion's shield evaporated.

"I can't keep doing that," said the prince, panting. "Even with the moons." He'd already expended an extraordinary amount of magic today. He needed to rest. But war didn't allow for breaks.

Vyrmyris had landed and was charging them, bellowing like a herd of nuu.

Fae grabbed Alysion's hand and pulled him to the side, hissing through his teeth as a spike on the tip of the dragon's wing slashed his shoulder. He glanced at Alysion and was relieved to see he was unscathed. The Elithar formed up around them.

Streaks of colour caught their attention. Something darted around Vyrmyris, casting all sorts of spells. Fear shot through Fae. Mellith couldn't take on the sapphire dragon alone.

With his fire and equally lethal tail, Vyrmyris easily drove them back.

"Wait here," said Alysion, wrenching his hand out of Fae's and sprinting towards them.

"Absolutely not! You're the one who told me to stay by your side!" Rainbow sword still in hand, he followed his prince into the chaos. The new wound on his arm throbbed, but he ignored it.

The two sorcerers and a handful of warriors set about pummelling the dragon with spells. Fae stepped forward with the sword but Alysion threw an arm out to stop him. "It's too dangerous, even with that. And you're hurt."

Fae ignored the stinging pain. "I fought Calandriel with it."

Alysion didn't seem to hear him and threw another spell at the dragon.

Well, he wasn't about to stand around. Vyrmyris' tail lashed out, deadly spikes heading straight for him. Fae leapt out of the way, narrowly avoiding being skewered. He swung his blade at the flailing appendage but missed, burying the tip in the ground. He wrenched it out and flung himself out of the way of Vyrmyris' leathery wing just in time.

A shape flew over them. Was that Ash on his friend's back? He didn't have time to process it—dragonfire was heading straight for him.

And Fae didn't have time to move. He instinctively ducked, but he didn't feel the lick of flames. Alysion stood beside him, shielding them both with a wall of earth.

"I told you to stay back," the prince hissed, focused on holding his spell.

Where was he supposed to go? The plains were pure chaos. Nowhere was safe.

The dragonfire died and left Alysion wavering before him, the constant use of powerful magic taking its toll on the prince. They needed to end this now.

"Where are the Elithar?" hollered Fae. They'd been surrounded by the warriors a moment ago. A quick look around showed him that most were now occupied with keeping other dragons at bay.

Vyrmyris crouched, about to launch himself into the air.

"We can't let him take off!" shouted Fae. They wouldn't stand a chance if that happened.

Alysion just grit his teeth.

"I'll distract him for you. Give you a clean shot," said Fae.

"What? No!" Alysion hollered. "Don't you dare!"

But Fae was already moving. He held up the sword, which gave off a bright rainbow light. Vyrmyris' great eyes locked onto him.

"Oi, over here! I'm the one you want."

Quick as a viper, Vyrmyris snapped at him.

Fae tucked into an awkward roll. A ball of flame smashed into the side of the dragon's head.

Vyrmyris roared in fury.

Fae rolled back onto his feet and jabbed his sword at the dragon's scaley neck. The blade flashed and sunk into scale like it was butter. Vyrmyris screamed, the sound nearly knocking Fae to his knees.

The dragon whipped his head around, jaws open.

Fae leapt over the bite that would have killed him instantly. He landed in one piece.

"I'm the crown prince. You want me!" Alysion shouted over the sound of battle.

The dragon turned away and loosed a sweeping breath of flame.

Bone-headed prince! Fae couldn't see him and could only pray that the prince was all right. He launched himself at Vyrmyris, swinging the sword.

They needed to find a way to end Vyrmyris quickly. But how?

Vyrmyris suddenly spun around, spiked tail whipping towards him.

Fae jumped, just managing to clear the scaled appendage. It struck an approaching elf, flinging them across the ground.

Vyrmyris roared and opened his massive wings, preparing to lift off.

• • ● ⬤ ● • •

"We need to get down there," Ranath hollered over the noise.

Xyrros angled their wings into a steep descent. Only they weren't aiming for the ground.

Ranath braced himself.

Talons reaching, mouth open in a ferocious snarl, Xyrros crashed into the sapphire dragon. Ranath was nearly thrown from the impact. It jarred his teeth

and rattled his skull, like running full-tilt into a wall. He shook his head to clear i
t.

Snarling, Xyrros bit and clawed at Vyrmyris. The larger dragon snaked his head around to bite them.

Ranath threw out a hand, conjuring a burst of bright light.

Vyrmyris jerked back, hissing, "Obnoxious thaliir."

"Cover!" Ranath yelled to the elves nearby. He threw a yellow ball at Vyrmyris' face. It exploded in a burst of light and heat.

Vyrmyris roared in pain, thrashing about as the spell burned his eyes.

Xyrros growled and dug their talons in to Vyrmyris' side, piercing through scale to stop them from being thrown.

The elves around them, his brother included, backed away from the flailing dragon.

"Damn you!" the blinded dragon screamed. He opened his maw, unleashing a stream of white-hot fire headed right for the elves.

An orb of water struck the flame, dousing it. Ranath looked around, spotting the prince and his companions through the haze. They were surrounded by a retinue of Elithar who all began to cast. Magical tethers shot forth and wrapped around Vrymyris' legs. He bellowed in fury and tried to lift off, but the gleaming chains held him in place.

Ranath nodded in thanks before turning his attention back to their enemy.

"They're holding him down for us!" he shouted at Xyrros before throwing another spell at Vyrmyris' ruined face.

"I will burn all of you!" Vyrmyris unleashed another torrent of flame, aiming wildly. The elves on the ground thew up magical shields. Thankfully the tethers held. But Ranath sensed the magic waning. The Luuya was ending.

Immediately, the prince's aura flared.

Ranath dared to peek. Fae had passed him the strange sword.

He really is the only one who can handle the crystals. Ranath had been a fool to believe he could ever harness their power. He pushed those thoughts away as an angry, fang-filled mouth tried to bite at Xyrros.

A powerful, fiery spell came for Vyrmyris' head. The dragon instinctively jerked back with a snarl, and Xyrros seized the opportunity to bury their fangs deep into the base of his neck. Vyrmyris let out an angry roar.

Ranath flicked his hand. A barrier of light appeared before them, shielding them from Vyrmyris' bites. Ranath punched into it, shooting out beams of light that struck the sapphire dragon. The spell weakened with each burst as the sky began to lighten.

They had to end this now.

Vyrmyris was covered in blood from their attacks, which only fuelled his fury. His thunderous roars rang in Ranath's ears, deafening him to anything else. Deflecting another flash of fire, he made cutting motions with his hands. Crescent-shaped bursts of light flew from his fading barrier, slicing at Vyrmyris' blue scales. Hot blood splattered his face as Vyrmyris screeched, the sound shaking him to the very core of his being.

By the Ancestors, what did they have to do to take this dragon down? He glanced at the prince. Alysion was using the sword to bombard the massive dragon with powerful magic that would have felled any other.

Still, Vyrmyris was weakening. He swayed beneath them, and his fire no longer burned as hot.

"Go for his throat—I'll cover you!" he hollered to Xyrros.

They wrenched their teeth out of Vyrmyris' neck, taking a mouthful of flesh with them.

Ranath slid from their back, dropping to the ground far below. He slid in the slush but managed to keep his footing as he ran around the trapped dragon, blasting him in the face as he went.

"What are you doing!" someone called above Vyrmyris' screeching. He ignored it, focused on keeping the sapphire dragon busy while Xyrros clawed their way up to his throat, their talons leaving a bloody mess behind.

"Insolent insects!" Vyrmyris raged.

"Get him!" Ranath hollered. He danced around the dragon, pelting him with bursts of stinging light.

Between his blindness and the tethers, all Vyrmyris could do was thrash like an angry uhaan, trying to throw Xyrros off his neck. But the amethyst dragon clung on like a prickly burr.

The prince threw spells at his wings, shredding them to tatters. Elves moved in to help him, launching spells at the enraged dragon. "Don't hit the small one! Hold your spells if you must!" Alysion commanded.

Vyrmyris suddenly reared up, ripping through his magical bonds. Xyrros had their mouth open, trying to get a hold of the softer flesh of his throat. Vyrmyris shook himself violently. Xyrros flew off, their claws leaving deep cuts in his throat as they lost their hold. Dark blood poured forth from the wounds.

"Xyrros!" Ranath screamed as the amethyst dragon hit the ground hard. Summoning every ounce of magic he had, he formed a spear of light, then ran towards Vyrmyris and threw it as hard as he could. A splurt of blood soaked him as it pierced the dragon's throat, illuminating the bleeding cuts.

Vyrmyris thrashed about, a horrible wet sound coming from his ruined throat. His mouth opened, a flicker of flame sparking and dying; no dragonfire erupted. Instead, blood sprayed from his mouth, raining down on the elves. They fled, not wanting to be trampled by the dragon in his death throes.

Ranath sprinted towards Xyrros' unmoving form. "Xyrros, wake up! We need to move!" They were going to get crushed. He began casting spells to try and rouse them, but most bounced off their scales. Fear gripped his heart.

"How can I help?"

Ranath looked up into the eyes of the prince.

"Just need to wake them," he said.

A shadow fell over them.

Alysion whipped around and threw up a shield just as Vyrmyris' lifeless bulk crashed down upon them. The shield stopped them from being crushed, but now Alysion was holding up part of the massive dead dragon. If he failed...Ranath saw the prince grit his teeth. Even with the crystals helping him, he was physically exhausted. His arms trembled.

Come on, Xyrros!

He tried more spells, but nothing was rousing the younger dragon.

"Just move them!" Alysion hissed. The barrier flickered. Ranath sensed him pull on more of the crystals' auras. The shield brightened, but the prince lacked the strength to push Vyrmyris away from them.

A horn sounded, but Ranath hardly heard it. Somewhere in the back of his mind, he realized it signalled the end of the fight.

Alysion dropped to a knee. "Hurry!" Sweat covered his brow, mixing with blood.

Ranath put every last bit he had into one final spell. If this didn't do it, then at least they would perish together.

He closed his eyes placed his hands on Xyrros' head and pushed as much aura as he could into them.

Xyrros eyes snapped open. They got to their feet just as the prince's spell failed.

Thirty-Two

Aftermath

Alysion woke to a pair of eyes he would know anywhere.

Fae.

He tried to say his name, but his throat was too dry. All that came out was a croak.

"Easy now." Fae straightened up and handed him a wooden cup of water.

Alysion eased himself up in bed—his own bed—and gratefully downed it. "What happened? How did I get here?" he croaked.

"The Elithar and your father brought us back. He carried you here."

He vaguely remembered his father showing up. "Is Xyrros all right?"

Fae nodded. "Your spell failed just as Ranath roused them. The Elithar stepped in and got all of you out there. Xyrros is still being tended to, but they don't appear to have any serious injuries. My brother is with them."

Alysion set the cup on the nightstand and sank back back into bed. Everything hurt. He felt like he'd been trampled by herd of nuu—no, an army of dragons.

"What happened with the dragons?" he asked.

"Are you sure you don't want to rest longer before we get into that?"

"Just give me the short version." His eyes roamed over his love. He could see some bandages peeking out from under Fae's clothes, but he didn't appear to be in pain.

"Once Vyrmyris fell, most of the dragons turned and fled. A few kept fighting, but they were quickly subdued."

"Killed?"

"I don't think so," said Fae. "I think Captain Anaril wants to interrogate them."

Ah, right. Of course they would. The dragons had managed to breach the Sky Peak wards. Everyone would want to know how that happened. And why they had attacked in the first place.

But Alysion knew. Because of his mother.

His *dead* mother.

Alysion's breath caught. His mother was dead. Calandriel had killed her. He clutched at the sheets as a flurry of emotions crashed over him. With all that had happened, he hadn't had the opportunity to process it.

Something wet dripped into his hands.

"Alysion?" said Fae, worried.

And suddenly he was crying. Crying over the loss of his mother, and what that meant for him as the prince. Crying over the fact that Calandriel had killed her, yet he couldn't fully blame the lost heir who had also been a victim. It was confusing. It was all too much. Shudders wracked his body as he buried his face in the blanket.

A warm arm wrapped around him, and a hand soothingly rubbed his back. Fae didn't say a word; him simply being there was enough.

Eventually, he looked up and dried his eyes on the sheets.

Someone knocked on the door.

"May I come in?"

His father.

The king wore a pained expression. He kept a respectful distance, not wanting to come between him and Fae. To his relief, he seemed to be all right; Alysion couldn't see any blood or bandages, and he was no longer in his armour. He looked just as exhausted as Alysion felt.

"When you are ready, everyone is waiting to begin," Illuven said. "We cannot delay the meeting any longer, as much as we may wish to."

Right. Alysion wiped his red eyes one last time and pushed back the blanket.

"Are you well enough?" Fae asked.

"I'm fine." He put his feet on the floor and stood. He was unsteady, but there was no point in delaying things.

"Meet us in the main council chamber." His father dipped his head and left the room.

Alysion let Fae help him change into something suitable, not feeling his usual embarrassment of being seen in a state of undress. That's how exhausted he was. This meeting was going to be torture.

He and Fae entered a circular room on the ground floor in one of the palatial trees. The polished walls were smooth, and vines hung from the ceiling. It was the same room Tarathiel had had his fate sealed by the queen decades ago. Knowing this did little to lift his mood, for neither his mother nor Tarathiel was alive anymore.

Alysion's heart hurt. His mother brought up so many conflicting emotions. She had never been kind to him. Her obsession with tradition had caused him to run away and meet Fae in the first place. The same obsession had pushed Tarathiel to do so many terrible things. And yet, she'd defied the very rules she seemed to care so much about when she'd lured an innocent dragon through the barrier and ensorcelled them into insanity.

And now she wasn't even here to deal with the consequences of that poor decision. It fell to him and his father to sort out this mess, just like at the Great Temple with Tarathiel's followers.

By the Ancestors, the Eburnas! They'd completely missed the ceremony! Instead, they'd gone to *war*. If the nobles needed any sign that the Brightstars were unfit to rule, this was it.

"Alysion?"

Alysion was brought back to the present. Everyone was looking at him.

"Are you sure you're all right?" his father asked from his throne at the head of the room. There were two equally ornate empty seats beside him.

He had stopped in the entrance. "Yes, I'm fine." He scanned the room. A crowd of elves stood before them, quietly whispering amongst themselves. Captain Anaril and a few of the Elithar were present, along with a handful of nobles—the heads of various families, and his parents' advisors. Mellith stood near the front of the crowd wearing fresh dark grey and sky blue robes. The windows were open. Xyrros poked their head in through one. Ranath stood beside them, away from the crowd.

"Princey!" A large red head appeared in another. Gale.

He nearly melted at the sight of her. He strode over to her before he could register what he was doing and wrapped his arms around her scaley head. "It's good to see you," he mumbled, ignoring the disapproving sounds of the nearest nobles.

"Same to you. Sorry we missed all the drama."

He stepped back to let Fae greet her. Then, they took their seats at the head of the chamber with his father.

Cane appeared in the window beside her. "We should meet outside next time," she said, looking at the king.

"It will be done," the king nodded. His face betrayed nothing, but Alysion could tell that his father hadn't been expecting so many draconic guests.

And thus the meeting began.

Having Gale and Cane there proved to be a great boon. They filled in all the gaps about Vyrmyris' actions that Xyrros and Ash were unsure about. Of course, they brought up what the queen had done so long ago. For many of the nobles present, this news came as a shock.

"Our queen wouldn't dare!" some insisted. "It must have been a trick of the dragons!"

To Alysion's relief, the three dragons did not react to these statements.

"More than enough evidence has been brought forth regarding the matter," said King Illuven calmly. "Might I remind everyone that I was present and injured during the attack." He turned to the dragons. "As the queen is no longer with us, and therefore cannot be tried, what sort of compensation do you desire?"

"To renegotiate the Sky Peak wards," said Gale without missing a beat. "Of course, now that Odenia has been populated by humans, we will require their input, as well as that of the dwarves'."

Alysion perked up at that. Right, the dwarves. Had they lost a ruler too? Urka had mentioned they had a council...

Angry muttering broke out amongst the nobles.

"That is the very least we can do," said Alysion before anyone could interject. All eyes turned to him. "The lands beyond the Sylandrian barrier no longer belong to us. We cannot make decisions for the people that call them home."

"All must be present for the negotiations," said Gale. "This meeting doesn't need to happen immediately. We can wait until everyone is ready."

"If you don't mind me asking," said Illuven, "what are you hoping to gain? Our missives will need to include your requests."

Gale and Cane exchanged a look.

"Ideally we would like the wards removed," said Cane. The hall went deathly silent.

Alysion's stomach jolted. A world with no barrier between them and the dragons? He couldn't imagine it.

The king didn't so much as blink. "Very well. I shall have messages sent out immediately." He nodded to one of the nobles who promptly left.

"And now we must move on to another matter of great importance." The king looked at Alysion.

Alysion's stomach twisted again. He had an idea of what was coming, and he almost wanted to be out fighting Vyrmyris again. *Almost.*

"With the death of our queen," the king started, "the one who carries the blood of our divine Ancestors, it falls to her son, our prince, to lead our people."

All eyes turned to him. Alysion wanted to sink into the floor and never come out. By the Ancestors, he wasn't ready to be king! A comforting hand gripped his. Fae.

"And yet, he has not yet undergone the Striiya and thus cannot accept the crown," said the king.

A small boon.

"But," his father continued, "both he and his partner Fae are of age."

Fae squeezed his hand.

Alysion looked up at his father. The king's expression was light, but Alysion could see the tension underneath. He didn't want to be speaking these words any more than Alysion wanted to hear them.

"The Striiya will take place after the wake for our queen."

There were some murmurs of agreement, but not all were happy.

"Do you really think the Ancestors will allow him to ascend to the throne? Look at the mess that's been made of our kingdom!" a noble said.

Some nodded.

"The Eburnas—which was supposed to help us regain favour with the Ancestors—turned into a war!" another roared. Suddenly, the nobles were all shouting and arguing.

"He must join with one of our thelim if we are to appease them!"

"His mother has brought nothing but ruin upon us!"

"The dragons came because the Ancestors have abandoned us!"

"His sera is nothing but a damsiri!"

Each comment Alysion caught drove a spike into his heart. If not for Fae's hand, he would have fled to his room. Instead he bit back tears. He knew he wasn't ready for the throne. He knew the Eburnas had gone terribly wrong. But he didn't think the Ancestors were upset. He didn't believe for a moment that taking anyone but Fae to be his mate would solve anything. By the Ancestors, how was Fae handling this so calmly? He sat still beside Alysion, expression unreadable.

It took the efforts of both the king and the captain to bring the room down to an angry murmuring.

"You are all dismissed for now," said King Illuven.

The nobles weren't pleased, but slowly filed out of the room. Soon only a handful of Elithar remained, including the captain. Mellith lingered by the door with a worried expression before leaving.

Alysion stared at his father, trying to stamp down his rising panic. "I'm not—I can't—" he stammered.

King Illuven rubbed a hand over his face, exhaustion filling it as he dropped his mask. "This is not an easy decision. I do not wish for you to ascend to the throne yet. But our people will not follow me. They have lost faith in our family and will only remain loyal to me for so long since I do not carry the Ancestors' blood."

Silence descended upon the room. Fae soothingly rubbed the back of his hand. It was the only thing keeping Alysion grounded. The Ancestors. Their people needed to stop worshipping them so much! He frowned. No, they weren't worshipping. They were using them as an excuse to push their personal agendas. And that was something he would work on as king once things settled down.

His guts twisted. Him, king. Though he'd suspected this might happen, he still couldn't fathom it.

"Alysion?" his father called in a tone that suggested he'd said his name a few times.

"Ah, yes?"

"We need to discuss your mother's wake," the king said solemnly. "It will be held tonight."

Alysion nodded, swallowing a lump in his throat.

THIRTY-THREE

THE FUTURE

Half a moon had passed since Queen Lymsia's wake. Odenia and the dwarves had yet to respond to the dragons' request to discuss the Sky Peak wards. Until replies were received and a date set, the three dragons stayed in Sylandris, much to the locals' displeasure. They mostly kept away from the cities, hunting in the wild, untamed Sylandrian woods. Fae visited with them as often as he could, something that was occurring less frequently as he prepared for the Striiya.

The Striiya only happened every few decades, as thelim were rare, and there wasn't always a royal heir as a participant. The city was determined to put on a good show, though Fae suspected it was to impress the dragons.

As if Gale and Master Cane would care.

Three elves were participating in the ceremony—himself, Alysion, and Ranath. He'd been worried the king would reject his request to let his twin participate, given his involvement with Tarathiel. But the king had agreed.

"It'll upset some of the nobles, but he was ultimately a victim of Tarathiel's machinations, and has since proven himself."

Ranath had been the one to deliver the final blow to Vyrmyris, though he would give Xyrros all the credit.

Fae's heart had leapt. He wouldn't have been able to go through it without him. He was doing his best to hold himself together, just as anxious as Alysion was about claiming the throne. Since he was Alysion's romantic partner, it put him in a strange position. Though he personally wouldn't bear the title of king until they were formally joined, something neither of them was ready for, he would still be considered a similar rank.

And that rubbed too many the wrong way, even with his participation in the war and stopping Calandriel in the canyon. But, he had won some over. The stares that followed him now were more curious than hostile. And more elves were bowing to him—something he swore he would never get used to, especially not after moons of being harassed and bullied.

The morning of the Striiya, he woke to find the bed empty. Alysion was already up and gone. Sad that the prince had left without him, he got up and threw on some clothes. They would change into some ceremonial robes later. He grabbed breakfast from the kitchen and went out to find his twin. Unfortunately, the palace couldn't accommodate Xyrros, so Ranath stayed with them in the forest.

When he arrived at the clearing, he was surprised to see all three dragons present.

"Are you planning on coming to the Striiya?" he asked them. The ceremony itself was private, but there would be a huge celebration afterward.

"We wouldn't be welcome," huffed Gale.

"Sorry, my boy. I wish we could," said Cane.

Fae's heart sank, but he understood. Hopefully, one day, their people would get along. But that was going to take time—a lot of time, given how long they all lived. Perhaps the coming meeting would help to foster some of those emotions.

"But we can still give you our blessing," continued Cane. She lowered her head until they were face to face and exhaled through her nostrils. A wave of hot, smoky air washed over him, blowing his hair back.

"Hey! I just brushed that!" But he was smiling. Fae closed his eyes and pressed his forehead to her silver nose. "Thank you."

Cane rumbled deep in her throat. "Not too long ago I found you near the wards. And look at you now!" She lifted her head. "I'm proud of you. We both are."

"And we know your parents would be too," added Gale. She lowered her head and exhaled over him as well.

Fae was glad she did, for it helped hide the tears that suddenly leaked out.

"Thank you," he murmured, throat tight. Would his parents be proud of him? Yes, they would be. He'd found Ranath and learned the truth about

Calandriel. And now he would be joined with a prince and hopefully mend the relationship between elves and dragons.

The ground lurched beneath him. It was a lot. He took a deep breath, eyes clearing. One thing at a time. First, he had to get through the Striiya.

"Where's Ranath?"

"I'm here," said a voice from behind Xyrros. He stepped out to face Fae, Cane and Gale wandered off into the trees, giving them some privacy.

"We need to return to the city to get ready."

"About that...I'm not going."

Fae blinked. "What do you mean?"

A mask slid over his brother's face, reminding Fae of the isidyll he'd once been.

"I have no intention of participating in the Striiya. The people don't trust me, and there is nothing for me here."

"There's lots for you here! I'm here and, and—"

Ranath shook his head. "My entire life here was a lie. I will never be accepted."

Fae clenched his hand. *But you killed Vyrmyris!* "Then what do you plan on doing?" He almost couldn't ask, afraid of the answer.

Ranath's mask dropped, pain taking its place. "I know you spent so long trying to find me. And I am grateful you did. Who knows how things would have turned out if you and the prince hadn't freed me from Tarathiel. But I can't stay here." He put a hand on Xyrros' neck and took a breath. "I want to return to Fiiraania with the dragons. Living with them has shown me a freedom I never knew was possible. A freedom I won't find anywhere else."

Fae stared at his brother. "You're serious?" he asked, fighting to keep his tone steady and neutral.

Ranath nodded.

Fae closed his eyes. He'd been so excited for Ranath to return from Fiiraania, to finally be with his brother again. But now...

"It's not like we won't see each other. If all goes well with the new treaties—"

Fae cut him off by wrapping his arms around him. Ranath stiffened at the touch.

"I won't stop you if this is what you want," Fae said into his ear, tears falling freely. "But I ask that you participate in the Striiya with me. It won't make up for all the time we've missed, but at least it's something."

Ranath hesitantly hugged him back. "All right," he said. "I'll come."

• • ● ⬤ ● • •

Dressed in only a light spider silk robe, the three of them stood in an open-air, nest-like room high up in one of the trees. Normally, this ceremony was performed at the Great Temple, but the temple was still undergoing repairs, and a new isidyl still had yet to be named. Bare footed, they stepped into the room and were met by King Illuven and two of the oldest elves Fae had ever seen. Their faces were heavily lined, and the shorter one was covered in tattoos. A ritual circle had been burned into the floor. They were careful not to step in it as they fanned out around the small space.

Fae suppressed a shiver. Their robes and bare feet did nothing to protect them from the chilly winter air.

"Step into the circle when your name is called," said the taller elf, their voice deep and clear. "We will begin with Ashm—Ranath."

Ranath did as he was told, and the circle began to glow with a gentle yellow light.

"Mm, a light-user. Rare."

The circle reacted to their magic? A jolt of panic shot through him. What did that mean for him? Fae pushed aside his worries and focused on his brother. The king would have warned him if he believed the ceremony would fail.

The circle flickered once as the tattooed elf joined Ranath. Ranath closed his eyes and pulled down the top of his robe, exposing his upper body. The tattooed elf pressed the tip of a finger to Ranath's chest, right over his damis.

Another flash of panic. *It will be fine.*

The elf started murmuring something that steadily grew louder as they traced a finger over Ranath's body. At first nothing seemed to be happening, but as their finger moved over his damis, the skin beneath it darkened like ink.

Alysion had told him that the designs and locations of the marks varied by elf. Most had theirs over their damis, but some had them over the heart or right in the center.

Fae glanced at his brother's face. He didn't appear to be in any pain. If anything, he looked relaxed.

The tattooed elf stepped back and left the circle. Ranath opened his eyes and dipped his head. Fae only caught a glimpse of his mark, something akin to a crescent moon, before he pulled up the robe and backed out of the circle. He caught Fae's eye and gave him an encouraging nod.

"Faeranduil."

Fae's throat went dry. Resisting the urge to turn and run, he stepped into the circle. His heart stopped. The circle wasn't glowing. Panicked, he looked up at the elves before him. The taller elf opened their mouth to speak but shut it when the circle flickered.

His feet went cold.

It flickered again, slowly lighting up. It was the same soft yellow light. The tattooed one cocked their head in thought as they approached. "We did not know what to expect from you," they said. "It appears someone in your past cast a powerful light spell upon you."

His stomach jolted.

"M-my father," he stammered. It must have been the spell he'd used to send Fae to Odenia when Tarathiel had attacked their home. He closed his eyes and bared his torso.

A hand gently grasped a lock of his hair. "That spell, it did this."

Fae's eyes nearly shot open.

"It's faint—a dying echo, but I can sense it. Whatever happened when the magic was cast, it changed your hair."

He bit his lip, fighting back tears. His father's spell was responsible for his hair? He'd thought it had always been like this. Even Ranath hadn't commented on it.

The tattooed elf let go and pressed their finger to his chest, not where his damis would be, but over his heart. Their finger was cold, making his skin prickle.

They began to draw.

The sensation was odd. It felt like water was flowing under his skin. He slowly got used to it and tried to relax, not realizing until then how tense he was. Soon, the elf stepped back. Fae opened his eyes and dipped his head in thanks. He resisted the urge to look at his chest as he pulled the robe back up and left the circle.

"Prince Alysion."

The circle flared with a fiery light, flecked by a rainbow of colour—a perfect reflection of the prince's abilities.

They repeated the same process for him, only his mark was centered on his chest.

"It's been a while since anyone was marked there," the old elf said as they stepped back. "It is a good sign. It shows a balance of heart and power. You shall be a great king, My Prince."

"Thank you."

Fae caught the subtle waver in his voice. Hardly anyone told Alysion that he would be great. Usually, they beat him down.

Alysion respectfully dipped his head. He fixed his robe and left the circle.

• • ● ● ● • •

The coronation ceremony was held less than a moon later. The nerves Alysion had felt before the Aubrillias paled in comparison to what he felt now. He had hardly slept the night before, and when Fae finally roused him in the morning (how was it morning already?), there were dark circles under his eyes.

"Hey, it's going to be okay," said Fae. His love sat up in the bed beside him and placed a soothing hand on his cheek. The prince closed his eyes and leaned into it. Fae's hand felt smoother; the calluses he'd built up from working in Cane's forge were disappearing.

"I can't do this," he whispered. "I'm not ready. I wasn't expecting to take the crown for many more decades. So many problems still need resolving, like the lack of isidyll, and handling the last of Tarathiel's followers..."

Fae kissed the top of his head.

Heat washed over his face, the tips of his ears tingling. By the gods, how he'd missed Fae the past few moons. Their bedtime activities last night hadn't been enough.

"You won't be alone. I'll be there, along with your father, the captain, and many more." Fae pulled him into a hug, skin touching skin.

"I wish we could just run away," Alysion mumbled, hugging him back.

"Mmm, me too. But we can't."

"Yeah…" His father and Tarathiel had longed to do the same ages ago, and he couldn't help but wonder what would have happened if they had. Would they have been happy, or would his mother have chased them to the end of the world?

"We have to get up soon," said Fae.

"I know. But a few moments won't hurt." He just wanted to lay back down and continue what they'd been doing last night. Fae had been able to make him momentarily forget about today's events.

They held each other until someone knocked on the door. "My Prince, it is time to prepare," said Layniir from the other side.

Alysion sighed. "We're up."

They got out of bed and helped each other dress in many layers of spider silk robes. Alysion's voluminous outfit was white with a lilac under robe. Silver stars and moons had been embroidered all over it. Fae's outfit didn't have as many layers. Traditionally, the sera wore grey, but when he'd pulled out his father's blue robe, Alysion had insisted he wear it instead.

"To honour your family."

Alysion busied himself with his sash while Fae blinked back tears.

"You look ethereal," said Fae once they were dressed. "Like a king."

Alysion turned around, taking him in. It was the first time he'd had seen Fae in any sort of formal wear. The blue brought out the depths of his brown eyes. Alysion could easily lose himself in them.

"Is something wrong?" Fae asked. "You're staring."

Alysion turned away quicky, ears burning. "No, everything is fine." He looked at himself in the mirror. *Humph, Fae looks more like a king than I do.* He felt like a thelim playing around with his parents' clothes. "Actually, I have something for you."

"Something for me? On the day of your coronation?" Fae's eyes gleamed.

"Don't remind me." He knelt, pulled something long and wrapped in silk from under his bed, and held it out to Fae. "You asked about this."

Fae accepted the bundle and slowly unwrapped it. He teared up again as a longsword was revealed. "Ama's sword."

"I hope it's an adequate replacement for the one that broke. And since the crystal sword has—" he was cut off by Fae throwing his arms around him. The sheathed sword whacked him in the back. But he didn't mind.

"Thank you," choked out Fae.

Alysion hugged him back.

"My Prince?" said Layniir from the hall.

Right, they had to finish getting ready. As they broke apart, he caught sight of Fae's expression in the mirror. "What?" he asked.

"I'm just admiring you. Those robes are a good colour," said Fae, staring at his reflection. "I can't wait to peel you out of them later. Layer by layer."

Alysion shivered, a flash of heat jolting through him. By the Ancestors! Clearly, Fae hadn't gotten enough of their antics last night, either.

Another urgent knock sounded at the door. "My Prince, we need to go!"

Fae held out his hand. "Are you ready?"

Alysion suppressed a snort as he turned around. "No, but I never will be. Let's go, my love." He pecked Fae on the cheek and took his hand.

Together, they walked towards their future.

EPILOGUE

The initial negotiations with the dragons had gone better than anticipated. It would be a while yet before anything was decided; the various parties had many conflicting options and desires that needed to be addressed and sorted. But, to their relief, the dwarves and Odenians were open to discussing rewriting the treaties signed at the end of the Syl-Raanian War. Luckily, the dwarves had sent Urka's mother, Melann, as one of their representatives. She personally believed it was time for a change and would be an instrumental player in the discussions. The Odenian representatives seemed a little in over their heads. After all, the humans hadn't been numerous in these lands during the war and most had never seen a real dragon before. They pushed for more time to think and to properly evaluate the situation.

One thing that *had* been decided on, much to Fae's delight, was that Ranath, Xyrros, Gale, Cane, and even Mitchy had been given the title of official representatives, meaning they could come and go through the wards as needed. Alysion had seen to this as one of his first duties as king.

"I don't want you two to be separated again," he told the brothers.

Clothes littered the floor, hastily flung off after a long day of negotiating. Bodies entwined, they fell onto the bed.

Alysion wrapped his arms around Fae and pulled him close. "I need you."

Hot desire surged through Fae. Their lips crashed together, rough and messy. Alysion was still inexperienced but that didn't bother them. They had the rest of their lives to figure it out.

His hand went low, causing the new king to make sounds that only added fuel to the flames.

By the gods.

They eventually collapsed, exhausted. Fae wrapped an arm around Alysion and pulled him close.

"You know," said Fae, "never in my wildest dreams did I ever imagine myself bedding a king."

Alysion snorted. "Hah! You'll soon be a king too once we're joined. King Faeranduil."

Fae's stomach jolted. "I'm never going to get used to that."

"Well, you'd better start. I'm not doing this by myself." There was a playful gleam in Alysion's emerald eyes. "My sweet King Fae," he said softly. He leaned forward and gently kissed him on the lips. "I love you."

"I love you too."

The End

ACKNOWLEDGMENTS

Thank you to everyone who helped make this book possible! To my amazing editor, Michaela Choi, for all your hard work shaping this into something readable. A loud shoutout to my beta readers Joel, Bee, and J.A.L. Solski (check out their queer indie elf novels), who gave be so much good feedback. And to Chery of Laughing Dog Studios (@laughingdogstudios on Instagram) for the stellar cover art.

ABOUT THE AUTHOR

R. Dawnraven is a formless entity who enjoys collecting shiny rocks, flailing about with swords, and creating all kinds of art. They live on Treaty 1 territory. *The Twin Moons* is their second novel.
Tiktok - Instagram - Twitter - Tumblr
@RDawnraven

Photo by author